Dedication

Julian Elsmore, the protagonist in this novel, is a man of integrity. He is thankful that women hold up half the sky. When the wicked winds blow, he bends but does not break. I write in compliment of all such steadfast men.

Full
Measure
of Love

a novel

Ann Hall Marshall

≈ 1564 Publishing ≈
Seattle, Washington

1564 Publishing ~ 3509 NE 98th St., Seattle, WA 98115

Cover illustration © Diana Marshall

ISBN: 978-1-6094404-0-4

Author's Note:

My gratitude goes to the many people who informed, critiqued,
edited, and corrected my writing. You were essential to this novel
and I thank you.

*Designed, printed, and bound by Vladimir Verano
at Third Place Press, Lake Forest Park,
on the Espresso Book Machine v.2.2.*
www.thirdplacepress.com

Chapter 1

WHEN JULIE DIED, when she was killed, many people knew about her death hours before her husband did. The people walking near her and the ones across the busy street, who watched in horror as the suddenly out-of-control car skidded onto the sidewalk and smashed her helpless body against a storefront, knew. The police, the ambulance technicians, the hospital staff, the people in the morgue, and the news reporters, they knew. Strangers they were to Julian and Julie, strangers who were shocked and saddened at such a bizarre accident and who perhaps pondered the fragility of life for a moment or two.

It was a detail in his rushing grief, but Julian found it inappropriate that these casual people knew Julie was dead while he was cheerfully on his way to meet her at the real estate office.

They had arrived in New York City almost breathless with excitement (although Julian tried to maintain his usual calm demeanor) on Friday afternoon and checked into the midtown hotel where they had reservations. They spent the weekend searching for an apartment and, although the rents seemed steep compared with Paducah, late on Saturday afternoon they found a place very much to their liking and within their price range. A bit above their price range actually, but, with Julian's promotion and with their children, Joy and Miles, launched (Joy married and Miles at West Point), they could afford it.

On Sunday, they went to church, reached a final decision, and called the leasing company saying they would come by and sign a one-year contract the next day. They had to laugh because they knew the real estate office in Paducah would be shut up tight on a Sunday. Well, they weren't in Kentucky. It was April 1978, and they were beginning a new phase of their lives. They were New Yorkers now.

"I just love that apartment," said Julie on Monday morning. "When our furniture gets here Thursday, we'll have the rest of the week to settle in and arrange things and buy new curtains and stuff, and we'll be Mr. and Mrs. Julian Elsmore, at home in New York City." She hugged herself in delight.

"I want to go to the office first thing this morning," Julian said. "Just for an hour or so to get a feel for it, meet the staff and the agents. The next few days, we'll do some sightseeing; have a little vacation for ourselves before the furniture gets here." He kissed her and twirled her about.

"Are you nervous about the agency?"

"Not really. I just want to see it. It's part of my settling in."

She nodded. "Okay. Remember, we sign the lease at eleven o'clock."

"Eleven. Shall I come back for you, and we'll go together?"

She pulled a map of the area out of her handbag. "Picked this up in the lobby." She inspected it for a few minutes. "The realtor is six blocks straight down this same street and then one block left. I can do it. I'll meet you there."

He smiled at her eagerness to cope with the big city. He was eager, too. Well, why wouldn't he be? He worked for a good, solid insurance company that he was proud of. Right after high school, he'd hired on at entry level and worked his way up, ambitious to observe and learn how successful men handled problems. He had been willing to work overtime, when needed, to fill in for a sick agent, to run the unexpected Saturday errand. Along the way, he took college courses so he could read profit and loss statements and understand actuarial tables. And then, just a month ago, at age forty-two, he was offered a promotion to district manager of the New York office. It was a plum. Both he and Julie knew it and knew that if he turned it down, such a chance would not likely come again.

"Well, we're here. Here in New York City. It's going to be great!"

He had dressed carefully for his visit to Reliance-Ryan Insurance Company. First impressions count, so he wore his almost-new, best suit of charcoal gray, a white shirt, and a light-blue tie with thin diagonal stripes of black. His suit was off-the-rack but of excellent quality. It fit smoothly across the shoulders and draped perfectly.

Julie admired him. "You look great. You look like the head honcho."

"Thanks." He turned from the full-length mirror, rather pleased with the man he saw there—five-eleven, a trim waist (he went to the gym twice a week), and good posture. His hair was brown with a bit of gray here and there, receding slightly, neatly trimmed. His eyes were a rich brown but not unusual. "What?" he said to Julie.

"I said, when we go shopping we should buy you some new ties, high-style New York ties, five new ones, maybe even a bow."

"Good idea, nix the bow. I'd feel silly. You should buy something special too, Julie, for yourself, to celebrate that life begins at forty-two. What would you like?"

"Oh boy! I'll give that some thought and get back to you." Her eyes were bright with speculation. "Something I would never have bought in Paducah." She suddenly sprang to her feet. "I know, oh, I know what I'll buy, Julian. I'll buy high-fashion boots. In Paducah, we wear boots when it rains or to muck around in the barn. Not my new boots. They'll be high-heeled, high-style New York boots; soft tan leather, maybe with little gold chains at the ankle. Nothing mucky. That's what I'll buy, and ties for you."

He kissed her then, nuzzling her cheek in his joy that Monday morning. "See you at eleven, and afterwards we'll find a good restaurant or maybe a New York deli and have lunch there. We'll ask the leasing agent."

She nodded. "Are you going to drive?"

"I'll walk. I want to know where I'm going before I take the car out in New York traffic."

"Likewise. I thought it was scary when we drove into the city, everything so fast and crowded, and the car so new."

He started to leave but turned back to kiss her one more time for luck. He supposed the doorman would have summoned a taxi for him, but then there was the question of how much to tip. How much for the doorman; how much for the cabbie? *Maybe you don't tip the doorman until you check out of the hotel,* he thought. There were many things to learn about this enormous city, things he would take pleasure in learning.

It was a short mile to the office. He had always walked to work in Paducah, so he stepped out jauntily, starting to whistle. Several people sent him an odd glance, but he knew there could be no law against it, so he whistled his way to work.

The Reliance-Ryan Building looked prosperous, as an insurance business should, but not at all ostentatious, just solid. The offices were carefully decorated in neutrals to convey a message of stability, relieved here and there by plants in big red pots or a pair of bright pictures. The message, overall, was one of reassurance.

The attractive, middle-aged receptionist was frowning at some papers, but she looked up immediately and greeted him with a pleasant, "May I help you?"

"Julian Elsmore to see Mr. Oberlin."

The woman did a quick double-take and put her finger on a phone button. "Mr. Elsmore! I'm sure Mr. Oberlin will be out right away to greet you." She spoke into the phone, nodded, and said, just a trifle flustered, "Welcome to our Reliance offices and to New York City, Mr. Elsmore. We've been expecting you." Julian noted that, despite the engraved-in-stone name on the front of the building, the receptionist did not use "Reliance-Ryan" but simply called the company "Reliance" as they did in Paducah. Good enough.

He thanked her for her welcome, observing to himself that she had the good sense not to offer him coffee or a chair. Of course he would want to be on his feet, hands free, when he met Stan Oberlin, who was temporarily in charge of the New York office.

He remembered being introduced to the man some five years ago at one of the company conventions, remembered being told that Stan had an enviable record with the company and was in line to be chief in New York.

That hadn't happened, and Julian wondered why. When Bill Redensfeld had keeled over with a heart attack a few months ago, why hadn't New York been handed over to Stan, who was, after all, right there on the spot? It would have been a smooth transition. *Why was it offered to me instead? I'll have to be careful.*

Stan came into the reception area and shook hands cordially. He took time to introduce Mrs. Abernathy ("our receptionist, who takes good care of us all") and suggested a quick tour of the suite. After Julian had met the agents who were in that morning and most of the support staff, Stan opened the door to an executive office. "This is yours. Shall we talk here?"

Julian walked across the carpet and sat down in the big swivel chair behind the glass-topped desk. He was the new district manager. It felt good, very good. Like coming to rest where he belonged.

Stan sank comfortably into the client chair opposite, and, almost immediately, a secretary appeared with coffee. The older man waved easily to a small table. "Put it there, Miss Rizzio. I'll pour."

He cocked an eyebrow at Julian, who said, "A bit of cream."

Julian noted the cup and saucer with approval. Fine china with a simple silver band, and the small cloth napkin was initialed with a bold, blue-on-white "RR". The coffee was fragrant with a whiff of vanilla.

"Stan," he began in his straightforward manner, "I can't help wondering why you aren't sitting in this chair."

"It was offered to me," the man answered, "and that was gratifying, of course. Ten years ago, maybe even five years ago, I would have taken it, been pleased. Now things have changed. My wife died a couple years back, my kids are on their own, my heart skips a beat now and then. I'm going to take early retirement. I'm content with that."

A moment ticked away as both men drank their hot coffee. Then Stan spoke again, "I'll stick around long enough to get my own clients transferred to another agent—some to you, perhaps—and to clue you in. It's just a lot of detail, record keeping, regional supervision, reports. Usually, the manager makes a visit to each office in the district at least once a month. Bill liked to drop in at random times, but the schedule's up to you now. I'll be glad to take you around, introduce you if you wish."

"I'm glad I can count on you."

"Absolutely. You can count on me, and the firm can count on me. I've been with Reliance over thirty-five years. Good times. Oh, once every so often, somebody sues us, but the company is fair, so we call in our lawyers and generally settle out of court. The office, in fact the whole Eastern Division, runs pretty smoothly. The rest of the country also, as far as I know."

"Sounds good."

"Any undercutting will come from a few agents who wanted the promotion for themselves. You treat them right, and they'll either settle down or leave for greener fields. You understand that these are guys who would have waited out my retirement to get another shot at the top job. You're too young for that. So any resignations won't be personal."

"I understand. I appreciate the heads up. Now, my wife and I just got into New York last Friday. We found an apartment over the weekend, and we're signing the lease later this morning. Our furniture will be here Thursday. I'll take the rest of the week to settle in." He almost asked if it was okay but, remembering in time that he was now the boss, "the head honcho," merely said, "So I'll see you first thing next Monday."

"Fine and dandy."

Julian stood up, leaving his half-filled cup on the desk. "Good coffee," he said with a smile and walked out.

He wanted to run, jump, or do cartwheels. Well, cartwheels in his head at least. He was happy that he had decided to visit the office and that the talk with Stan had gone so well, with no maneuvering or hidden agenda that he could detect.

He said a warm goodbye to Mrs. Abernathy and promised himself that, in a few weeks, he would gently point out to her that she should never (even though she probably could) predict to anyone her boss's action. He would point out that instead of saying "I'm sure he'll be right out" or "I'll have him call you," it was her role to say "I'll let him know you're here" or "I'll give him your message." She was not in charge, and that should be clear.

Small points, he reflected. At the same time, he would compliment her on her job performance. She was clearly an asset to the office. Nevertheless, he wanted Mrs. Abernathy to represent the company as perfectly as possible. He wanted that for himself.

He strolled along to the realtor's office, whistling again, admiring New York in the thin, promising sun of early April, thinking he was in good time, thinking life was full of possibilities, wondering if a New York

Reuben would taste better than a Paducah Reuben, never thinking, not for a single moment, that Julie was already dead. No premonition. No sense of life—his, hers, theirs—ending. He mourned that failure later. He mourned that, totally unaware of her death, he had been giddy with happiness, his head full of plans and dreams.

When Julie's heart stopped beating, when the bright light faded from her eyes, how could he not have known?

Chapter 2

IT TOOK THE NEW YORK CITY POLICE a couple hours to identify Julie and over two more hours to locate her husband. The card in her wallet said that she was a resident of Paducah, Kentucky, so the cops assumed that she was a hick tourist. When they called the phone number in Paducah, however, the phone was disconnected. They thought this odd because a person doesn't have her phone taken out when she goes on a short vacation. The cops were mildly suspicious.

Neighbors, contacted by the police, knew that the house had been sold a month ago and that the Elsmores had left late last week. Julian and Julie, they told the police without hesitation, had been their good friends for years, good people. They were sorry to see them move. Already, they missed the Elsmores.

"Julian worked for Reliance Insurance," one woman volunteered. "They left, you know, because he was promoted. He's running the company's New York City office now. You could ask there...Is something wrong?"

Tight-lipped but methodic, the police kept checking. There was absolutely no police record for the Elsmores in Paducah, not so much as a parking ticket. One of the officers there said that he knew the couple personally. "Mr. and Mrs. Clean," he described them as and "very public-spirited too."

At Reliance Insurance in New York, Stan Oberlin said that, yes, Mr. Elsmore had been in but was not expected again for a week. He remembered that Mr. Elsmore had said he was going to meet his wife and that they were signing a lease on an apartment. He didn't know where. He was sure that Julian hadn't mentioned the name of the realtor or of his hotel. Mrs. Abernathy, who was also questioned, had nothing to add. She was sorry Reliance Insurance couldn't be of more assistance. Privately, she was curious.

The cops found Julie's little area map, imprinted with the name of the hotel, in a side pocket of her purse. They phoned the hotel. Yes, the desk said, Julie Elsmore was registered, she and her husband Julian, but both keys were gone. The Elsmores listed New York City itself as their address with a bouncy little note that read "Here to stay!"

"No," the police said, "do not leave a message that we called. Do not." A few minutes later, the young man they had spoken to went off duty.

Following Stan Oberlin's clue and their own plodding protocols, the cops checked the real estate agencies in the area and finally got a hit. Yes, Julian Elsmore was there that morning. He had waited almost an hour, expecting his wife to show up. He had said, "I guess she got lost, after all. Maybe the map was wrong." He had signed the lease himself and left.

Scarcely more than an hour after returning to his hotel, Julian called the police in a panic and reported his wife missing. "She'll probably show up any minute," the clerk told him easily, "probably just shopping and lost track of time."

Julian knew that wasn't true.

When, working through their many departments in their own mysterious way, the police finally connected Julian to the dead woman from Paducah, they sent a man to escort him to the morgue. Julian was almost too paralyzed to even nod his head when they turned the sheet back so he could identify Julie's poor, battered body.

There was much to do. Julian moved through the arrangements in a daze of disbelief. He couldn't bear to send Julie's remains—no, he couldn't bear that word "remains" either—couldn't bear to send Julie's body back to Paducah, so far away from him. In an immense city where he had no connections, he picked a funeral home, a coffin, a cemetery, and a day and time for the funeral. He notified his family, making arrangements for them to stay at his hotel. Stan Oberlin knew a retired minister who would preside. The funeral director, even though he was a stranger recommended by a stranger, was very helpful.

Julian managed it all with a firm jaw and dead eyes. Part of him knew that eventually he would have to awaken from this impossible nightmare. *It has to be a bad dream.* Part of him knew otherwise, but he could not bring himself to the truth that Julie was dead.

She was buried on Wednesday afternoon. On Thursday morning, their furniture arrived, and, in a way, it was a relief. Decisions had to be made. Put the high-backed sofa in the living room facing the fireplace, maybe seven or eight feet back, the wing chairs on either side, the trunk in the master bedroom under the big window, all those boxes in the spare room. He checked out of the hotel, pretending not to see the sympathy in the desk clerk's eyes.

He had sent Joy, who was six months pregnant, and her husband, Brian, home right after the funeral. The young couple was distraught with sorrow. *All this grief, the constant tears, can't be good for the baby. Don't risk Julie's grandchild,* he had thought. *Go home to Philadelphia, Joy, and try to get back to normal.*

Miles' voice was heavy with sorrow. "I wish I could stay. I wish I could think of a way to help somehow, Dad, to help us all. There doesn't seem to be anything that anyone can say at a time like this, but I wish I could stay anyhow, be with you." He put his arm around his father's shoulders. He was big and a bit clumsy, anxious to be comforting, needing to be comforted. "You know I'd stay if I could, don't you? I've got to get back to West Point. Exams are coming up. At least Pop-Pop will be here."

Julian's father remained with him in the apartment. Together they composed an obituary for the Paducah papers. Mostly they were silent, enduring.

They asked the apartment manager for the nearest place to buy groceries, and they brought in coffee, orange juice, cereal, bread, butter, and paper plates. It took them a while to find the toaster and the coffee maker. Julie would have known where they were. Julian was sure of that, and he thought for one glorious, unbalanced moment that, when she came back, *she* could unpack the rest of the kitchen stuff. He was immediately angry at his silly illusion, at Julie for not being there to help, and at his empty life. He snapped at his father, with sudden violence, that the pictures could stay crated. *How should I be expected to know where to hang them?*

The movers set up the bed. Julian unpacked the sheets and found the pillows, but he slept fitfully. When he reached out in the night to gather his wife close to him, he would suddenly come fully awake to find his arms empty, himself frantic, and sleep impossible.

He and Julie had been together since birth. They hadn't met at a high school dance when they were fifteen or been introduced ten years later at an office party. Their parents were friends before they were born, the Elsmores and the Kronks, and they had simply always been together—in their strollers, at play group, through school, marriage, jobs, parenthood, and the move to the big city. Now she was dead, and he should be with her. He should be dead too. It was wrong, wrong for him to be alive, required to eat and talk, to shower and put on fresh clothes, and to make decisions about where to hang pictures without talking it over. And he had to do it all with a heart that had been split in two, the Julie half buried with her.

When night came after each of those first long and desperate days, when his father was asleep in the second bedroom of the unsettled apartment, a thought beat in his head. *She was my life. My glow, my wife. And now my beloved is dead.* A chant followed, and he couldn't stop it. *Nothing, nothing, nothing,* pulsed the refrain. *Nothing but sadness and blackness, nothing.* It became a mantra, an ugly, reverse mantra because it did not soothe him. It agitated him. Life was a hopeless mess. He wept and was ashamed of weeping.

Cards and notes of sympathy came from Paducah. He treasured them, especially the ones that spoke of Julie's merry laugh, of her volunteer work, or of a funny memory. He thought of reaching out to those old friends, but the phone wasn't yet installed. And, even if it were, what would he say? What would *they* say? He knew that he could not stand to hear their awkward condolences. Nor could he chitchat about, say, the weather in New York or his solo plans for the future. He had no plans. Julie had been torn viciously from his arms, and he could think of nothing else.

By Monday, a week after Julie had died, he knew that he had to go to work. Work was *real*. The New York office was still an unfamiliar place to him, but it was the only sure place in all of New York City where he could function. He walked in at eight o'clock a.m. on Tuesday, having just seen his father off for Paducah.

Why, dear Lord, did Julie and I ever leave there?

He said pleasantly, "Good morning, Mrs. Abernathy."

AT THE CEMETERY

Late May, 1978

He stood there very quietly, a neatly dressed nice-looking, middle-aged man. He stood on the little rise in the cemetery where Julie lay buried. It was Sunday morning, unusually hot. He was composed or appeared to be. Actually, although he had come to talk with Julie, he couldn't seem to put any words together. Would she want to know that he had ordered a marker for her grave? Or did she know? He was sweating slightly. His heart was hammering, and the loud beat, pounding out that he was alive while she was dead, was disgusting. What had he come to say?

Fifteen minutes later, when he began moving, silent and defeated, down the slope he finally gathered together a thought:

> *I loved you all my life, Julie.*
> *I loved you with all my heart.*
> *I still do.*

He left the cemetery and drove back to his empty apartment.

Chapter 3

———————————

IT WAS STAN WHO HAD INDIRECTLY recommended Dr. Glazer. At first, right after the funeral, he had recognized Julian's need to grieve and had limited his sympathy to support and small kindnesses at the office. Julian, he noted, was able to immerse himself in learning the people and routines of the New York City District Reliance Insurance office and, while concentrating on that, seemed able to keep his sorrow at bay.

Two months after the tragedy, thinking how isolated Julian was in the big city, Stan suggested in an offhand way, "A bunch of us usually wind up at O'Reilly's after work on Friday for Happy Hour. I'm going this evening. Why don't you come along? It's nearby."

"No, but thank you for asking. Maybe some other time." He was perfectly polite, as usual, even with a small smile, but his tone told Stan that further urging was useless.

Three weeks later, clearing the last few things from his desk as he prepared for retirement, Stan tried again. "Why don't you come along to O'Reilly's with me after work? Just for an hour or so. It's a nice crowd, and I hear there'll be a little good-bye ceremony for me. I'd like you to be there."

Julian just shook his head. "I can't, Stan. I certainly wish you well, I appreciate all your help since I got here, but I can't go to O'Reilly's."

Presuming on his position as an older man, Stan said, "When Virgie passed, I couldn't imagine myself going anywhere without her, so I just stayed home. It was grief at first, but then it was just moping. Most nights I'd pick up a sandwich on my way home, get a beer out of the fridge, and sit there in the dark and eat. After a while, I knew, if I didn't stir myself, I was doomed to be one of the walking dead for the rest of my life. Julian, what do you do when you get back to your apartment and close the door?"

"The usual. I remember things. Sometimes I take a sleeping pill."

"You've lost weight. Do you eat?"

"Sure. Most of the time."

"Listen, when I was so sunk after losing Virgie—we'd been married nearly forty years, good years—I started seeing a shrink. Oh, I'd heard the jokes. I didn't really like the idea, thought it was sissy to pay someone to listen to your problems, a sign of weakness. But Dr. Glazer was just what I needed. Very down to earth. I remember he suggested simple things: that I turn on the lights when I got home at night, that I get someone to clean the house, that I get a puppy. And he checked that I did it. Good beginnings. It took about six months of small steps up out of the pit, but I finally stopped feeling so sorry for myself all the time, started remembering the good things. I got back to living a pretty normal life. Worth every penny."

"Maybe," said Julian, but there was no promise in his voice.

"Here's his number. If you look in the phone book, you'll see there are two Dr. Glazers, both psychiatrists. The other one is his daughter, Victoria Glazer. Her clients are all women, so be sure you see Henry."

Julian thanked him in his usual courteous, noncommittal manner, but he did tuck the little white card under his blotter.

A few days later, Julian sat staring at the name and number Stan had given him. "I suppose I do need to talk to someone." He realized he had spoken aloud, and, embarrassed, although there was no one else in his office and the door was shut, he pushed the card out of sight again.

That night, depressed and semi-hungry in the apartment, he looked up Glazer in the phone book. There was Henry, and farther down was Victoria Glazer. Not "V Glazer," he noticed, but "Victoria." He said it out loud, a good, strong name.

"I need to talk to someone," he said. "There's Joy of course. She'd understand, but the baby is due in just a couple of weeks now, and I don't want to burden her." Sighing, he put the card out of sight again, but not before he had written down Victoria Glazer's phone number. "I need to talk to a woman." The notion that had entered his mind was as fragile as the memory of a kiss. Stan had said that all her patients are women. *Maybe among all those women...*His thought was too feeble to be called a plan. Suddenly resolute, he reached for the phone. "Why not?" he muttered.

He was surprised to get an appointment for after work on the following Friday, surprised and not entirely pleased that it was so soon. He didn't feel ready to plunge into icy waters but still needed some time to ruminate. *Maybe people with psychological problems need to be seen at once, like how a dentist will see someone with an abscessed tooth right away.*

Julian did not think of himself as a person needing psychiatric care. He was grieving, that was it, and he needed to talk to a woman because women have a special gift for understanding.

Chapter 4

JULIAN AND DR. VICTORIA GLAZER SAT in comfortable, blue upholstered chairs, not quite face to face but at a little angle. She wore a trim, dark suit and held a small leather notebook on the broad tapestry-covered arm of the chair. *She doesn't look like a doctor* he thought, but he had checked in the dictionary just to be sure and a psychiatrist was indeed a medical doctor. He had imagined that she would wear a white coat, have a stethoscope hung around her neck and would immediately detect his broken heart.

"Your chair is a recliner," she said casually, "in case you would be more comfortable leaning back."

"No," he said. "No, thank you." He knew he needed to stay alert if he was to accomplish what he had come for. *All her patients are women.*

She glanced at the few notes that her secretary had jotted. She saw that Julian Elsmore had recently moved to New York City from Paducah, Kentucky, to manage the regional office of Reliance-Ryan Insurance. He had volunteered that he was a very recent widower. Vicki guessed that he was in his early forties, near her own age. *Grief-stricken? Perhaps guilty about something?* He seemed tense.

"We will have a conversation," she told him. "Every word spoken here is forever confidential. The conversation will be lopsided because it is your job to talk while I am a friendly listener. If I ask a question, try to answer it, Julian. I ask only because I seek to understand, to help."

He nodded vaguely. He could scarcely believe he was in the office of a shrink, could think of nothing to say.

The first conversation between Julian Elsmore and Dr. Victoria Glazer:

She began, "Tell me about your wife,"

"My beloved is dead."

"She died when?"

"Almost three months ago. On April 10. Three days after we got to New York." He shut his mouth tightly.

She persisted. "How long had you been married?"

"Twenty-four years."

"Children?"

"Two."

"They're grown up?"

"Joy is married and lives near Philadelphia. She's expecting a baby later this month. My son, Miles, is in his third year at West Point."

"Did you and your wife have a happy marriage?"

"Her name is Julie."

"Julian and Julie," the doctor observed.

"It was always that way." Suddenly, the floodgates opened, and, beginning at the beginning, despite having decided to merely outline his life with Julie, he talked for over twenty minutes.

"Our families, the Elsmores and the Kronks, were next-door neighbors and best friends. We were born three days apart in June of 1936. I was first, but Julie and I were in the nursery at the hospital together. Always together. The country was recovering from the Great Depression, and, though we kids didn't know it, it was a fine time for America."

"And was it pleasant for you?"

"Very. We lived in a neighborhood of new, little houses. Nothing pretentious. Two bedrooms, one bath, a rumpus room in the basement. The lots were rather small, but all the back yards in the whole development were separated from each other by a fence or hedge. Except ours. Our parents planned it that way, planned that their children would play together. There was no barrier between our yards. Julie and I shared a big sandbox and one big swing set and, as we got older, one jungle gym and one tent where the sandbox had been."

"So you and Julie played together constantly?"

"There were other children in the neighborhood, of course. We would invite them to come and play in our yard."

"Did you and Julie always get along? Ever fight?"

"My very first clear memory is playing in the sandbox with her. It must have been the summer we turned four. I was making a castle, and I had carefully packed damp sand into our bucket and turned out two side-by-side cones. While I waited for them to dry a bit, I was making a path to the castle. I told Julie to get some little stones. Instead she grabbed the pail and began to fill it, saying she'd make the upstairs."

I told her she couldn't, that she'd spoil it, that she'd knock the castle down.

"Will not," she said, "Gimme the pail." We tussled over the handle, and then she fell sideways, and she did squash the two cones.

"Look what you've done!" I yelled.

Our mothers were sunning themselves and drinking iced tea nearby. "Children, children."

"I'll build it back." She grabbed the pail and started to fill it.

"You don't know how, dumb girl." I yanked the bucket away from her and dumped out her sand.

"Mine, mine!" she screamed and started banging on the pail with our little shovel. "Let go, it's mine."

Mrs. Kronk came over then. She saw that both of us had our hands clamped on the pail and were tugging angrily. "Julie, honey, it's nice to take turns."

He paused a moment. "I remember that Julie looked up at Mrs. Kronk with the sweetest, most reasonable smile in the world and said, 'I *am* taking turns, Mommy. He had it last. He had it for about a million years. Now it's *my* turn.' My little finger was bleeding where she had hit it with the shovel. I stuck it in my mouth to hide it."

"You didn't protest?"

"Well, how could I? It *was* her turn. That's the first clear memory—a whole incident, you know—that I remember."

She made a quick note in her little leather book. "Where did you live growing up?"

"Paducah, Kentucky." She smiled a little, obviously unimpressed.

"It's quite an historic town," he informed her, "founded in 1827 by William Clark, brother of George, as in Lewis and Clark."

"I see," she said. "Paducah. And you lived there until you moved to New York?"

"Julie and I always lived in Paducah. Side by side in Paducah."

"But when did you come to New York?"

"Three months ago. Exactly three months ago. On April 7."

She paused a long moment but he said nothing more. "Why did you move here?"

"My company had an opening here, and it was offered to me. A promotion, you know."

"So you jumped at the opportunity?"

"Not really. Not exactly jumped. Julie and I thought it over, pros and cons, you know. We'd be nearer to Joy. Who knows where the Army will station Miles? Our parents are dead, except my dad. He's seeing a widow back there in Paducah and didn't want to move with us. But he's never been to New York, so he said he'd probably come to visit, maybe *they* would visit."

"Have they?"

"He came for the funeral. He loved Julie. Everyone did. He stayed for a week."

"And you've been alone ever since?"

"Both the children came for the funeral too, but Joy was six months pregnant, and her doctor didn't really like the stress she was under or her traveling. The baby's due the nineteenth of this month. If it's a baby girl, they'll name her Julie." His eyes misted. "Julie, my Julie, would have loved having a grandchild."

"And your son?"

"Miles had to get back to his classes." Julian couldn't help bragging a little. "Miles is a smart boy. Valedictorian of his high school class. He has a Congressional appointment to West Point."

"Did you and Julie have many disagreements?" she asked suddenly.

"A few, some big, some small." He half-smiled, remembering. "But we always worked things out because," he said, leaning forward in his chair, "we had to, Doctor. We were together for all our lives. We had to be together, and we both knew it." He drew in a slow breath, pushed his lightly salted hair back from his high forehead, and looked about as if dazed, searching for something. "Only now she's gone; we're not together."

"Did Julie," she asked, careful to use his wife's name, "always win your arguments? Did you always give in?"

"Oh no, it wasn't like that. She was cute—curly blond hair, a little wispy, dimples—and, when she set her mind on something, she was very serious about it. She'd write her arguments down on a three-by-five card so she wouldn't forget an important point. That made me smile."

"And *then* you would give in?"

"Not always. Don't try to make it like that. Sometimes it was her turn, or maybe it didn't really matter to me, like what color to paint the living room or when to buy a new car. If I thought it was important to do it my way, like take out more life insurance rather than some fancy vacation, you know, then that's how we did it in the end. Mostly though, we would talk things over and agree. She was a good wife, a before-women's-lib-wife. We were happy."

"Julian, if it seemed to you that I was suggesting something—a moment ago, you said, 'don't try to make it like that'—I apologize. It's not my job to put ideas in your head. I see that it might have sounded that way, and I'm sorry. Please think of me as a listener only. A sympathetic listener while you work through your grief. Now, we have just a few more minutes. Is there something in particular you'd like to speak of?"

"Yes," he said, "there is, but I've taken so much time telling you about Julie, well, may I have another appointment? I'll try to be more organized."

"Organization isn't the point, just remembering, maybe random backcasting. Let's say this same time next week, if that's good for you. I believe my secretary has left, so I'll walk out with you and check the appointment book. I seldom schedule five o'clock conversations, but, in your case…well, no matter."

She rose gracefully, a tall, attractive, dark-haired woman with a round, pleasant face, calm blue eyes, and good legs. He didn't really notice. He didn't know that she was intrigued to have a male patient.

AT THE CEMETERY

July 9, 1978

Stan said I should see a shrink or I'll live out the rest of my life just going through the motions like a zombie. He gave me a reference.

Is it okay with you, Julie? That I'm seeing Dr. Glazer? I had to do something. Only I should tell you, Stan's shrink was Dr. Henry Glazer. I'm seeing his daughter. Her name is Dr. Victoria Glazer. I found her in the phone book.

He put his hand on the handsome granite marker for a moment. Under Julie's name, it read:

BELOVED WIFE AND MOTHER

He wandered down the little hill, stumbled but didn't fall, got into his car and drove back to his empty apartment.

🙠 🙠 🙠

Chapter 5

THIS IS ONE OF THE STORIES Julian told Dr. Victoria Glazer:

There was a big sweet cherry tree in our back yard and the way the branches grew there was one where Julie and I could sit and lean back against another. It was like a sofa up in the air. We would read and talk and eat apples or saltines and pretend anything we wanted to. When they were ripe, we'd pick the cherries and have spitting contests with the pits. One day we were reciting the multiplication table, which we had to learn in third grade, sometimes chanting it out, sometimes shouting it out for fun. But she kept making a mistake, saying six times nine was fifty-six, and then we'd have to go back to the beginning.

I reached over and pinched her, a twisting pinch. "You dumb, skinny girl, can't you ever get it right? Six times nine is fifty-four."

She shoved me hard then, and I fell out of the tree. It was only about seven feet to the ground, but I flung out my arm as I went down and crashed it against a lower branch. I landed flat with a thump, and the wind was knocked out of me. Our mothers heard Julie yelling and came running. They pulled me up to sitting and raised my arms over my head so I'd catch my breath. As soon as I managed to get some air, I started screaming, too, because my right arm was broken.

"Oh, Julian. Oh, honey," my mother said as she very gently let my arm down. It hung twisted below the elbow, and I kept on screaming with the pain. "Oh, poor honey," she said again and she put me in the car and drove to the hospital. My mother was always calm and capable in an emergency. When we were driving away, I saw Julie waving from our yard. She mouthed a "sorry" and I thought she should have been sorry.

"You were about eight?"

"We were both eight."

"Did you stay in the hospital?"

"No, it was a simple break."

He went on with the story:

About four hours later, Mom and I were back home. I had a cast, a sling, and enough pain medicine to allow me to enjoy being a martyr. My mother installed me on the couch, plumping pillows and bringing a damp washcloth to wipe my sweaty face.

Almost at once, Julie and her mom showed up. Her mother brought a pitcher of lemonade, and Julie carried a plate of cookies. "Chocolate chip," Julie said, holding them out to me. "I know you like chocolate chip. I helped make them while you were at the hospital. We had to walk to that little store three blocks over for the chips."

I took a couple of cookies and ate them without comment.

My mother stepped into the little silence. "That was very nice of you, Julie. They just hit the spot, I'm sure."

Julie often latched onto grown-up phrases. "It was the least I could do, Mrs. Elsmore," she told my mother seriously, "because I pushed Julian and made him fall."

"But it wasn't intentional. You didn't intend that he should break his arm."

"No, of course not." Julie, her eyes glistening with sudden tears, passed the cookie plate to me again. "Will you let me sign your cast, Julian? Please? I'll go home and get my red pencil if it's okay. Or maybe my paint box."

"Oh, I suppose," I said and reached for another cookie. "I'd like some more lemonade, too."

It was Mrs. Kronk who refilled my glass because Julie was already skipping toward her house.

Julie drew a red rectangle on my cast. It was pretty big, about three inches long, and she carefully wrote her name. She added a flourish here and there and then drew a flower in each corner. Our mothers admired it. Julie tapped her red pencil against her teeth and then added a tiny heart at the end of her name.

I looked at it and said crossly, "You can go home now. I'm sleepy and my arm hurts again."

She glanced up from her artwork and her face clouded. "You bet I'm going home." She sounded angry all of a sudden. "Who wants to stay with a clumsy boy who doesn't even say thank you for the cookies? Seven times eight is fifty-six, so there, stupid!" She flounced off.

I only heard the "fifty-six."

"No, no it is not. Not, not, not. Six times nine is fifty-four. You're the stupid one. You're just a dopey ..." Then I realized what she had said, and I swallowed the rest of my sentence. She laughed because she had changed the equation from six times nine to seven times eight. That made fifty-six the right answer.

Julie tore up the steps of her back porch, taking them two at a time. She had tricked me. My arm hurt. I didn't even have the energy to reach for another cookie.

My mother and Mrs. Kronk sent each other eye signals.

Chapter 6

FOR THE FIRST SEVERAL WEEKS when he visited Dr. Glazer, Julian talked mostly about his childhood with Julie in Paducah. He thought the stories weren't especially important, yet somehow he looked forward to telling them, even found himself searching his memory and choosing an episode to relate at his next appointment.

During one of his first "conversations" in early July, he told this story:

Julie and I were close to celebrating our thirteenth birthdays and were playing on our jungle gym, when Julie suddenly dropped to the ground and said, "I hate my name. Do you know that? I hate, hate, hate my name."

"Julie?" I was surprised. "Why do you hate 'Julie'? It's a good name."

"Not 'Julie,' dumbo. I hate 'Kronk.' It sounds like *thud*. I hate, hate, hate it."

I was bewildered. I protested, "'Kronk' doesn't sound like *thud*. They don't rhyme or anything. What's ticked you off?"

"How would you like to be 'Julian Kronk' or 'Julian Thud' or 'Julian Dropdead'?"

"Well …" I started to consider the matter, but Julie didn't really want an answer. I could tell she had been brooding about her name for who knows how long and now she was raving.

"I wish I could change my name. I will change it as soon as I'm old enough. I'll change it to something pretty like 'Starr' or maybe some high-class English name like 'Churchill' or 'Lancaster.'

"'Julie K. Lancaster.' How does that sound? Or maybe I'll spell out the K, you know, 'Julie Kaye Lancaster.' Do you like that?"

"Well, maybe, but what will your parents say?" I knew she was distressed and, even though it was all of a sudden, I wanted to help.

"I don't care. I don't care what they say." Her color was high because she was so vehement. "It's an awful name. I think *they* should have changed it. Why haven't they changed it? Tell me that. Do *they* like it? How could they like it?"

Then the storm died, and Julie said in a small, sad voice, "You don't even know what I'm talking about, do you? You're my best friend, but you've a nice name, so you don't know. 'Elsmore' is a very nice name. You never get embarrassed by it. I get embarrassed by 'Kronk' whenever I have to say it. It's a dumb, dumb name. A thuddy name." She started to cry.

I opened my mouth to say that 'Kronk' was a fine, solid name, but then I had a better idea. "Julie," I said, "if you like my name, we can get married as soon as we're out of high school, and then you'll be 'Julie Elsmore' forever. That'll work slick."

"Maybe."

She perked up a little and seemed to consider my offer seriously. "Okay, Julian, that's nice of you. Maybe, I don't know how, but maybe I can bear to be 'Kronk' for a few more years. After that," she said, beginning to smile at the idea, "I'll be 'Julie Elsmore' forever."

I was glad that her mood had suddenly swung, as it so often did. I never knew what to expect, and it was happening more often of late. My mother said it was because Julie was growing up.

"I'm growing up too," I said. My mother just smiled that mysterious woman smile.

Somehow, I must have said the right thing to Julie because she was suddenly all sunshine. After a moment, her dimples flashed and she said, "Thanks."

"You're welcome."

Julian told Dr. Glazer in a serious voice, "We were twelve years old and that's how we got engaged."

AT THE CEMETERY

July 16, 1978

We have a baby granddaughter, born early this morning. Seven pounds and two ounces. Brian says she is perfect.

Her name is Julie, for you. I guess you know that.

It was raining. He didn't have an umbrella.

Remember that time, right before Joy was born, we got caught in the rain as we were out walking? You were too big—too big with our child—for us to make a run home, but you said, "Never mind. Rain is good. It makes things grow. Baby's growing."

By the time we got home, you were soaking wet. We stripped off your clothes and wrapped you in my big woolly robe because your robe wouldn't close around you, and I rubbed your hair with a couple of washcloths and combed it out until it was dry and blond again.

He choked up, turned abruptly down the hill, and drove back to his empty apartment.

Chapter 7

"I DON'T REALLY KNOW HOW JULIE DIED," Julian told Dr. Glazer on his fourth visit. It wasn't how he had meant to begin. He really had had a purpose in scheduling these sessions, a question for the doctor. He wanted to ask it, but worried that she might think him crazy and would no longer see him. She might even think him dangerous and might refer him to some other kind of doctor. He knew he wouldn't like that, so he delayed the question. He found it oddly soothing to talk to her of Julie.

Dr. Glazer was startled for a moment, but then she asked, in her soft, professional tone, "How do you think she died, Julian?"

"That's just it. I don't know. When that car careened up onto the sidewalk, it smashed her against a plate glass window. The window frame rested on a low wall of brick, and, when the window broke, Julie sort of pitched through and lay there prone, her shoulders hunched, her head hanging partway into the building."

The way he described the episode, the words he chose, "careen" and "prone," told Dr. Glazer that, in his mind, he had rehearsed the telling of the incident countless times. Perhaps he had never voiced it to anyone before but simply turned it over in his mind, repeating it silently to himself, stroking and editing it.

Dear God, she prayed silently, *help me help him.* She was astonished at her own emotion which, she scolded herself, was quite unprofessional.

"I know that," Julian went on, "because there was a tourist just ahead of her, and he turned back and took a picture. Later he gave it to the police, and I saw it. Her left leg was twisted around, obviously broken, her shoe lying a few feet away. There was blood from the glass cuts. Maybe she was still alive then, breathing. I couldn't tell from the snapshot, but maybe she was still alive, and I should have been there to gather her up, get her to the emergency room, sit by her bed, and, when she opened her eyes, comfort her, tell her she was going to be all right, her leg would mend, her cuts would heal, her bruises would fade. Tell her she'd be pretty again. I don't know. And maybe it's just a fantasy, but maybe it could have happened that way.

"But I wasn't there, you see. And, just a few minutes later, it must have been right after the snapshot was taken, that heavy, broken windowpane slid down in its frame and cut off her head." His tone was sodden with pain. "I knew Julie all of our lives, together since we were babies. I knew everything about her, even when she got her first period. We were both a bit embarrassed by that. Sort of proud too. Now my beloved is dead, and I don't know how she died. Was she crushed to death, or was she beheaded? Guillotined?" He looked bleakly at Dr. Glazer. "I think it's very strange that I don't know that."

Her training called for her to say something bland, calming, or probing, perhaps. *Why is it so important to you to know?* But she lost her professional poise. In a totally uncharacteristic burst of feeling, and with a sound of sympathy in her throat, she leaned forward and put a hand on his arm. "Oh, my dear. Oh, Julian." It was a lapse on her part, but he seemed scarcely to notice.

"The undertaker asked me to bring a dress for her to wear in her coffin. You see, the suit she had been wearing when she died wasn't ..." he searched for a word before continuing, "wasn't okay. I said that our clothes were mostly in a moving van, but that I'd look in the suitcases we had brought and bring a dress in the next day.

"He said, 'Bring a pretty scarf to put around her neck too, something I can fluff out.'

"Well, when I unpacked, I found another suit, a soft, blue one that she had loved and that I thought would do quite nicely. I was still pretty much in shock, you know, but then I couldn't find her scarves. I flung stuff all over the hotel room, and then I dumped both our suitcases on the floor and searched through the piles. Nothing. If she had ever owned a scarf at all, and I knew she had, it wasn't in those suitcases. And I felt that I had failed her all over again. I couldn't find a scarf to dress up her beautiful blue suit and to hide her ruined neck. I sat down on the bed in that alien room, in the midst of her personal things. I sat in the midst of her sweaters and bras and nylons, her toothbrush, her little leather jewel case, the tampons she carried, even though she had started menopause, and I bawled for Julie. I hadn't cried before, but I suddenly realized that she would never wear these clothes, never fasten the amber beads around her neck, never brush her teeth again. I wanted to die, too. I really didn't want to live."

"But you *are* alive, Julian. It seems unfair, but we have to go on living."

He looked at her in surprise. He had forgotten that she was listening. But she had been listening, and she understood. He was grateful for that and repeated, "Yes, we have to go on living. That's the hard part."

"Did you feel guilty?"

He thought about that. For a long moment, it seemed as if he wouldn't, or couldn't, answer. Finally he said, "I didn't feel guilty about her death; I hadn't caused it. I felt guilty because I wasn't dead." He bowed his head, then snapped it up again with a despairing glance at her. "My heart had been ripped out, and I felt dead. But there I was, breathing in and out and thinking about where to go shopping, thinking that if you wanted to make yourself dead, how would you do it? I could go out and buy a rope or a gun or maybe a bottle of sleeping pills. But first I had to go shopping for a scarf and take it to the funeral home. I had to go shopping; I had to go to the funeral; I had to have the phone installed."

She recovered her professional rhythm. "Is that what you did next?"

"Yes, I went out and bought a scarf. She needed one. It had lots of twisting lines, like twining ivy, all shades of blue and grey, with a pink touch here and there, and sometimes it looked like scrolls or seashells. The saleswoman had a name for it—'praise lace' or something."

"A paisley pattern," she told him softly, and he nodded.

"It was a long scarf that could be looped over itself under her chin. It hid the damage very well. It looked nice."

"The scarf was important to you?"

He nodded again. "It was something I could do for her. She was a pretty woman, and I wanted her to look pretty in her coffin. I didn't want to see that she had been beheaded. I didn't want anyone to see that.

"Not that there were a lot of people at the funeral. My father, my son and daughter, and my daughter's husband Brian. Stan Oberlin, Mrs. Abernathy, and a few other people came from the firm. But of course there were no cousins or neighbors or people from our church. It rained that day."

"But you were pleased that she wore a pretty scarf?"

His elbow rested on the arm of the blue chair. He held up his right hand, looked at it vaguely, and turned it from side to side. He regarded it with cheerless eyes. "I wonder, when a person's head is cut off, how does the undertaker keep it—the head, you know—from rolling around in the coffin? Do you know how that's done, Doctor? Did he sew Julie back together? Or use some kind of glue? Or clips? Or little braces, like bookends, you know, that her hair would have hidden? What?"

"I don't know how it's done. You didn't ask at the funeral home?"

"I didn't even think about it then. A week later, I began to think about it." He suddenly realized that he was talking too much. He was there to talk of course, but he couldn't reveal to her how he had obsessed for months over the question of Julie's head. *She'll write me off as a nutcase. Well, I suppose I was just about crazy then. And then I won't be able to ask...*

He heard her calm voice. "Try to remember how pretty Julie was, how much you loved her. Remember her looking pretty in her coffin, wearing the scarf you picked out to hide her ..." she started to say 'neck' and then switched to 'wound.' Neither seemed quite right, so she repeated, "It's hard, I know, but you've told me there are good things to remember, too."

"Yes," he said, "there are." He knew this wasn't the time to raise the question that he wanted to raise. He would postpone it. He made an effort to pull himself together, and, although she hadn't really asked him anything, he said in the most cooperative voice he could summon, "Yes, Doctor, that's what I'll try to do."

In her little notebook, Dr. Glazer wrote "Depressed. Intense. Suffering. Obsessed with details of accident and death."

AT THE CEMETERY

Early August 1978

I copied out a poem to put here by your grave, Julie. I needed a stone to hold it down. You'd laugh at how hard it is to find a big loose rock when you live in an apartment house in New York City. I went to a garden shop and bought a paving stone.

I wonder if the author of the poem lost someone who was as dear to him as you are to me.

I wonder if God ever makes a mistake.

I wonder a lot of things.

Anyway, here's the poem:

> **Joy is a partnership.**
> **Grief weeps alone;**
> **Many guests had Cana,**
> **Gethsemane had one.**
>
> ~Frederic L. Knowles

My heart feels like the stone I couldn't find. I weep alone.

Chapter 8

PATIENTS ENTERED DR. GLAZER'S OFFICE suite through the door to the reception room, the door with her name and degree lettered on the frosted glass in gold and black. The room was pleasing, done in relaxing earth colors and subdued lighting. It held a few recent copies of *Smithsonian*.

The receptionist, Mimi Dunnowitz, greeted patients warmly. If they were a bit early, she asked them to be seated. If the doctor was waiting, she waved them down the corridor.

"Go right in. Dr. Glazer is expecting you."

The corridor, about ten feet long, was a buffer between the office and the inner sanctum, between business and the intensely personal. It was a rather narrow passageway with soft, recessed lighting, designed to reassure patients and to signal that they were stepping into a private world where every word they spoke would be held in the strictest confidence.

Actually, the space on either side of the corridor was practical. On the left, behind paneled and polished sliding wooden doors, were closets, storage areas, and file cabinets. On the right was a unisex bathroom where another closet held Victoria Glazer's coat and spare umbrella, after-work clothes, a box of accessories, and a small tray of cosmetics.

Patients leaving the office, after their session (or their "conversation," as the doctor preferred to call it), exited directly from her office by a door marked "Private." This discreet arrangement protected the privacy of all patients. They did not pass each other coming or going. There was never a need for the small, embarrassed nod or half-smile of recognition.

Julian, however, followed a different routine. During his first visit, he had asked Dr. Glazer for another appointment, and, because the receptionist had left for the day, the doctor walked to the front office with him to check the book herself. From then on, he was always the last appointment on Friday afternoons, and he continued to leave by the main door. Dr. Glazer double-bolted it after him, returned to her office, made final notes, added a splashy scarf or clever piece of jewelry to her professional outfit and brightened her lipstick. Usually, she had plans for some social event on Friday evenings.

Chapter 9

JULIAN HAD BEEN SEEING DR. GLAZER for almost three months when, after his usual Friday session, he walked into the front office with her and saw a young woman, about twenty years old he guessed, sitting there quietly.

Mimi Dunnowitz talked frantically on the phone. "Yes, Mrs. Bellington, Lori's here; she's fine. She came back to the office when your chauffeur didn't show up. Yes, I told her. The problem is how to get her home. A taxi…yes, I understand your concern, but the cab company says their foreign drivers are very reliable. Well then, could she ride the subway? It's just a block over. Mrs. Bellington, I don't know what to do. But I'm already fifteen minutes late leaving here, and I have an appointment I can't miss. Oh, here's Dr. Glazer now."

With relief, Mimi clapped her hand over the receiver. "The chauffeur had an accident after he dropped Lori off. The roads are slippery, and someone skidded into him. He's in the hospital, the limo's in the repair shop, and Mrs. Bellington is demanding, I mean *demanding*, that something be done." She handed over the phone, grabbed her pocketbook from her desk drawer, and, with a glance of harried apology, went out the door.

Lori spoke up, "Mr. Dempsey's been driving for Grandma forever. She thinks a limo is the only way to go. I could certainly get myself home by subway, but Grandma really isn't strong, and she might keel over from high blood pressure before I got there."

Dr. Glazer, who had hastily covered the receiver, now removed her hand and said soothingly, "No, we don't have a doorman at this building, Mrs. Bellington. I'm sorry I can't bring her myself, but I'm catching a train in just a few minutes. No, no, don't call an escort service. Those escort services in the phone book aren't really what you want. There's just no one available to bring Lori home, but it's still fairly light out, and this is a safe neighborhood. No, I don't think the police do private transporting. Oh wait …"

With a "may I?" gesture, Julian reached for the phone. "Mrs. Bellington, my name is Julian Elsmore. I'm a friend of Dr. Glazer's. She'll vouch for me, I'm sure. I happen to be here at the office, I have a car and free time, and I'll be glad to give your granddaughter a ride home." He listened a moment and said, "Certainly." He passed the phone back to Dr. Glazer and, pulling out his wallet, handed her his driver's license.

"Several months. Absolutely dependable. Head of the Reliance-Ryan Insurance office here in Manhattan. Yes, a fine, old-line company. Mrs. Bellington, I'm going to read you the numbers on Mr. Elsmore's driver's license, and then," Dr. Glazer, looking at the slip of paper that Julian had quickly scratched on and handed to her, continued, "I'll give you his license plate number, just for your peace of mind, and we can all be on our way. Lori should be home in less than half an hour. What? Oh." She pulled a comic face, winked at Julian, and said solemnly, "Episcopalian, I believe." Briskly then, she hung up the phone.

"Thank you," said Lori. "I'm sorry to be so much trouble. Grandma likes to run things her way."

"No trouble at all," said Julian kindly, "but we'd better get going."

The doctor, fidgeting to be gone herself, told Lori, "Accidents are upsetting, even second-hand ones. Take it easy." Then she patted Julian on the shoulder and murmured, "A knight to the rescue."

He was surprised to find himself wondering about his psychiatrist's plans for the weekend.

Chapter 10

───────────

JULIAN ELSMORE LOOKED AT THE YOUNG WOMAN he was squiring to his car. She had an oval face, clear skin, and even features. She wore no make-up. Her hair was clean, medium brown and straight, and pulled back in a ponytail. Her jeans were nondescript, frayed at the hem, and the flannel work shirt that topped them was an uninspired, small plaid. Obviously, she had taken no pains with her appearance. He wondered if it was just indifference or if she was making a statement.

Mindful that she customarily traveled in a limousine, he asked politely, "Where would you like to sit, front or back?"

"Front," she said without hesitation. He helped her in and, as soon as he himself was settled into the driver's seat, told her, "There's a map of the city in the glove compartment. Will you get it, please, and show me where you live?"

"It's not far, about twenty minutes. I think I could direct you."

Nevertheless, he asked her for the street and number and traced the route with his finger. "We don't have time to get lost."

She nodded. "Grandma will have the police out hunting for us if we're late."

He eased out into traffic, and, after a few blocks, she said amiably, "This is a nice car." It was a one-year-old Buick Le Sabre, sober black but jazzed up by a dark red leather interior. The chrome was discreet. He kept the car very clean.

"Yes, I like it," he said. "My wife picked it out."

"She has good taste."

"Yes," he said again. "She does. Have you always lived with your grandmother?"

She was startled by the abrupt questioning but responded easily enough, "Oh, no, just for the past four months."

"Because?" he prompted.

"You don't have to make conversation."

"I was just wondering why a normal-looking young woman doesn't wear make-up and sees a psychiatrist."

"You're pretty blunt." She smiled wryly. "It's not a scandal, not even a secret. I just turned nineteen. My fiancé, that's Bill Letterson, we went to high school together, and I wanted to get married right after we graduated, but my parents think I should go to college. They don't have anything against Bill, really. They hardly know him, but they say life has lots to offer and I shouldn't be tying myself down to a blue-collar guy when I'm so young."

"Parents are like that."

"I guess. My mom sort of enjoys poor health, and I try not to upset her. And Dad, he's a high school teacher. Anyway, we compromised. I agreed to come live with my Grandma in exciting New York City for a year. I thought it might be sort of fun, actually. Anyhow, I didn't want to quarrel; quarreling upsets Mom and she faints. When I'm twenty, Bill and I can be formally engaged, and we can be married on my twenty-first birthday."

"It *is* an exciting city," he said and immediately thought that he didn't really know that firsthand. Worse, he sounded like a parent. He cleared his throat. "And are you having fun?" he asked Lori. He thought that she looked and sounded rather sad.

"Well, not *fun* exactly. It's okay here with Grandma, you know, different. I miss my parents. Mom doesn't like the phone, so I write to them twice a week. But my Grandma and I have sort of clicked too, and she seems pleased to have me around. She's opinionated, in a funny sort of way. We're just getting to know each other.

"I'm taking a couple of courses at a community college. And I babysit a neighbor's twins, a boy and a girl almost three years old, every Wednesday afternoon so she can get a break, you know. And I see Dr. Glazer, just someone to talk to. Her father, Dr. Henry Glazer, and Grandma have known each other forever and Grandma thinks Dr. Vicki will help me 'adjust.' She doesn't say what I'm adjusting to, but I like Dr. Vicki so it's okay. Grandma pays for it.

"What courses are you taking?"

"Biology 101 and History of England."

"Biology? That's a surprise."

"It was that or basket weaving. No, excuse me, not really. I took biology in high school, see, but we had a substitute teacher almost the whole year. She didn't really know any biology, so we didn't learn anything. But we had a great time goofing off, and she gave everyone either an A or a B, so no one complained."

"My question was, are you having fun in this big city?"

She thought about that. "Well, not really *fun*. When you were nineteen, were you having fun?"

He was startled. "That was different. When I was nineteen, I was married. My wife and I were expecting our first baby, happy about it. It was a serious time." Running alongside his words, memories came rushing, which he thought was strange. He remembered those years with a sudden, bright clarity, as he had not let himself remember happiness since Julie's death, and he smiled. "Yes, I was delighted with our life. Sometimes we did silly things."

"Oh, doofus me, I let you drive by the entrance." She indicated a gracious, white Victorian home set deep in a grove of old maples. "That's where I live. Well, never mind. Just take the next turn, right here. It's a circular drive, see?"

He swung the car smoothly into the drive that she indicated but then slowed to a crawl. "Will I get a ticket for entering at an exit?" he asked solemnly. She looked blank for a moment. "You know, is it as depraved as walking up the down staircase?"

She giggled. He liked hearing her giggle. "Drive on. I'll vouch for you."

He walked her to the door and said, "I'd like to meet your grandmother. I'll reassure her. Don't you think I look sober and honest?"

"Well, maybe, but you're Episcopalian."

"That's not good?"

"It's not exactly bad, but Methodist would be better. Grandma has always been a pillar of Trinity Methodist Church."

"Amazing. Actually, I grew up Methodist in Paducah. Back there, *my mother* was the pillar."

She looked at him suspiciously, but, before she could inquire further, the door swung open. "Hi, Munchkin," she said. "How's Mr. Dempsey?"

"Left leg's broken. But he feels worse about the car. Crumpled fender. He never had an accident before. Not even a scratch in fifty years." The butler shook his head dolefully and muttered, "Poor old lad. Doctor says a week in the hospital, and he won't be driving for at least six weeks. I think maybe never again. Clean break, though. I'm glad you weren't involved, Miss Lori."

"Thanks, Munchkin. Ask Grandmother if I may bring Mr. Elsmore in to meet her, will you please?"

The butler departed at a dignified pace, and Julian looked around the massive foyer. "Are you always so formal?"

"Pretty much so. Grandma's coming up on ninety years, and her world is even older."

"Is the...uh, butler really named 'Munchkin'?"

She giggled, "His name is Mr. Munchen, but I just can't resist. Either he thinks it's funny too, or he hears what he expects to hear. We're good friends, you know. I wouldn't hurt his feelings for the world. Listen now, when I introduce you to Grandma, don't put your hand out to shake unless she puts hers out first."

"Ye gods," was all he said.

Mrs. Bellington received Julian with a genial nod. She didn't offer her hand, but she expressed sincere thanks for his bringing Lori home safely. "New York is a dangerous city," she commented, "full of marvelous sights and experiences, of course, but dangerous."

"Always has been."

"Which is why careful families always see to it that their daughters or granddaughters are properly accompanied when they go out." She stated it as a fact, and Julian thought that she was a woman accustomed to making statements. It was perhaps also a way of explaining her earlier apprehension about taxicabs and subways. She looked Julian up and down and made a decision. "Won't you sit down, Mr. Elsmore?"

Julian sat with a murmured *thank you* and wondered where he could take the conversation. He wondered if he should explain that he wasn't Episcopalian and didn't want to sail under false colors. *Or is that too personal?*

No need to wonder. Mrs. Bellington, adept in social situations and responsible for directing the conversation, noted his slight southern drawl and probed in a most courteous manner, "Are you native to New York, Mr. Elsmore?"

"Not at all, ma'am. I moved here about six months ago from Paducah, Kentucky." He decided against mentioning that William Clark founded the city and asked himself what a careful grandmother would want to know. *Ah!* "It came about as a transfer from the Reliance office in Paducah, where I'd worked since I was a young man, to the New York City office." No need for him to add that it was a promotion. She would deduce that. Also, it told her that he was stable, responsible, and respected. *Not bad*, he thought.

"And did your family move with you from Paducah, Mr. Elsmore?"

"Both my daughter and son are young adults, Mrs. Bellington, and out on their own. My wife," he took a deep breath and continued, "was struck by an automobile shortly after we moved to New York. She died as a result."

"Oh my, how very sad. My condolences. Then you are in mourning still?"

"Yes, I am mourning."

"This must be a very hard year for you. A sad year."

"Yes."

"We need our faith, need to believe that God has a plan, don't we?" She paused and bowed her head for a moment, then moved the conversation along briskly, moved it to closure. "Mr. Elsmore, I do want to say again how very much I appreciate you bringing Lori home. So fortunate that you were at dear Vicki's office."

Whoa. She thinks I'm a friend of Dr. Glazer's—well, I told her that myself, a little stretch—and an Episcopalian besides. "Ma'am, I don't want to leave you under a false impression. I am a patient of Dr. Glazer's—because of my wife, you understand. We had been in the city only a few days when my wife was killed. We had had no time to make friends here in New York. I needed someone to talk to, a confidant, as it were. So... anyway, I was thinking, since your chauffeur will be laid up for several weeks, and since I see Dr. Glazer every Friday, just as Lori does, I'd like to offer transport for her appointments, both ways, until things get back to normal."

Mrs. Bellington hesitated. *What can I say to reassure her?* "I also need to clarify that Dr. Glazer was guessing when she told you I was Episcopalian. I was raised Methodist."

"Oh really? And have you joined a church here in New York City?"

"I've been thinking I should do that."

"Indeed, you should. I belong to Trinity Methodist, myself. I know the congregation—some fine people, both Dr. Glazers are members—and I know they are most welcoming to newcomers. Gabriel Wellington is the pastor. "

"Thank you. What a great name for a minister." He stood and waited. "About...?"

"About Lori? Well, if you're sure it's not too great an inconvenience, Mr. Elsmore, thank you. It will certainly ease my mind until we can make other arrangements. I hate to feel rushed, and it's so hard to find good help these days." For a moment, he thought that last line was said jokingly but realized immediately that the old lady was sincere, even somewhat indignant.

She put out her hand then to show him, he surmised, that he was not considered "help," good or otherwise. He shook her hand lightly but firmly in return, careful not to press her gorgeous rings into her frail fingers.

"Lori will see you to the door."

Lori did, and he was surprised by a ripple of merriment in her voice. It contrasted with her sober clothes and indifferent manner. "Wow, you're a hit. I can tell that Grandma thinks you're a proper young fellow."

He gave a little snort, cast her a sidelong look, and thought that she would be quite pretty if she made any effort. He arranged a time to pick her up on the next Friday. He would have to leave the office a half hour early, which gave a bad example, but, since he was the boss, it was doable.

He was positive that Mrs. B, in her role as a careful grandmother, would call Dr. Glazer and confirm her quick estimate that he was "a proper young fellow," that he was not some sort of pervert. *Who knows why anyone sees a shrink?*

AT THE CEMETERY

Mid-October 1978

A few weeks ago, I met a woman who reminds me of you, Julie, the way you were when we finished high school and got married. She lives here in New York with her grandmother but she says she engaged to a boy back home. Her name is Lori Seever. She's sort of cute but very young—only nineteen. She sees Dr. Glazer just as I do but I don't really know why. I drive her to her appointments. It's kind of complicated how that happened.

I've met Lori's grandmother, too. She's not a feeble old lady who rocks and knits and plays bingo. More a benevolent dictator. Interesting. Very rich, I think. Very old.

Julie, you were never too young or too old. You were always just right. How I wish you were here, still "just right."

Without further comment, frowning a little, he walked down to his car and drove back to his empty apartment.

🌺   🌺   🌺

Chapter 11

"Mr. Elsmore?"

"Speaking."

"This is Mimi Dunnowitz from Dr. Victoria Glazer's office. Dr. Glazer finds it necessary to cancel all her appointments for the present. We'll be in touch to reschedule in about a week. Sorry for any inconvenience."

"Wait, don't hang up," he said. "What's wrong?"

"Nothing, Mr. Elsmore, I assure you. We'll be in touch very soon."

"May I speak to the doctor, please?"

"Why, she's not here. She's...uh. "

"What's wrong, Mimi? Is she sick?"

"Well, not really sick. I'll call you when she can start seeing patients again."

"Mimi," he said, "what's up? Don't give me the runaround. Dr. Glazer wouldn't cancel her appointments without a reason." Then he asked an outrageous question, knowing it might produce some information. "Is she having a midlife crisis?"

Mimi denied it with an indignant gasp. "Of course not. Mr. Elsmore, I've got a bunch more calls to make, so please let me get on with it."

But he continued to be provocative. "For the checks I write, I think I ought to know why she's canceling."

Mimi sighed. "Dr. Glazer had an emergency appendectomy two nights ago. I'll call you later." Then she did hang up.

It took only a few minutes for Julian to locate the hospital where Dr. Glazer was "doing as well as could be expected" and learn their visiting hours. Then he called Lori. "Dr. Glazer has cancelled us for tomorrow."

"I just heard. Do you know why?"

"An emergency operation. She had her appendix out at St. Luke's. Now, here's what I suggest …" He was thinking fast, not as carefully as he usually did. Somehow, he simply didn't want his soothing, placid Friday routine to be whirled away. *Can this Friday be saved?* he asked himself facetiously, remembering a *Ladies' Home Journal* series that Julie had often quoted. *Or is it off to O'Reilly's at last?* Somehow, it seemed important, as if Friday and Dr. Glazer were an anchor in his life.

"Lori, I remember you said your grandmother is family friends with the Glazers. And we're both her patients. Shouldn't we pay her a quick get-well visit? If it's okay with your grandmother, I could pick you up at the regular time tomorrow, and we'll stop for flowers or something, and afterwards we could grab a hamburger or pizza or whatever. Think you can work it out?"

"I can try. Grandmother likes you, so maybe yes. Fun in New York City. Oh, I don't mean 'fun' that Dr. Glazer is in the hospital; that wouldn't be nice of me at all. But since she is in the hospital, well, you know, something different."

"I understand. Call me back as soon as you can." He gave her his office number and added, "Remind your grandmother—I'm sure you can do it adroitly—that visiting the sick is a Christian work of mercy."

"Adroitly? You mean, not make a major point, just slip it in sidewise?" She reproved him, "You Methodists are certainly sneaky."

"Just good tactics, nothing sneaky about it," he replied, his voice a bit piqued, but he was satisfied with himself when he hung up.

Chapter 12

THEY STOOD, LOOKING AROUND the large florist shop. There were all sorts of containers, and such a choice of blooms! Julian wondered why a flower shop also sold a variety of exotic teas and herbal soaps. *A little surprise to tuck into a bouquet perhaps? Wouldn't the flavors, well, the odors, no...the scents, that was it, fight each other?*

"What do you like?" he asked Lori. "I know what we don't want: one of those silver baskets with a high handle and lots of gladioli and fern." *The last time I ordered flowers, it was for my wife's funeral, and that's what I ordered, the big, silver basket of gladioli and a blanket of yellow roses for the casket. Am I morbid, thinking of that now? I've got to stop. Julie has been dead over six months. I've got to stop.*

Instead he remembered that the clerk, sensing his confusion, had murmured that the silver basket was a very appropriate choice and had suggested that he might like a casket blanket of roses. "We have white, pink, yellow, or red."

"White," he had said and then immediately countermanded it. "No, yellow, I think. Julie liked color." *What does it matter?* he had thought at the time. *Will she know or care whether they're white or yellow. Black,* he had thought, *black roses would be appropriate. It didn't matter. Nothing did.*

Wandering ahead, unaware of her companion's sudden melancholy, Lori spotted a display of dish gardens. "These are nice...Oh, look, look here, Julian. I bet Dr. Glazer would like this one, see, there's a wee elf sitting right next to that little cactus. See his red cap? He has a flute, too."

He looked. The container was grey-green pottery, irregularly shaped, probably hand thrown, and only about three inches deep. It was filled with plants in a variety of heights, and, sure enough, there in the middle, was a tiny ceramic elf dressed in a green and brown jerkin and wearing a red cap with a tiny feather in it.

He managed a chuckle, more at her enthusiasm than at the dish garden itself. "So shall we take it?"

And she said gravely, "I vote for that."

"I'll make it unanimous." He signed the card that the clerk handed him without trying to be witty. It already said "Best Wishes," and he simply added their names, "Lori Seever and Julian Elsmore."

Chapter 13

JULIAN SAW SURPRISE AND PLEASURE in Victoria Glazer's eyes when he and Lori walked into her hospital room. It was just past the dinner hour. She was looking a bit washed out in a white hospital gown, but her hair was neatly combed, and she wore soft lipstick.

"What a nice treat to see you." she said smiling.

Julian shrugged. "Well, it's Friday. We always see you on Friday, and we didn't want to let a misbehaving appendix stop us."

"Yes, Mimi told me you had *tricked*—I believe was the word she used—her into giving out more information than I authorized."

"An inflamed appendix isn't a scandal, is it?"

"No, but it doesn't build a professional image either, especially if you had seen me a few days ago, bent double in agony and screaming for help."

Lori was instantly sympathetic. "You're feeling better now?"

"Better, but not tip-top. I need a few more days of rest, and that's why I've canceled my appointments for the next week."

"Well, we aren't here as patients, you know," Julian said. "Mrs. Bellington thinks our visit is a Christian work of mercy. As for Mimi, the guard dog, we won't snitch if you don't. This is just a friendly visit, all right?"

"Good enough. And for my part, I won't tell Mimi you called her a dog."

He blanched. "Ye gods, I never intended…I put my foot in it, didn't I?"

With a light push on his arm, Lori took charge. *Just like her grandmother*, he thought. *I'm surprised. Very smooth. Yes, like her grandmother. Or like Julie.*

"We won't stay long or tire you," she said. "We just wanted to see how you're feeling and bring you this." She put the dish garden on the bed tray, swinging it so that Victoria could undo the green wrappings.

"Beautiful!" she exclaimed when the planter was revealed. "Just beautiful, and oh look, there's an elf—isn't he darling? Or is he a pixie?"

"He's whatever you want him to be," said Julian. "He's here to cheer you up. Well, if you canceled all next week, then that means …"

A whirlwind burst through the door, a whirlwind preceded by a huge bouquet of red roses. "Vicki, my dahling, I came as soon as I heard. What have you done to yourself? They say you'll live. Is that true?" He blew her a kiss.

"Rance, you're home again." She blew him a return kiss. "Yes, in all probability, I'll live. It was just an appendectomy."

"I heard, I heard. I couldn't believe it. So banal. You, my sweet, are an exotic flower, and, if you are going to be ill, it should be some mysterious disease blown in on zephyrs from the Orient, a bafflement to your doctors. But an inflamed appendix! How commonplace! I repeat, how banal! How humiliating! I can't believe it of you."

"Rance, for goodness sakes, hush. Just do something with all these flowers. They're lovely, thank you, but they'll make me sneeze."

"Your wish is my command." He turned to Lori, noticing her for the first time. "Perhaps this delightful young lady, or …" As an aide came through the door, he said, "Angel of Mercy, can you find a vase for these blooms?"

"I'm here to fill the water pitcher. There are vases under the sink."

Ransom DeVoe smiled charmingly at Lori, who, somewhat reluctantly, found a vase, filled it with water, and observed, "The stems are too long. Anyone have a scissors?" The aide finished her task and whisked out the door as if she hadn't heard the question.

Victoria seized the moment to make introductions. With a noncommittal 'How do you do?' nod to Ransom DeVoe, Julian pulled out his pocketknife and walked over to stand beside Lori at the sink. He folded up a bunch of paper towels to make a cutting surface, picked up two flowers, and sliced about eight inches off, cutting diagonally. "Will that do?"

"Sure, whatever."

"I'll leave the ferns taller," Julian said, continuing to trim rose stems. Lori jammed the ferns in behind the roses, and Julian carried the bouquet to the far windowsill.

Ransom beamed on them and continued his chatter. He was just back from Istanbul by way of Paris. "Istanbul," he noted, "was a surprisingly modern city in parts, but, oh, it had its dark, dangerous, twisting streets too. Perilous, even for a photographer with a well-paid guide." "But," he finished, "I got some great pictures, and my editor is happy."

He turned negligently to Julian to mention that editors make a point of being dour and breezed on to say that Paris, now, was a city he loved, always and forever. He asked if they had ever been there, not waiting for an answer.

Victoria was looking exhausted. *Why wouldn't she be?* Julian thought. He rose to leave, and she thanked him and Lori again for the dish garden. "I'll probably be here until next Wednesday. Please come again. I'll be stronger. More up to a visit."

Just as they walked out, Victoria sneezed once, heartily. And then again. Julian, somewhat irritated, hoped that it didn't tear her stitches, or her staples, or whatever.

"Ransom. What kind of name is that?' he scoffed as he walked down the corridor beside Lori. "She should call him Rancid for short. She should."

"And I think you're a little jealous, Julian." Then, before he could deny it, she went on, "Rance is his nickname, just 'Rance.' It's rather a dashing name, Julian. Southern, I think. Sounds like it anyway. But red roses," she said and sniffed disdainfully, "How terribly, terribly commonplace! How banal!"

He looked at her sideways, "Then we did good?"

"We did. We certainly did."

Chapter 14

EARLY IN NOVEMBER, Mrs. Abernathy had told Julian that Reliance Insurance always hosted a Christmas party. "Nothing rowdy or wild, like some companies, but most everyone attends and brings their spouse or another friend, and kids, if they have kids, of course. We have a fine buffet and exchange of gifts."

"Who plans it?"

"Well, I've done it for the past twelve years, and Carmie Rizzio helps, and Mr. Redensfeld always approved the invoices immediately so the vendors got paid before Christmas. Only now, well, it'll be up to you; that is, if you intend to continue the party. I'll be glad to help however you want."

"By all means, let's continue. You take charge, whatever you did other years," he said. "I'm sure you do a fine job. Give me some details. Is there a regular date?"

"Not the Friday before Christmas, but the Friday before that. We knock off at one, so the buffet is really lunch—steamed, seasoned shrimp, little pigs in blankets, tiny potatoes dipped in cheese, mushrooms and scallops wrapped in bacon ..." She stopped because he held up his hand in mock defense.

"I'm getting hungry. Sounds great. This is all catered?"

"Except dessert. We ask people to bring a favorite goody. Makes it interesting. People bring everything from brownies to snickerdoodles.

Bachelors tend to show up with petits fours or cupcakes from the bakery. We've used the same caterer for years now. Very satisfactory."

"And the gifts?"

"The exchange gifts are something general, under five dollars. A Christmas tree ornament, a box of chocolates, a two-pound tinned ham… And then the company always gives each employee a gift, everyone the same."

"Like what?"

"Something quite nice…in the thirty-five dollar range. Last year a snow globe with a Currier and Ives winter scene, and, let me see, the year before, a lovely, white wool scarf from Iceland. It can be something very practical, like a coffee maker, or something unusual and special. Anyway, it's for you to decide or maybe ask your…" She stopped abruptly and then finished lamely, "Or maybe you could appoint a committee."

Realizing her embarrassment, he said quickly, "I'll figure out something. Don't worry."

"Mr. Elsmore, will you actually come to the Christmas party? You don't socialize much. You're all business, which is good in its way, but…"

Her question was soft, and Julian remembered Stan saying, when he introduced her, that Mrs. Abernathy "takes care of us all." He hesitated over his answer, and she went on, "I know you are in mourning—it's only a half year since your wife's death—but please come. Everyone will be disappointed if you don't."

"Day after tomorrow," he said. "Day after tomorrow, it will be seven months exactly since Julie's death." It was somehow important that the time be precise. "Well, Mrs. Abernathy, I can promise to stick around at the party for a couple of hours, although I have an appointment every Friday at five. I'll bring an exchange present, and I'll make a short list of suggestions for the company gift and get it to you by the end of the week. Anything else? Do I have to make a speech?"

"Just a few words. 'Good to be enjoying this time together,' 'happy holidays,' that sort of thing; unless, of course, you want to say more." She drew a careful breath and, made bold by her long tenure at Reliance, added, "Mr. Elsmore, do you ever think that it's better to mourn a good marriage than to live a failed one?"

"What?"

"Well, so many marriages—and relationships too—turn out to be miserable. You were…How long were you married? Over twenty years?"

"Nearly twenty-four years."

"Happily?"

"Very happily." He spoke reluctantly. He didn't want to be drawn into this personal conversation. When Julie and he were married, they knew they were happy; there was no need for words or any kind of analyses. Their friends in Paducah knew, and some perhaps envied them. And since her death, well, how could he talk to strangers about their marriage? He was barely able to talk to Dr. Victoria Glazer about it. Mrs. Abernathy was a business associate and clearly a kind woman, but he didn't want to discuss the state of his heart with her.

As he turned away, he heard her say, "I didn't even have two happy years."

He almost hated his own need to be polite. He turned back towards her and, through gritted teeth, asked, "Why was that?"

"Joe couldn't stand the babies, twins," she said simply. "The crying, the burping, the diapers. He loved the girls, I think, but, at the same time, he couldn't stand them, couldn't stand being home with them all the time and me being so busy with them. He wasn't the type to help, so he started running around on me. On our second anniversary, he packed a suitcase and left. That was the end of my marriage. He died a few years back."

"He left you? With two babies?"

"And no money." She smiled grimly at the bad memory. "Those were tough times. But you see what I'm saying? You and your wife had a good marriage for twenty-four years. You raised a terrific son and daughter. I've seen their pictures on your desk. And hers there too, such a pretty woman. You've a lot to be thankful for. Twenty-four years."

"And a lot to grieve over," he blurted out with a thickness in his throat.

"Your choice," she told him almost flippantly and hurried off, as if sorry that she had spoken.

He wondered if he should thank her for her caring, for the glimmer of truth she had shown him. "Oh, Mrs. Abernathy!" he called after her, but, if she heard him, she did not turn. *Well,* he thought, *I hadn't really wanted to continue that particular conversation. I'm lonely, at loose ends.*

I'm weary of grieving. I know that. It would be a comfort to talk to Mrs. Abernathy about Julie, just a low-key, ten-minute chat, maybe. But, no, I'll not get involved in an office friendship. That would be stupid.

He couldn't help wondering how Mrs. Abernathy had managed to survive and who had helped. *She must have had help,* he thought. *Someday I'll ask her.* She was generous-hearted and strong. He admired her.

He made his way to his office, sat down, and made a note on his "to do" pad: "Decide on office Christmas gift by Friday." On his mental notepad: *Think about blessings.* He wondered about chatting with Mrs. Abernathy and wondered if she could keep a confidence. Once again, he cut off the thought abruptly. *Don't go there. Talk to Dr. Glazer.* Office associations, he had observed, could easily grow over-friendly and were usually ill-fated.

Chapter 15

"Did you ever go out with any other girl?" Dr. Glazer had asked.

"No."

"Before you were married? After you were married?"

"No, I didn't even think about it."

"And Julie? Did she ever date anyone else?"

He took a moment to reflect. He considered where to begin and how to explain Julie, his lovely, never-fully-netted butterfly. "One day when we were sixteen, just starting our junior year in high school, Julie announced in a sort of careless manner that she was going to try dating some other guys. I asked her why, and she told me it was just for fun.

"'Might be interesting,' she said. 'Or maybe I just want to see if I can. I think I'll try Fats Moffat.'

"Fats was a senior football star, a really big man on campus. And good looking. All the girls were after him. He wasn't fat at all; that was just a funny nickname because once some fan had yelled, 'Yay for Mur fee Mof fat-fat-fat-fat.' And it caught on. He was 'Fats' like Robin Hood's big, brawny pal was 'Little John.'

"Anyway, I asked Julie how she thought she would get a date with Fats.

"'Watch and see,' was all she said, flinging her words over her shoulder as she hurried off to Social Studies.

"I thought the whole idea was sort of revolting. Well, I did watch, and all I saw was the next day at lunch she stopped by Fats' table to whisper to one of the girls there, and then she looked straight at Fats and laughed and batted her eyes at him. When she and I went to the movies on Friday like we always did, Julie told me not to come over to her house the next night because she had a date with Fats.

"'Just going out for a drive along the river,' she said. I told her to be careful. That he was fast.

'I'll be careful,' she promised.

"When I saw her out in the yard on Sunday afternoon, I walked out and asked her how her date went. 'Not bad,' she said. 'Well, not good either. Fats got really mad when I wouldn't let him put his hand up my skirt.'

"I was appalled. 'How'd you stop him?'

"'I told him not on the first date,' she said.

"I thought about that for a minute. He was a big guy, but so was I. Actually, he was about two inches taller and on the football team, a good athlete. I was on the boxing team, in good shape and probably knew some tricks he didn't. 'I could beat him up for you,' I offered seriously, and I was so furious with him in my heart that, if she had simply nodded, I would have been glad to rip his face off.

"'Don't you touch him, Julian. We're going to the movies together next Saturday.'

"That sort of stunned me. When I asked her why, she just looked wicked. 'I want to see that flick. And I want to teach the big jerk a lesson. I'll wear my skintight jeans. Hard to get on and hard to get off. The fly doesn't have a zipper; it has buttons.'

"'Fats can't do buttons?' I asked.

"'And I'll have my little can of Mace along if I need it, or I could put my finger in his eye or…Look, I took a course in self-defense, you know,' she said.

"'It won't be a first date. He'll be expecting…something.'

"'He won't get anything; that's the point.' She spit her defiance out with a funny, little laugh that worried me.

"He *was* a very big, strong guy. According to the scuttlebutt, he was used to girls who would go all the way. Julie's self-confidence worried me. 'I wish you wouldn't go out with him,' I told her.

"'I guess I could stick my finger down my throat and throw up all over his precious car if I had to,' she said.

"In my mind's eye, I pictured Julie on her back, in the front seat, helpless, clawing at Fats and screaming, 'No, I said no!' So I said again, 'Julie, listen, please don't go out with him.'

"'Stop worrying,' she said. 'I'll handle the pig. Anyway, I really do want to see that movie.'

"'If that's all, I'll take you to the damn movie.'

"'Julian,' she exclaimed, "wash your mouth out! No, that isn't all. Before we get married, I really want to know what it's like to date some other guys. And you should go out with some other girls, Julian. Just for the experience. Don't you ever think about it?'

"'No, thank you,' I snapped. 'I know what I want.'

"All of a sudden, in one of those abrupt changes of mood that I was never really prepared for, her voice was soft and coaxing, almost seductive. 'What do *you* want?' she asked, and then, by golly, she batted her big blue eyes at *me*.

"'I want you,' I said, my voice rough, and I stamped off in a huff. And I thought, *Go ahead and have your 'experience' with that big stinker. Maybe you can't handle him, Miss Know-it-all. Serve you right.*

"Such a terrible, terrible thought! I immediately hated myself for it. Oh, why couldn't we suddenly have been eighteen and graduated and married? Sixteen was supposed to be a great age, but it wasn't. It was a neither/nor age, and I distrusted it. I turned back. 'Julie, can't you just skip these "experiences"? They scare me.'

"She laughed. 'Julian, believe me, you look soooo good beside other guys.'

"But that wasn't what worried me, and she probably knew it. She was always pretty perceptive. Then she kissed her fingertips to me and floated serenely into the house, leaving me to deal with my raging adolescent hormones. And I thought, *Like she doesn't know I'm jealous. Maybe part of her 'experience' is to make me jealous.* I hated that thought too, even though, somehow, in a peculiar way, it was flattering."

Dr. Glazer looked up from what had seemed like a reverie. "And did Julie continue to date Fats?"

"No, just those two dates. She told me she wasn't going out with him again, and then her voice got sort of tight, and she said he probably wouldn't ask her. Too bad, because she'd love to turn him down, the big fink. That's all she said, which was okay by me. And we went back to our routine. Movies every Friday night, and on Saturday we'd get together with some of our gang and play Monopoly or make fudge or maybe have a wiener roast and sing around the bonfire in our backyard."

"Ah, I do remember the Fabulous Fifties with pleasure," said the doctor.

"Julie and I had a secret ritual for each weekend too. Right after we got engaged, we each bought a piggy bank, and on Friday nights we would get together and solemnly add to our savings. 'For your engagement ring,' I would say, and she would say, 'For our honeymoon,' and we would drop our money in our banks. At first we only saved a dime or a quarter, but, by the time we were sixteen, we put in a dollar or more every week. Julie was babysitting quite a bit, and I was working after school at the Dairy Queen. I worked ten hours a week and got paid three dollars. I put one dollar in the bank, and, for another dollar, Julie and I could go to the Tivoli, which was a second-run movie house, and afterward I could get us each a sandwich and a milk shake. Hard to believe that today, isn't it?"

"Wow! What did you do with your third dollar?"

"Told my parents I now had pocket money and they needn't give me an allowance anymore. That felt good."

"Did Julie ever date anyone else?"

"Yes. I didn't like it, but, almost at once, she told me she was going to go out with Jim Bean. We called him 'Bean the Brain.'"

"He was a classmate?"

He nodded. "Very smart. She asked him to help her with her chemistry homework, and, next thing I knew, they went on a hike. I could have helped her with chemistry, but I knew she didn't really need any tutoring. It was a trick, you see, so she could be with him. Julie had a streak of mischief, a sort of wildness sometimes. I don't know exactly what it was."

"And did anything come of that?"

"She said he was okay but boring and awkward, although, with time, he might improve. She acted very mature about it. We went back to our easy-going relationship, except I made a special effort to surprise her every now and then—with something unusual like a nutty joke or a little gift, sometimes a few flowers, even some bad poetry that made her laugh.

"Anyway, I learned to never take her for granted. When we were seniors, she had her ears pierced. Right after Thanksgiving, no special occasion, I gave her tiny, sparkly Christmas tree earrings. Nothing expensive but kinda cute. She wore them to all the Christmas parties and let everyone know I had given them to her. Maybe that's what she wanted all along—not to be taken for granted."

Chapter 16

JULIAN AND LORI WENT TO THE HOSPITAL again on Tuesday to visit Dr. Glazer. She was more like her usual self. She told them that she had been walking up and down the hallways some and was going home the next day but would not be seeing patients until the following Monday. By then she felt sure she'd be back at peak energy.

"Good, that's good, but we'll miss coming to you on Friday."

"I thought about that. I'm going to write you a prescription for Friday. I had Mimi bring in my pad." She fished for it in a tote bag, which sat at her bedside. "I prescribe a boat ride around Manhattan. You tourists need to see some of our sights. When we have our next conversation, you can tell me about it—the Statue of Liberty, the other people taking the tour, the smells.

"Lori, tell your grandmother I said this will be good for you. You're looking a bit pale. No, 'peaked.' That's a word she'll understand. Tell her I said you were looking peaked. Also, tell her it's perfectly safe; Julian will be with you."

"That will help. She has decided that Julian is very reliable."

"As I most certainly am," said Julian.

"Dr. Glazer," asked Lori, "why is 'peaked' better than 'pale'?"

"When your grandmother was growing up, around the turn of the century, young ladies from well-to-do families were fashionably pale. Farm girls who worked in the fields had the great tans that we strive for today.

Anyway, pale skin was beautiful, but your grandmother certainly wouldn't want to hear that you look peaked, as if you were getting sick. You might actually be going into a 'decline,' another great, old-fashioned word."

Julian glanced around the room. "Where are your roses?"

"I sent them down to the nurses' station. They did give me sneezies... or maybe the ferns did it. It was sweet of Rance to bring flowers, and he'll never know I passed them on. May they brighten the staff. He's off to the west coast on a new assignment."

Julian said, "Humph. Good for Rancid."

"I saw those roses when we walked by the desk." Lori sniffed. "They aren't holding up. Kinda droopy."

"Listen, you two, Rance is a friend from childhood, a good friend. He's flamboyant and extremely talented, often impossible, and quite rude sometimes. I know that. He's also quite gay, and his longtime companion died recently. I wouldn't hurt him, ever. Life's been tough enough."

Julian had the grace to redden slightly, and Lori said, "Oh...well, sorry. We didn't realize ..."

"But, as you can see, my little elf is still here. A well-behaved lad, just sits there quietly, except, when I'm drifting off to sleep, he plays a tune on his tiny flute for me. Did you tell him to do that? It's very soothing."

They both laughed, a little self-consciously, and then practical Julian recovered enough to do his part to change the subject. "Is there someone to take care of you when you get home?"

"My neighbor, next apartment over, says she'll come and fix dinner and eat with me until I'm tired of either her or her cooking. Otherwise, I'll just be careful. I'm pretty mobile, but if I feel lazy, I'll conduct an experiment in doing nothing. Some of my meals I'll order in, just because I've never done that. I'll catch some z's in front of the TV for a few days. That will be new to me too. I've never in my life had time to waste time. It will expand my professional understanding of a couch potato." At their rather blank looks, she murmured, "Means really, really, really lazy. Don't worry. I have my father and a few friends I can call if I need to."

Visiting hours were over, so they started to leave, but, when they had reached the door, Victoria called Lori back. "Just a suggestion, woman to woman. When you go on the boat ride, wear some lipstick so you won't look peaked."

As she and Julian walked toward the car, Lori spoke from deep thought, "Dr. Glazer is a very nice person."

"I think so too, even though we don't really know much about her."

"We know lots, Julian. She's nice, she lives in an apartment, she's not married, and we know she doesn't have a live-in boyfriend to take care of her. Those are important things."

"You're right. Good points, all." He reached over and squeezed her hand.

Chapter 17

"ARE YOU RECOVERED?" he asked as he settled into the blue recliner. Dr. Glazer nodded. "The boat ride was a good idea," Julian continued.

"Tell me what you saw," she prompted.

He told her:

"We saw a marvelous New York skyline, a better view than from Times Square. Lots of other boats and ferries. The Statue of Liberty. Ellis Island. We had a guidebook and followed it pretty closely."

"What else?"

"The trip put color in Lori's cheeks. She looked alive. There were lots of people, lots of couples, a bit crowded. Because it was Friday, maybe."

She waited, and, after a moment, he continued, "I can't tell you why, but I felt good. Better than I have in a long time. Then, right at the end, as we were docking, this weird thing happened."

"Tell me."

"We weren't in any hurry, so we waited until most of the other passengers had gone ahead, and then we started walking toward the gangplank, and Lori stopped suddenly and said, 'Julian, look, there's a baby.' I looked around, and, sure enough, there on the port side, on a bench, was an infant sleeping in a little old basket. It was a sort of ratty looking basket, but, when I walked over, I saw she was tucked up nice and warm. She wore a little, pink bonnet."

"Where's her mommy?" Lori asked.

"I don't know. Did you see a mommy?"

"Yes, I think so." Lori ran to the railing and scanned the passengers walking away from the ferryboat. "I see her, I'm almost sure. That girl hurrying off, see, with the long ponytail, navy windbreaker. Oh, Julian," she continued in a shocked voice, "that woman forgot her baby. How can we catch up with her?"

I told her, "It looks like she left the baby on purpose, dumped her, I'd say. There's a note." I fished out a paper napkin, rather crumpled, tucked alongside the blanket. I read it and passed it to Lori.

> *baby Elena 4 monts good baby.*
> *sory no job no $ for baby las botel*
> *she like you sing*
> *mama*

And Lori said, "Oh, poor baby. Poor little darling. Julian, isn't she sweet? What will we do?"

"A man in a uniform came hurrying towards us, telling everyone, 'all ashore'."

I told him, "This baby seems to have been abandoned."

"Seems what?" he asked.

"Someone just left her here. Dumped her."

"Not your baby?"

"No, indeed," I said.

Lori added, "Her name's Elena."

I shot her a warning look of "don't offer information." And, with that, the darling baby woke, opened her sweet, little mouth, and screamed.

"Well, damn it to hell four ways," said the uniformed man. He pulled out his walkie-talkie. "Chief, it's Jack. We got a lost baby down here, little baby in a basket, and two people, a couple, who say she ain't theirs. Okay, okay."

Elena kept wailing, and Lori asked me, "What's the matter with her? Oh, Julian, what's wrong with her?"

"This baby," I was the voice of experience, "is probably hungry, probably wet or worse, probably wants to be cuddled and sung to."

"Shall I pick her up then?"

"Maybe there's a bottle, the last bottle." I rummaged along the side of the basket and drew out a cylinder wrapped in cloth diapers. I stripped off my cashmere scarf. "Fold it into a pad," I told Lori. Then I said to the baby, "Help is on the way, sweetie." The baby howled all the louder.

I stripped off the nipple cover, shook a few drops of formula onto my wrist, sniffed to see that it was fresh. I handed it to Lori to hold for a minute. I turned the baby onto her side, thinking how you never forget certain things. Then I put the bottle on top of the wadded up scarf and slid the nipple into the baby's mouth. Instant silence. "Hah, that plugged you, little Elena."

Then Jack, the uniformed man, said, "Folks, the captain says we should get on up to the cabin right away." Jack looked at the little basket dubiously, so I reached to pick it up. When the handle started to give way, I simply gathered the basket into my arms, and we moved to the stern of the ferry. Elena lost the nipple en route, but I slid it back into her mouth before she could wind up again. I was alarmed that the bottle was already almost a third empty. And only two diapers. I was glad I had risked getting my scarf sopped rather than getting the diapers wet. Dry diapers would be needed soon, I knew.

Jack led us to the small office but stood aside for us to enter. I set the basket carefully on a bench and glanced around.

"Well, well." The captain was clearly suspicious. "You guys say it's not your baby? You know whose baby it is?"

"No, but there was a note in the basket," I said and handed the paper napkin to the captain, who read it and grumped, "Of all the ferries, she had to pick mine. You sure you guys don't know anything about this kid?"

I told him, "Not a thing. We just happened to be the ones who found her."

Lori hovered, her eyes never leaving the infant except to glance at me. She understood my message, "keep quiet."

The captain reached for the phone. "Let the cops sort it out."

Elena's sucking had slowed somewhat, and her eyes began to droop, but, as I well remembered, that didn't mean a thing. *Yes, indeed*, I thought, *let the cops sort it out.*

Lori was horrified, "You're calling the cops? Where will they take her, Julian? What do cops know about babies? Don't let them take her!"

"The police will handle it. Don't jump to conclusions," I said.

"The police know what to do, there's regulations," the captain explained. "They'll probably call social services or drive her to a hospital where people will take care of her. Don't you fret, little lady, she'll be all right." He spoke into the phone and then informed us, with relief in his voice, "There's a squad car in the area. Be here in five minutes, ten tops."

"Can we stay until they get here?"

"Well, see here, I've got another sailing yet today, loading," he looked at his watch, "in about four minutes." He called to the man outside the door, "Jack, get these folks off the ferry and up to the ticket office. They can wait there. And get back here on the double."

I picked up the basket and followed Jack ashore. Lori tagged after us. We were a strange little group, watched silently by the people waiting behind the chain to board the last tour of the day.

Just before we reached the ticket office, we heard a short toot from the boat. Jack spun around. "I gotta go, folks. Good luck."

Lori and I entered the office to blank looks. The woman behind the desk huffed, "You want to make this last tour, you gotta hustle. Babies don't need a ticket."

"We just took the tour," I said. "When we were leaving, heading ashore, you know, we found this baby all alone in a basket on a bench. The captain phoned the police, and they're coming here to get the child." I fished the crumpled napkin from the basket and handed it over.

"No one called me." The woman looked at us as if we were criminals and then read the note. "Hey, Ray!" she called. "C'mere, will ya?"

Ray came and read the note aloud. "I'll be damned. You say the police are on the way? This ain't your kid?"

"We took the tour. We were among the last to go ashore. We saw this baby. Someone had left her behind. We're just trying to do our duty as good citizens. The captain told us to come here and wait for the police," I said.

"Sure, sure he did. Dumped it on us." Just then, thankfully, a squad car pulled up, and two cops got out. Their arrival did nothing to make the little office friendlier.

"Julian," Lori spoke almost in a whisper, "can I pick her up and burp her?"

"Let sleeping babies sleep," I replied.

"Well, can I take her home, just 'til the cops find her mommy?"

"No. Shhh." I knew that I sounded exasperated, but my heart told me that she's so terribly, terribly young. I didn't mean the infant. I meant Lori. *Young and inexperienced,* I thought, *a little bit lonely, and of an age to want a baby of her own.*

"You see the baby's mother?" the older cop asked me.

"Lori may have."

"Can you describe her, miss?" he turned to Lori.

Lori was surprised when I gave her a tiny nod. She told the officer, "I'm not sure it was her mommy, but there was a young woman standing right by her …"

"How young?" the cop asked.

"Maybe my age—I'm nineteen. Skinny, less than medium height, black hair, wore jeans and a navy blue windbreaker, ponytail. Her hair …" Lori paused. "Well, it didn't look real clean, a little oily maybe. I noticed her because she'd been crying."

"She say anything?"

"Not to me. And then she was gone. I ran to the rail and saw her—I think that's who it was—leaving the boat in a big hurry."

"Notice anything else?" the cop asked.

"Just that the baby is wrapped up warmly, and her mommy left a bottle and some clean diapers," Lori said.

"The basket is falling apart," I added. "The baby just finished the bottle."

Elena didn't seem to wake, but she squirmed, got red in the face, and gave several significant grunts. "I'm not taking care of *that,*" said the woman behind the desk and she told the police. "She's your problem."

"No one asked you to help, ma'am. She'll be okay for a few more minutes." The older cop pushed a little notebook at me, "I need your names and your address and phone number."

I wrote and Lori hung over the basket and mourned. "Oh, Julian, no one wants her. Please find out where they're taking her. Find out if I can visit her, maybe in a day or two."

I handed my business card to the policeman. "If I can be of help, reach me here. This young lady is Lori Seever. She lives with her grandmother,

Mrs. Clarissa Bellington. I'm a family friend. I've written Lori's name and Mrs. Bellington's address and phone number in your notebook. If there's nothing else, we'll be on our way."

I moved to the basket to get my scarf but instead just patted the little girl. "This handle is loose, officer, it won't hold," I said.

"Noted."

"Let's go, Lori."

Lori's eyes were wet and doubtful. "You will take good care of her, won't you?" she asked the cop.

"Sure thing. That's our job," he said.

"Oh, I almost forgot,' I said. "I need to call Mrs. Bellington. May I use your phone?"

The woman at the desk was irritated. She glared at me. "This isn't a public phone. There's a pay booth outside to the left."

I went outside, found some coins, and made my call. "Mr. Munchen, Lori and I have been delayed. Please assure Mrs. Bellington that Lori is perfectly all right. Absolutely all right. It just happened that there was an incident as we left the ferry. We weren't involved—not personally—except we were witnesses, so we had to give our statements to the police." I listened, then continued, "Just emphasize that Lori is okay. We're hungry so we're going to get a bite to eat now. I'll have her home in about an hour and a half. Thanks, Mr. Munchen." In silence, we walked to my car. When we were settled in the front seat, I turned, looked at Lori's wet face, and asked, "What?"

She blew her nose.

"I don't understand. Why didn't you want me to talk to the ferry people?"

I explained, "They had the basic facts. You were the one person there who might possibly be the baby's mother. They'd wonder how come you knew the baby's name."

"Well, it was written right there in the note."

"And who wrote the note?" I said. "Anyone might have. That's how police think, Lori. I didn't want you to give them any ideas or display any emotion that they could speculate about. I didn't want you to be needlessly involved."

"But, poor Elena," Lori said.

"Yes, poor baby. But let the cops handle it. They'll get her to where she'll be taken care of. They'll look for her mother. You know, it's a crime to abandon a child. I'm not sure just how the New York laws read but the cops know and they'll handle it."

"They'll arrest Elena's mommy?" Lori's tears flowed again. "That's not right."

"No, no," I assured her. "They'll probably find some help for her. Listen, Lori, there's a fast-food place up ahead a few blocks. Let's get something to eat and maybe a milk shake, and we'll discuss all this." She sniffed and blew again, which I took for an 'okay.'

Over hot, greasy hamburgers (they were delicious), I explained what I thought would probably happen. Elena would be taken to a hospital and be checked over. Then Social Services or Child Services, whatever, would find a foster home for her while the police searched for the mother.

"Most likely the mother will stay right here in the New York area," I continued. "They'll look in the barrio, but it's unlikely she has relatives in this country. Hispanics have a strong family system, and normally the extended family would manage to keep the child even if they scolded the mama for getting pregnant. Just guessing, but I think she doesn't have family in this country, not in New York anyway, and her boyfriend must have skipped. She probably had a job, but now she can't work and take care of her baby too. Anyway, it's likely she doesn't have the resources to go much of anywhere, so she's probably nearby. She needs a job, food. There are lots of ways of tracking her, lots of places to look."

"If they find her, will they arrest her?" Lori asked.

"I don't know. Maybe, just to keep an eye on her, you know, detain her until they arrange help. Look, Lori, don't start crying again. It won't do any good, and it will scare your grandmother. That's one reason I didn't want to take you home straightaway, all red-eyed and drippy-nosed."

"Oh, good thinking, I guess." A little embarrassed, she sat up straight and dried her eyes. "But, Julian, I want to know what happens. I feel connected, like it *is* my business, and I should know what happens to that baby. Is there a way to find out?"

"Doubtful, but maybe," I told her. "On Monday I'll see what I can do."

"Why Monday? Why not tomorrow?" she wanted to know.

"Tomorrow is Saturday. Don't bother people on the weekend and expect them to be jolly. But on Monday it will seem perfectly reasonable to want to recover my scarf—it's an expensive scarf, cashmere—that I put in the basket to prop the baby's bottle."

I gave her a sideways look of amusement. "See, I was going to take it back, get it dry cleaned, but I left it there because I had a notion you'd want to follow up."

Her eyes widened. "What a hoot. You Methodists *are* sneaky."

"Not at all. I'm just a nice, helpful guy. So I'll chat a bit at the police station, and they'll probably tell me they think the scarf was still in the basket when they dropped Elena at such and such hospital. That will be my next stop."

"But what if someone at the police station helped himself to your scarf?" Lori asked.

"Doesn't matter," I said. "They'll tell me that it went along with the baby. See, Lori, I'm not really going to be looking for the scarf." *Not even though Julie gave it to me*, I thought and then continued, "The scarf is just an excuse to make inquiries and find out which hospital or office to go to next."

"Oh." She was quiet for a few minutes, sucking on her straw and noisily slurping up the last of her chocolate milk shake.

"Hey," I asked, "did anyone ever tell you what a straw is for?"

"'What?' she asked.

"It makes that noise to let a nice, young lady know when she has drunk it all."

"Oh, Julian!" She hit me on the shoulder. I reached out and put my hand on her arm as we left the restaurant.

"Listen. We had an adventure. Remember that. Make it a good story when you tell your grandmother. Tell about the note; the little, pink bonnet; and that uptight gal at the ticket office who was so afraid she'd be asked to do something extra. Make it a good story, but not scary or you won't be allowed out with me again." I nosed the Le Sabre into the night traffic.

"Okay, I'll make it good." She was quiet until just before we turned into the circular drive. Then she said, "Julian, I'll make it really good. I like going out with you."

Chapter 18

JULIAN CONTINUED TELLING HIS STORY to Dr. Glazer:

We were returning earlier than I had predicted, but Mr. Munchen had been watching for us. He swung the door open as we came up the stairs and scanned Lori with troubled eyes. "Are you all right, Miss Lori?" he asked.

"Fine and dandy, Munchkin. You shouldn't have worried."

"We didn't exactly worry, seeing that Mr. Elsmore was with you. Still, we're pleased that you're home. Your grandmother asked that you come to her in the back parlor right away."

"Of course. Bye, Julian, and thanks. I'll make it good."

"Do. I'm counting on you."

My hand was on the door when I heard, "Mr. Elsmore, if you have a moment, Mrs. Bellington would like to speak to you also."

"Oh…well certainly."

"Perhaps you would like to clean up a bit first. The lavatory is just down that side hall, sir, first door on the right."

"*Wow*, I thought as I followed directions. *Do I smell like baby? A bit of spilled formula, perhaps? Or was it part of a butler's job to know when a man's bladder was about to burst and make discreet arrangements?*

"Thanks, Munchkin." I laughed and then laughed once again because I had unintentionally used Lori's pet name for the solemn old man.

A few minutes later, I was asking, "Tell me true, Mr. Munchen, am I in hot water for bringing Lori home late?"

"That's not for me to say, sir." The tall man straightened with authority, and the handsome, old head nodded wisely, "But I rather think not."

"Mr. Elsmore, good evening. Please sit down. Lori has been telling me of your incident on the ferry. A remarkable episode, quite exciting." Mrs. Bellington's old eyes sparkled.

"Yes, ma'am. Quite," I said, thinking, *Ye gods, I sound like Munchkin.*

"I've not finished the story, Grandmother, but I can wrap it up for you later. I really wanted to bring Elena home, but Julian said no, and he's going to try to find out next week where they've taken her, and maybe I can go visit. Do you think, maybe?'

"We'll see."

Julian stopped his story to Dr. Glazer abruptly, as if maybe he was saying too much. Vicki just laughed and summed it up. "Well, that was unexpected, but it turned out okay, didn't it? It's a great story, a bonus."

"Yes, we certainly had an adventure."

"Is there more?"

"Not much. Just that Mrs. Bellington didn't seem at all upset. She thanked me and invited me to stay for dinner when I bring Lori home tonight."

Victoria Glazer's eyes widened. "My goodness. Did Lori tell you it's apt to be four or five courses?"

"For Friday night dinner? I was thinking pizza; well, maybe not, not a pizza household, but Mrs. Bellington said it would be informal."

"Did she? I've eaten there, and four courses is what she would call informal. *She* never eats dinner, you know. She 'dines.' Always has and always will—even when she gets to Heaven, and Heaven better have the table set properly. Well, good luck. You realize this may be something of a test?"

"Ye gods, of what? My table manners? I've been eating a lot of those TV dinners lately, but I think I can remember which fork to use." He frowned. "You're scaring me."

"Maybe you should be scared. I think she has her eye on you." She shooed him towards the door. "Go along. Lori is waiting, and tardiness is frowned on."

As he walked down the little hallway, all that Julian hadn't told his therapist flashed through his mind.

Mrs. Bellington, ramrod straight in her chair, had said, "Mr. Elsmore, I find myself once again in your debt for looking after my granddaughter. What a comfort to know she's with a competent man and that she listens to you. Perhaps when you bring Lori home next Friday, you'll stay and dine with us. We'll want to hear if you've discovered anything about the baby during the week."

Julian was startled by the invitation. When Lori gave him a high sign from behind her grandmother's chair, he almost stuttered. He finally managed to say 'thank you' and added, "That will be a treat for me."

"Good then. We dine at seven. We're quite informal," she said.

And he thought, *Informal like this parlor is informal? All antique furniture, Persian rugs, beveled mirrors in gilt frames, and paintings worth many thousands?* But he reassured himself that an informal meal would surely mean something like spaghetti or, more likely, since this was a formal household, elegant sandwiches, salad, and a brownie. *No, a petit four*, he thought.

"Good night, Mrs. Bellington." He shook the hand she offered. Right at that moment, it would have seemed more appropriate to bend and kiss it. As before, he was careful not to press her diamond rings into her flesh.

Once again, Lori showed him out. They walked down a long and gracious corridor, past a sitting room on one side, a breakfast room and library on the other. Lori giggled. (He liked her giggles, he realized, and found himself trying to say things that would bring them on.)

"Did you see how Grandma shuddered when I said I had wanted to bring Elena home but you wouldn't let me? You got points for that," Lori said.

"Is dinner really informal?"

She considered, assessing him. "It's informal by Grandmother's standards. That outfit you're wearing is okay for a boat trip; I like it, but you would never wear a zipped jacket to dinner, even a navy blue like that. Khakis won't do, either. A business suit will be fine and dress shoes with a spit polish. Conservative."

"Okay, I'm set then. That's my regular outfit that I wear to the office. See you next Friday." He ran down the steps then turned at the bottom to glance up at her. Backlit by the immense chandelier in the reception room, her color high, she looked quite pretty. He wondered if "informal dress" meant that she would actually wear a dress instead of her usual jeans.

She blew him a kiss and smiled as she closed the door. "Good night, Julian. See you next Friday. Thanks."

Chapter 19

"ARE YOU FEELING FULLY RECOVERED?" Julian asked politely as he settled into the blue recliner. It was Julian's second meeting with Dr. Glazer since the hospital visit on Friday and the ferry excursion the following Friday, and he sensed that there had been a change, although he couldn't pin it down. "You look okay now," he observed. "I mean, you look good."

"Thank you. But, since we're meeting professionally, I'm the one who's supposed to ask, 'How are *you* feeling?'"

"Okay, I guess. I went to see Joy. That's my daughter, you remember, and her baby, little Julie." She waited for more. "Well, you asked me a couple of times when was I going to see my granddaughter, but I kept putting it off, and then the Saturday after Elena, I just woke up and called Joy and drove to Philadelphia."

"Why did you do that?"

"Elena, I guess. The baby left on the ferry, you know. She was an abandoned child, and, all of a sudden, I felt that I had abandoned little Julie." Again, she waited. "I hadn't really abandoned her, you know. I've thought about little Julie, dreamed about her. I started a college fund for her, took out another life insurance policy with her as beneficiary, had a top-of-the-line high chair delivered, even though she won't be sitting up for a while, ordered a big rag doll and some soft books from a catalog."

"But you didn't go see her."

"I wanted to."

"But you didn't."

"No. At the last minute, I even cancelled on her christening," he said, and Victoria watched him intently. "I love Joy. I love my granddaughter. But I didn't go see them. I was afraid."

"Tell me about it."

He hesitated. "I'm not sure I can."

"Find a first sentence, Julian, maybe whatever day it was, and keep going. Ramble...or whatever suits you. You know I'm simply a quiet listener. I will never judge you or think ill of you."

"It's not that," he said. "But it was scary. There was a long period—several months—after Julie's death when I was afraid to go to sleep at night because the dreams were so scary. I'd have to take a sleeping pill and, even then, sometimes the dreams would come. But I noticed they were coming less often. I thought I was managing to heal, to accept, you know, that my Julie, my beloved, is dead...gone from me forever.

"But when the baby was born, little Julie, you know, the nightmares started up again, and they were...well, fierce. They terrorized me."

For the first time in the months that Julian had been talking to Dr. Glazer, he tipped the recliner back and raised his eyes to the ceiling. He was agitated. He took several slow breaths to calm himself.

"When my granddaughter was born, my Julie had been dead three months and six days. The nightmares since her death had been terrible, like I said, but they were growing less frequent. Sometimes I would even have a happy dream, nothing elaborate, more like a snapshot, of our kids playing with a kitten or of Julie and me bowling with friends.

"I dreamed that I held my baby granddaughter in my arms. She was a healthy, beautiful child—beautiful—and I was so pleased and so proud. I put her on my shoulder and patted her little back and smelled that special talcum smell, and I crooned to her that Granddaddy would always love her and take care of her.

"Suddenly, she slipped through my arms and fell to the floor, sort of bouncing once as she hit her head, and then...and then her little head rolled off into a corner, like my Julie's." He shuddered. "Other times, I'd be holding her and she would simply evaporate out of my arms.

"I'd wake up, clutching air, my heart pounding, hurting, and I'd weep. Sometimes I couldn't breathe; a giant hand would choke me, and I'd be gasping and struggling, and, at the same time, some little part of me would wonder why I didn't just stop breathing. I couldn't hold onto my grandchild...I hadn't held onto my wife, my Julie."

"When you actually saw your granddaughter, how did it go?" She was back in her professional mode.

He didn't say anything for a few minutes, apparently reviewing the visit in his mind, while he returned the chair to an upright position. A small smile touched his mouth. "It was absolutely wonderful to hold her, wonderful! She's such a solid little person, almost ten pounds now, and she felt just right in my arms. I... Well, I put her on my left shoulder so she lay over my heart. That was good, very good. I felt at peace, healed in some way."

"You didn't feel scared, as if she might slip away?"

"Not a bit of it. When I was driving into Philadelphia, I worried about that, but, once I had my little Julie in my arms, there was no fear at all. I *knew* I had her safe."

"Have you had any nightmares about the baby since?"

"Not one."

"Nightmares about your wife?"

"Almost none."

"Will you go see little Julie and your daughter again?"

"Tomorrow. I thought I'd go every other Saturday. Just day trips. I don't want to get in the way or be a pest to Joy."

She waited, thinking that he was a kind and loving man, suspecting that what he would really, really like would be to live next door to his little granddaughter as she grew up.

"I was thinking too, I suppose I could stay over at a motel every so often, then maybe watch the baby Sunday morning while Joy and Brian go to church, maybe brunch afterwards. It would give them a break." He looked at her, his face solemn, then poked fun at himself. "Am I trying to kid you or me? I *want* to be little Julie's babysitter."

They talked then about his dinner with Lori and Mrs. Bellington the Friday before. "You were right. It was four courses."

And she couldn't resist teasing him. "Told you so, didn't I?" *What is happening with me and this man? I talk to him as if he is more friend than patient.*

"But simple." He ticked off on his fingers and said, "Tomato juice, Caesar salad, a main dish of haddock filet, asparagus and rolls, key lime pie for dessert, and caramelized pecans in a cut glass candy dish. All very good. All served by a middle-aged maid named Elsa."

"My parents," she told him, "moved in the same social circles as Mrs. Bellington. They were almost a generation younger, but they knew the stories. She's so proper now, but my mom said she was truly a madcap debutante, an honest-to-goodness flapper with bobbed hair, short skirts, plenty of fringe here and there, and a rope of pearls hanging to below her waist."

"I wouldn't have guessed. She seems so, well, maybe 'reserved' is the word."

"After she married the Colonel, who was at least eight years her senior, she settled down to being a proper socialite, and among the city's Four Hundred, she was very powerful, an arbiter of fashion, too."

"I can believe that. Even when she is not expecting any guests, like that first time when I brought Lori home from your office, she was perfectly dressed as if expecting company. She's not one to lounge around in her bathrobe."

"In the nineteenth century, her century, she would have been 'properly gowned.' Get with it, Julian. 'Getting dressed' includes putting on undergarments. No lady used a sexy term like 'getting dressed' when conversing with a male."

"I just meant that she's never caught hanging out in her bathrobe."

"Oh, Julian, Mrs. B has never even worn or mentioned a bathrobe. Once in a while, a hot summer day perhaps, she might wear 'a morning gown.'"

"'Bathrobe' was a no-no word? You're kidding."

"Think about it. Associated thought: bath/naked."

"Wow! What a lot of inhibitions."

"You understand I'm talking about 'ladies' and polite conversation. My mother knew a woman who served 'limb of lamb,' wouldn't utter the word 'leg.' Of course, common women, as opposed to ladies, you understand, washer women and scullery maids and ladies of the night, for example, had a different vocabulary, including some pretty salty language."

"I find Mrs. B and the way she phrases things quite charming."

"There aren't many of her generation left. They have mostly faded away, leaving her lonely, although she would never admit it. Having Lori there has put a new spark in her life. She enjoys Lori."

"Somehow, I feel a sense of power in Mrs. B. I've noticed that, in her own, very nice way, Mrs. B moves people around on a chess board until everything is suitable according to her lights. She's a born organizer, but sometimes it makes me feel a bit itchy."

"Don't begrudge. What's left to her but power? I've seen her in my mother's scrapbook. She was a beauty. There were constant headlines about her dinner parties, her balls, her charities, even her wisecracks. When she heard that Prohibition had become law, she was shocked. 'But what are we to do? We simply can't have cocktail parties without cocktails.'

"Enough of this, Julian. We've gone off track with all this history. Tell me, what did you talk about when you dined with Mrs. Bellington and Lori?"

"One more question. When was Lori's mother born?"

"Alexis was, for the times, a late baby. Born around the mid-twenties. A much quieter era. And Lexie—that's what they called her—was a much quieter type than her mother. Introspective, I guess you could say. Read a lot of poetry. Married late. Now, tell me, did you report on Elena?"

"Not until supper was served. I knew Lori was bursting to ask me while we drove from your office, but she held off until her grandmother could listen, too. She's thoughtful that way. As soon as grace had been said, Lori asked if I had found Elena. I said I knew where she was."

"Where? Tell me," Lori demanded.

"With her mother."

"But her mother doesn't want her."

"Her mother's name is Maria, and she always wanted Elena."

"Didn't seem that way."

"Moms want their babies, Lori. Besides, I talked to the social worker who handled the case. Moms give up their babies when they realize they can't take care of them, can't give them all the things that babies need.

Maria is only seventeen, even younger than we guessed. She didn't know how to get help. She doesn't speak English well. She panicked."

Mrs. Bellington asked, "This mother and child have found shelter then?"

"Maria is living at a group home with three other young women who are expecting babies or already have infants. Sort of a cooperative. There's a resident manager who oversees the program, but the girls rotate the jobs: cooking, cleaning, laundry. They share childcare."

"Can I go visit?" Lori asked.

"Certainly not now. It's not allowed."

"Why not?"

Julian explained that Maria was very young, very busy building a new life, and needed no distractions from her old life. "I think that rule is meant to protect the young women from their boyfriends who want to get back together or from abusive husbands. But it covers us as well. I suppose we can send things, however, things to support the program."

"Like what?"

He reached into his experience. "Disposable diapers, baby powder and lotion, toys and books, money." Lori's eyes brightened, and he thought again, *She's of an age to want a baby of her own.*

"It would be fun to pick out some toys. Or some cute, little outfits."

"What about Maria's education?" asked Mrs. Bellington.

"That's part of the program." He reflected that Mrs. B, tutored by the Great Depression, by widowhood, and by her church work, was far removed from her debutante days. Once, she would have thought a husband would be the solution to Maria's problems. Times had changed, not necessarily for the better, in Mrs. B's opinion, but she recognized that Maria needed some way to make a living if she was to raise a child in a tough world.

Julian wondered if he should answer the question about Maria's education in greater detail. He sensed that both women were genuinely interested, and so he told them what he knew about Maria's program. "Babies need constant care, Lori. No weekends or vacations for mommy. You can't put a baby on a shelf and tell it to stay there, safe and sound, while you go to class, no matter how important the class is. Childcare classes are taught right there, at the shelter, and the girls who have babies bring them along."

"That's certainly 'hands-on' learning."

"Yes, and then Maria goes out to ESOL classes three times a week. She arranges for another girl to take care of Elena while she's gone. None of the girls can afford to pay for help, so it has to be an exchange of services, a sort of barter. Maria is learning to use the resources she has, to be organized and responsible, to set goals. It's all under the eye of the resident manager, who is a qualified social worker."

Mrs. B looked a trifle befuddled, which was unusual for her. "I can appreciate that Maria needs to learn childcare. What is the class she goes out for?"

"It's called ESOL, English for Speakers of Other Languages."

"ESOL. That's new to me."

"It's a government program. Fairly recent. Free. Available wherever it's needed across the country. Immigrants need to learn English in order to become American citizens."

"That program sounds complicated—and expensive. It must be almost private tutoring for some people. Spanish, well, I can understand classes for Spanish, especially in New York City. But suppose the immigrant is from, say, Latvia? Or Senegal? I should think it would even be a chore, maybe an impossibility, to find a competent teacher. Who would know if a person from Latvia even speaks their own language correctly? Maybe there are Latvian hillbillies who have their own dialect." She giggled and he thought that Lori had inherited her giggle. "I don't even know if there are hills in Latvia," Mrs. B went on. "I'll have to look it up. In any event, how would you go about finding a person competent in each one of, for example, the African dialects? How would you ever?"

"That's the beauty of ESOL, Mrs. Bellington. Each student may have a different original language. That's what they call them: 'original' or 'first' languages. The teacher's only language may be English, but that's what she or he needs to teach."

"You mean a teacher can…How is it done?"

Julian was remembering. "A lot of mime. A lot of pictures. A lot of imagination. It's amazing to watch."

"You visited the class?" Lori was indignant, feeling she had been left out.

"Not Maria's class, Lori. Back in Paducah there was a Literacy Council that petitioned to teach an ESOL class in our parish center. I was a councilman at the time. I was asked to look into it and make a recommendation, so I observed a class in another part of town. As I said, it amazed me."

"The instructor doesn't speak the language, the original language, of any of her students? How can that work?" Mrs. Bellington persisted, and Julian wondered what explanation he could provide. *Something very simple*, he decided. He yearned for an easel and a huge blank pad but had to start without props. Five minutes later, he had walked them through a basic lesson.

"The teacher draws two figures on the board, clearly a man and a woman. She labels them, points to one, and says 'woman,' points to the other and says 'man.' She cups her ear, points again, and they repeat after her 'woman, man.' She puts her hand on her chest and says 'I am woman.' They go around the room, saying to each other 'I am man' or 'I am woman.' The teacher draws a circle, or maybe a heart, enclosing the stick figures, and goes on to say 'husband, wife.' If there is a married couple in her class, she uses them too. She has deliberately drawn the circle wide, and, eventually, there is a child, then children. She circles them all once again with her chalk. 'Family.' Family is a universal concept, so the students catch on quickly and are pleased with themselves."

"But they *must* learn to read and write," Mrs. Bellington said firmly.

"Well, yes, but speaking comes first, just as all of us spoke English first before we went to school."

Mrs. Bellington considered. "That's true. We don't learn to talk in school. We learn to talk when we are very young, without teachers or rules."

"But, for newcomers who don't understand English, learning to talk, to communicate, is essential. How can you ask directions, apply for a job, explain a sickness or why the rent money will be late if you can't talk? So we have ESOL."

"Julian," said Lori, "teach us something in ESOL. How do you do it?"

He demurred and thought that perhaps he was boring them. "I'm not an ESOL teacher, Lori. I've just observed a couple of classes."

"You could do what you observed."

He hesitated again, but, when he looked at Mrs. B, her eyes were as bright with interest as Lori's were, and she nodded in encouragement. "Well then," said Julian, and he stood up. At a signal from Mrs. B, Elsa, the maid, hastened to remove the dinner plate in front of him. "You're my ESOL class. It's very important that immigrants learn about money." He pulled out his wallet, extracted two dollar bills, and held one up in his hand. "Dollar," he said and beckoned them to repeat.

Still holding the bill in one hand, Julian held up the index finger of the other hand and said, "One dollar." They repeated.

"You have already learned to count, so I can move right on to 'two dollars,' taking the opportunity to review both numbers and plurals." He turned to an imaginary blackboard, mimed a dollar sign there while he pronounced it, and had them say "dollar sign."

"Each student would have a notebook and pencil. In my own notebook, I would copy from the board a big dollar sign and turn my notebook so they could see it, and I would cup my hand behind my ear so they would all say 'dollar sign.'

"The teacher of that class I observed told me that students need to hear it, say it, see it, and write it—to involve all four language skills. Then I would point that they should copy the sign in their notebooks and turn the notebooks to me so I could check."

Julian looked in his wallet again and found more bills. "See the '5' on this bill? I'll write '$5' and '$5.00' on the board. You students copy in your notebook." He mimed writing to them. "See the '20' here?"

"Julian, why don't you teach an ESOL class? I could be your aide. Maybe we'd even see Maria," said Lori.

"We're not trained, Lori. It takes more than good intentions. For example, the teacher I watched used the equal sign, wrote it on the board. She had taught it earlier, I guess." And Julian mimed writing, '$1 = $1.00 = one dollar.' You see, Lori, I have no idea how you teach the equal sign to people who don't know the English word 'equal.' Would you know how?"

"We could surely learn how to do it. Someone could teach *us*, couldn't they?" She sounded annoyed, and Julian, dismayed to see the disappointment written on her face, struggled to finish on a warm note.

"Near the end of class, this teacher produced a jumbo candy bar. Some of the class, especially those with kids, already knew 'candy bar.' They were quite happy, almost relieved, to see an object that they already could call by name.

"Well, then the teacher showed a picture of a grocery store, and then she gave the candy bar to a student with a whispered instruction. She stepped out of the room, taking her pocketbook, then came back immediately and said distinctly as she opened her purse, 'I want to buy a candy bar.' She put her finger on the candy and asked, 'How much?' The 'clerk' replied, 'One dollar.' The teacher wrote '$1' in her notebook and held it up. The exchange was made, and then the role-play was practiced by other students. Finally the teacher pulled a sack of Hershey kisses from her tote, saying with gestures, 'I give you a kiss.'

"The students were smiling. I gathered they had done something like this before. They responded, 'Thank you for the kiss.'

"Whew." Julian sat down. "That's all I know. This class is dismissed."

"Very, very interesting," Mrs. Bellington complimented with a smile. Then, pronouncing her words carefully, encouraging them to respond, and nodding to Elsa, all in one graceful gesture, she said, "I-offer-you-a-piece-of-pie."

Julian played the game. "Thank-you-for-the-piece-of-pie."

Mischievous Lori, her usual good spirits restored, joined in. "Pie-is-good. We-are-fresh-out-of-kisses."

"Well," said Victoria Glazer when Julian finished his account of dinner at the Bellington's. "Well, well. You seem pretty bland on first acquaintance, Julian, but that's not true, is it? Still waters and all that... You're full of surprises. Here's a question. Do you think this is a good connection for you with Mrs. Bellington and Lori?"

"I think we are becoming friends, my first real friends in New York. After dinner last Friday, Lori and I visited with Mr. Dempsey, the chauffeur, you remember. He always lived over the garage, but, after the accident,

Mrs. B had him moved into the big house because he couldn't manage the garage stairs. He's mending, getting around slowly with a walker, but he's pretty old."

"And what did Mr. Dempsey have to say? Is he alert?"

"Well, we just talked about the limo. He's certainly right on top of that. It's a classic, a Lincoln Model L. Very special. Fifty years old now. It was in the shop after the accident, but the man who serviced it says it still runs like a charm. Mr. Dempsey's proud of it. He's the only one who ever drove it, but he knows he'll probably never drive again, and he worries how Mrs. B and Lori will get around. Not that Mrs. B goes out much."

"And Lori?"

"You mean, suppose she has to go to the dentist or something, how will she get there, especially since Mrs. B has no faith in taxi drivers? I can't answer that. I'll do what I can, of course, but it's an open question. We'll see, I guess.

"Yes, of course, but it's really not your problem, Julian."

The coolness in her voice floated past him.

He said, "Meanwhile, Lori drops in to see Dempsey every day, brings him a little treat or a new magazine, sometimes a gardening catalog. Dempsey is the yardman too. She stays and chats for a few minutes."

"Good for her."

"I'm invited for dinner again tonight."

"Well, let me ask you another question. Are you thinking of teaching ESOL?"

"Maybe. It's in my mind. It was in my mind, and Julie was interested too, back in Paducah."

"We'll talk about it later, if you wish. Time's up for today."

She walked to the outer office with him. Lori was reading, sitting beside the table that held the dish garden that they had given her. The plant was thriving. They both thanked her and wished her good night. As she locked the door after them, she mulled over Julian's comment, "We're becoming friends."

"*So?*" she told herself shortly. "*He needs friends.*"

Chapter 20

JULIAN, SEATED IN THE TRINITY METHODIST CHURCH's Fellowship Hall, sniffed the good smell of roast turkey and stuffing and the brown sugar aroma of baked ham. All about him were smiling people plying him with food and drink and snippets of conversation. The sign that hung from the ceiling at the far end of the big room read "ANNUAL HARVEST DINNER." He looked in the other direction and saw another banner that read "BOUNTIFUL GOD, WE GIVE THANKS FOR FOOD AND FRIENDS."

Humm, he thought, *and just how did I wind up here?* There wasn't really any question. He knew exactly how it had happened—arrangements by Mrs. Bellington, social engineer. Now she sat across from him, obviously delighted to be here and to be chatting with old friends. Lori sat beside her, dressed as conservatively as a teenager could manage, eyes bright, and hair softly curled. *Pretty Lori*, thought Julian, and he was glad that the young woman had fixed herself up to please her grandmother.

Mrs. B was clearly proud to introduce Lori to all of the friends who stopped by. From time to time, when she thought it appropriate, she introduced Julian too, but not so often that he didn't have an opportunity to eat. She herself, he noticed, ate very little.

The maneuver had begun the week before, when he had been enjoying another of those congenial, "informal" dinners with Mrs. Bellington and

Lori. It was now pretty much taken for granted that, when he brought Lori home from Dr. Glazer's on Friday night, he would stay and dine with them.

"Next week is our Annual Harvest Dinner at my church," Mrs. B had said. "I used to attend regularly, even volunteered when I was younger, but then, well, these last few years, I just didn't feel up to it. But it's always quite festive, and Lori's never gone, so I was thinking—since it's on Friday—if you would kindly be our guest and escort, we might make a night of it. It's a fundraiser for the missions."

What could he possibly have said? He was cordially invited on a night when she knew he was free. He was clearly needed as driver and escort. It was a good cause, the missions. *And maybe*, he thought, *my attendance would be a small way of repaying Mrs. B for her invitations to dinner.*

He had begun to look forward each week to Friday night when he had the pleasure of eating dinner with friends, so he said, "Thank you. Sounds good to me." They discussed details. So, here he was. Lori passed him a bowl of stuffing, and, as he helped himself, a very young man, clearly a church worker, appeared with a gravy pitcher.

"Best gravy in all New York," he announced. "Get it while it's hot. Our pastor makes it himself."

"Everything tastes good. Just like our church dinners back home."

"Where's home?"

"Paducah."

"Where's Pah-*doo*-kuh?" But the young man was laughing in a friendly way.

"Paducah, Kain-tucky. You'll learn that next year in sixth grade."

"Ouch! I'm in tenth grade, Mr. Paducah, and I'm old enough and smart enough to know I should move on right now. Anyway, here come the raffle kids. Thank you, sir, for eating with us."

A trio of high school kids approached the table. A girl and a sheepish boy were carrying a big tray. It held an elaborately frosted flat cake, which was shaped like the church, bell tower and all, as if someone had taken a snapshot of the church from the front.

The third teenager, clearly the spokeswoman for the group, announced with missionary zeal, "We're raffling off the church. Fifty cents a chance or, our special for this evening, two chances for a dollar."

Lori laughed and produced a dollar. Mrs. B did the same. Julian pulled a twenty from his wallet, saying, "Don't bother with change."

"Julian, you'll have forty tickets."

"I'm in to win." (That was as close as Julian ever came to a lie.) "I'm counting on you to help me keep track of those tickets, Lori." Later he took chances on a quilt stitched by the Ladies Guild and still more chances on a clock radio. He hoped that he wouldn't win. He was just trying to support the church.

Despite the many chances that Julian held, someone else won the quilt and someone else won the clock radio. But, when the numbers for the cake were read, the luck he'd been counting on to keep him winless ran out, and he heard Lori squeal, "I have that stub. It's one of yours, Julian. You've won the cake!"

The parishioner running the raffle hustled up. "Hi, I'm Harry. May I see your ticket please?" He took it from Lori, checked the numbers, and then, using a big spoon as a gavel, he rapped loudly on the table. "Folks, we have a winner! Kids, bring the church over here. This cake goes to Mister…" He turned to Julian, who obligingly filled in the blank. "To Julian Elsmore. And where are you from, sir?"

"I'm from here in New York and am delighted to have won this beautiful cake. It's truly a work of art." There was a round of hearty applause and, under the cover of it, Julian made a quick decision and leaned in to speak softly to Harry, who nodded and rapped with his big spoon again.

Julian stood and cleared his throat. He seemed quite at ease, and his deep voice carried to every corner of the big, quiet room. "I moved to New York City just last April. I have not yet joined a church, but Mrs. Bellington, who kindly invited me here this evening, has certainly recommended Trinity Methodist. And I've been thinking about it." He looked down at the cake. "Winning this cake—this church cake—is a sign, don't you think? I hope someone from the membership committee will give me a call in the next day or two. Reach me at Reliance Insurance."

There was another round of hearty applause. Mrs. Bellington smiled benignly. "One more thing," Julian continued, and he managed to keep his voice steady. "I live alone. There's not much freezer space in my refrigerator. I don't even think there's enough counter space in my apartment to hold this magnificent cake, so I have suggested to Harry that he raffle it off again. But I do want a sample, so I ask that whoever wins it, please cut me a piece to take home." Julian sat.

Harry took over, shook up his bag of tickets, and held it out to Mrs. Bellington. "Oh my," she said as she reached in for one of the little green pieces. "What an honor."

Harry called out the number, and there was a happy shout, "I won, I won! Over here."

Julian returned to his stuffing and gravy. Someone hurried along to refill his coffee cup and to say, "Welcome to our congregation."

Mrs. B beamed and said, "What a remarkable evening this is turning out to be."

Lori looked across the table and spoke admiringly, "Julian, you said all the right things."

"I hope so."

"Just on the spur of the moment, you said all the right things. You even got in a plug for Reliance. How do you do that?"

He shrugged, smiled, and helped himself to a little more ham. No reason to point out that he was twenty-three years older than she, that the years had given him time to take a Dale Carnegie course and many opportunities to practice. He was enjoying the meal. Except for Friday nights at the Bellington's, there had been only TV dinners in his life recently.

Just then a rather breathless woman bustled up to the table, two adolescent boys in tow. "Hi, Mrs. Bellington. What a nice man you brought to our dinner." She turned to Julian. "I'm Elsie Lindly, the winner after you, and these are two of my five greedy children. They thank you." She gave the boys a look, and they chorused a thank you. She handed Julian the knife and plate that she had brought. "I want to be sure you get your piece before they carry it off and round up their friends and demolish it."

"Where should I cut?" he asked.

She eyed the cake carefully. "Anywhere you like. Even the bell tower if you really want it."

"No no. I think a piece of the foundation."

"Take the cornerstone, why don't you?" It was Lori's suggestion.

He looked at her. "Good idea. Symbolic." He cut his piece from the cake, and the teens immediately grabbed the tray, one of them so eager that he mushed a green frosting shrub with his thumb.

"Hold it, Bub," he ordered his brother. With a smart-aleck grin for his mother, he scraped up the entire ruined bush and licked it from his thumb. "Let's get out of here."

Mrs. Lindly sighed indignantly, "That Les. I've been trying to civilize him for fifteen years, and one of these days ..." Pausing only a moment more to welcome Julian, she tore after her offspring.

Mrs. B was pleased. "Now you'll always have a special connection to the Lindly family. Fine people. They own an office supply store and a bookstore. Amazing, isn't it, how things turn out?"

"Amazing grace." *Perhaps Reliance Insurance can steer some business to the Lindlys.* He'd check it out.

Next came a plump woman who announced that she was the baker of the cake. "It had required three bowls of batter," she told him proudly, "and over an hour to frost." Then she added, "I have a little business decorating cakes for special occasions; here's my card." She observed that, if they had started selling tickets again for the second drawing, they could have made more money.

Julian managed to murmur, "I should have thought of that."

Ms. Cake Decorator (it was weeks later that he learned her true name) moved on, and his hand was grasped by a tall, distinguished-looking man. "I'm Henry Glazer, Mr. Elsmore. Welcome to you. Neat speech. It added to the evening. You made everyone feel good." He turned to Mrs. B. "Clarissa, dear lady, I heard you were here. I've been on duty in the kitchen and never want to see another green bean. Just caught a break. It's wonderful to see you out and about. And this is your only granddaughter, Lori, is it?" He reached across the table and gave the girl's hand a formal shake.

"Lori, dear, meet an old friend, Dr. Glazer, Vicki's father."

Julian suddenly made the connection, but, not knowing how confidential his status was as Vicki's patient, he said nothing.

"Have you had your dinner, Henry?"

"Years ago it seems; I vaguely remember." He surveyed the table. "I'll just make up a ham sandwich and see if I can get a cup of coffee."

Even as he reached for a roll and looked around for a server, one showed up, cup and saucer in hand, saying, "If you'd rather decaf, I can be right back with it."

"No no, this is fine." Dr. Glazer, genial but commanding, was a presence not easily ignored. *I bet it's always been like that for him,* thought Julian in easy admiration. *He attracts people, just as his daughter does.*

While Dr. Glazer and Mrs. Bellington murmured of past times, the pastor arrived to introduce himself and welcome Julian. Julian produced a smile and a business card to give to the man. At the same time, another corner of his mind realized that Lori was signaling him. He raised a questioning eyebrow. With a slight tick of her head in her grandmother's direction, Lori mouthed, "Let's go."

"Well, yes, I suppose," he said, but he was unsure how to suggest that they leave. He put his napkin down, rose, and moved around the table. A closer look made him realize that Mrs. B was indeed fading.

Lori was direct. "Grandmother, I think we should call it a night."

"I believe you're right, dear. I confess I find myself a bit weary. Pleased with the evening, but tired." She put her hands on the arms of her chair and raised her body slowly, then leaned against the table until she found her balance.

Julian thought he heard her knees creak into place, and, for the first time, he realized that she was truly old. Almost ninety, Lori had said. *An indomitable spirit, yes, but a weary body. Time to go home.* He noticed that Lori was getting their coats and her grandmother's cane from the hooks along the wall.

"Wait here, I'll bring the car to the front," he offered.

Mrs. B, one hand still flat on the table for support, raised her eyes to Henry Glazer. "So very nice to have talked to you this evening, Henry dear. I hope you'll come and dine with me one of these days."

She raised her free hand, rings flashing, to touch his face, but he caught the hand against his heart and bent and kissed her cheek. "I'll come. I'll phone you."

Mrs. B carried her cane in her right hand and confidently put her left through the crook in Henry's elbow. He guided her carefully to the door just as Julian drew the car up to the end of the chrysanthemum-bordered path and jumped out to help her get seated.

Lori was right there too, carrying the piece of cake that Julian had all but forgotten.

Chapter 21

JULIAN WENT TO BED THAT NIGHT in a mellow mood. *The evening*, he thought, *went well*. He was pleased that he had committed to the church, something he had felt a need to do. People had been friendly, as Mrs. B had predicted, and he knew that it had been a real outing, a treat for her. That pleased him, too.

He had liked meeting Victoria's father. Lori had been a joy to watch also. He felt an odd sort of pride. Although it surely wasn't the most exciting Friday night for a nineteen-year-old girl, Lori had seemed quite happy. She had been attentive to her grandmother, charming to her grandmother's friends, and elated when she had called out that he had won the church cake. *And so pretty she looked*, he thought, *with just a touch of lipstick and her brown hair curling softly.*

Julian woke at four-thirty in the morning in a furious state of mind. Sitting straight up in bed, he said, in a hissing whisper, "She should have been there. Julie should have been there."

He pictured his wife. He pictured her sitting in Lori's place, wide-eyed at a story that Mrs. B was telling. He pictured her leaning over, afterwards, to tease Henry about something, then suddenly remembering that she was supposed to be watching the stubs spread out before her and laughing. He pictured her saying, "I must pay attention here. What if Julian wins something?"

He got out of bed, trembling. His voice was hoarse and angry in the empty room. "Julie should have been there."

He knew about the stages of grief, knew that denial came first and anger second. The reasoning part of his mind asked, *Why am I angry now, this very morning, months after her death? Maybe I'll call Victoria. She's supposed to know about these things.*

Instead he stewed around the apartment in just his pajama pants. He made a pot of coffee and drank most of it, although it had a bitter taste. He peeled an orange, remembering when Julie would peel an orange and share it with him, slice by slice. "One for you and one for me." When it came to the last slice, even if it was her turn, she'd laugh, pop it into his mouth, and say, "For you, because I love you." *She should have been there last night; she should have been there.*

The truth that he wouldn't face, couldn't bear to face, was that he had enjoyed the Harvest Dinner. Of course he wished that Julie had been there, but he had enjoyed himself without her. *Forgive me, beloved. I didn't think I'd ever again enjoy anything without you. Forgive me.*

He wondered if the pleasure and the fellowship that he had felt there at the dinner with Mrs. B, Lori, and Henry Glazer, and with winning the cake and all, had been a sign of healing. *I could use some healing; I want to heal. I want to enjoy life again, and, Julie, I know you want that for me too because you love me. Why do I feel so ill, so rotten, so depressed, so...guilty?*

He dozed off for a few hours, sleeping restlessly, and again came awake with a start He knew that the mother of a young baby should be awake by eight o'clock, so he called Joy then and told her that he wouldn't be driving to Philadelphia after all. "Not feeling well today," he said.

"Oh dear. You sound a bit hoarse; are you coming down with a cold?"

"I went to a church dinner last night. Could have caught a cold, but I probably ate too much."

"Do you have something on hand? Alka Seltzer or something?"

"Sure, don't worry. I'll take care of it."

"We'll miss seeing you, Dad. I love your visits. Baby Julie will miss playing with you."

Already, he was regretting his decision. "Well, listen, I'm going to hang up now. See you next Saturday, Joy. Kiss the baby." He put the phone gently back it its cradle and mopped sweat from his forehead. Maybe he *was* coming down with something after all. *Not likely. I could still go, call Joy back, save the weekend, still play "Where's the baby?" with little Julie. But with this foul mood I'm in, I probably shouldn't be on the road. And, if I am getting a cold, I'm contagious now, so no visiting anyone. What a mess!*

He thought again about calling Dr. Victoria Glazer, not really for advice but just to hear her calm voice, but again he decided not to and shoved the phone aside.

Chapter 22

WHEN THEY LEFT DR. GLAZER'S OFFICE one Friday night, Lori asked Julian if he would let her off at a friend's house. "It's just before we get to Grandmother's. I'll show you where. I've an errand I must do. I told Grandmother, and she said we'd plan to eat at seven-thirty, just half an hour later than usual, okay?"

"Of course it's okay. But perhaps I could just park and wait for you. Or go with you if that would help."

"No." She looked at her watch. "You go on and keep Grandmother company. I just need to drop in on these people, neighbors, you know, something I promised to do, and they live close by. I'll cut across the lawns coming home, and I'll tell you all about it while we eat dinner."

So that's what they did, and, ten minutes later, Julian was sitting in the Bellington's old-fashioned parlor in a chair that wore antimacassars gracefully. He was drinking white wine from a slim, crystal glass, while Mrs. B probed delicately. "You were very generous at the Harvest Dinner, Julian." (He was glad that she had dropped the 'Mr. Elsmore' a few weeks earlier.) "Buying all those chances," she said.

"My pleasure. Happy to support the church."

"But I hope you didn't think you had any obligation to do so. By being my guest, you made it possible for me to attend, which I very much appreciated and enjoyed. There was no expectation that you would buy chances."

He said slowly, "I do believe that each of us should support the religion we belong to, and, since my wife's death, I have been remiss. The chances I bought were just a little way of catching up. Now that I've formally joined the congregation, I plan to do much more."

"Well, that's good then. It's just friendly curiosity, you understand, but I couldn't help observing how freely you spent at the Harvest Dinner. I hope you didn't inconvenience your purse."

My soul, what a quaint expression. "Inconvenience your purse." Right out of the 1890s. He said gravely, "Do not concern yourself, Mrs. Bellington. I am comfortably well-off."

"Thank you for letting me know. And here's Lori. How are the twins, dear?"

"Adorably wicked. Hadn't we better eat, or Cook will ..."

"Yes, if she's not cranky by now, she will be soon." Mrs. B took Julian's arm and remarked, with a quiet smile, as they walked into the dining room, "Cook's old and entitled to be cranky. Sometimes, you know, we old people have these little faults—we're cranky and creaky and sometimes curious."

It was an apology for her earlier prying, and, as Julian seated her, he murmured, "I can understand that." Actually, he thought it was rather comforting to have someone in this big, lonesome city care about him and his "purse."

When grace had been said, Julian shook out his napkin and asked Lori, "Who are the twins?"

"Matthew and Matilda, almost three, and the most beautiful children in the whole, wide world. Also, quite a handful. I'm in love with them."

"And you're their regular sitter?"

"Every Wednesday afternoon. But Connie, that's their mother, asked me to sit tonight too because she and Bob wanted to go out to dinner to celebrate their fifth anniversary. Bob's mother was willing to come, and she's there now, but she really isn't fast enough to take care of the twins by herself. I couldn't do it tonight of course, but I got a friend from my biology class, a very steady girl, eldest in a large family, to come, and I told both her and Connie that I'd look in a little after six just to check. Now I'm starved." She dipped into her bowl of seafood chowder.

While Julian tried to sort out all this information, Mrs. B asked, "And how are they managing?"

"Looking a bit frazzled, but no real difficulties. I suggested Bob's mother take a half-hour break while I was there and have her dinner in the other room. Suz, that's my friend, and I fed the kids, which is always a riot. They're probably in the bathtub right now. They love to splash, and Bob's mother loves to watch them and gather them up in a big, fluffy towel and powder them and sing them to sleep."

She frowned. "You know, when I see Matthew and Matilda, who are so cherished by everybody and who will grow up with advantages, with a head start in life, I think of little Elena. It's not fair, is it, that some children have so much and another darling baby gets abandoned on a ferry boat in a rickety, old basket?"

Cook served mushroom omelets on a bed of thinly sliced Canadian bacon with melted Gorgonzola cheese on top and fresh asparagus on the side. There was also a tasty rhubarb chutney. As they buttered warm crescent rolls, all three diners felt a twinge of guilt.

Life certainly isn't fair, not fair at all. What will become of poor little Elena and her mother? Julian cleared his throat and broke the silence. "Next week I'll check and see how Maria and Elena are getting along. I'll let you know."

The conversation moved along then. There was a reprise of the Harvest Dinner. Mrs. B told them that Henry Glazer had phoned, as he had promised, and that he would be joining them for Friday night dinner the following week. "I sent an invitation to Victoria too, but I haven't heard yet."

"Oh, I hope she comes. Julian and I like her a lot. Wonder if she has a boyfriend? She's certainly good-looking. Did you ever hear anything about that, Grandmother? Surely she must have had lots of men after her. Or maybe she had a tragic romance and buried herself in medical school and gave up on the opposite sex. What do you think?"

"I have no idea," said her grandmother primly, but Julian glimpsed a spark of curiosity in her old eyes and wasn't surprised when she added, "If she comes for supper, maybe we can find out." He rather hoped they would. It would be interesting to know.

Feeling mellow, the three of them lingered over apple cobbler and coffee. Lori waxed on about the twins. "When I said they're a handful, I didn't mean that they're really naughty, you know. They're just at an age where they want to explore everything, test everyone, and, well, there are two of them, and you can't forget that even for a minute. They keep me on my toes, but I look forward to Wednesdays."

She paused, turned thoughtful. "I shall miss them terribly when I go home. Maybe Suz will be their regular sitter then. Do you know, I'm jealous when I even think about that." She laughed at herself. "It's just that they're so bright and beautiful!"

And you, Julian thought, aware of the yearning in her eyes, *are bright and beautiful too, my young friend, and of an age to want babies of your own. You've transferred all that longing to Matthew and Matilda and maybe even to Elena, and you don't even know it's just a matter of biology.*

Chapter 23

LATER, IN HIS APARTMENT, hanging up his clothes, laying out tomorrow's outfit, brushing his teeth, and, checking the radio alarm (he set it an hour earlier than usual so that he could be on the road to Philadelphia in good time), he thought back on Mrs. B's probing and thoughtfully reviewed his financial situation.

He was a careful man, and he had known that he could pretty much spend whatever he wanted to. Yet, when he actually summoned enough interest to sit at the kitchen table and jot the figures down for the first time since Julie's death, he was mildly surprised to see that he was almost a millionaire.

Julie had been well-insured, of course. Her life policy had a double indemnity clause, and the company that insured the car that smashed her to death had made an impressive settlement. (Reliance Insurance's own in-house counsel had seen to that, and Julian had been glad to put the whole matter in the man's capable hands.) In addition, Julian had the proceeds from the sale of the Paducah house socked away in safe CDs and several healthy-looking mutual funds that he had begun with small investments twenty-five years ago. Every month his salary exceeded his expenses. Every year there was a substantial Christmas bonus through the company's profit-sharing plan.

He thought that he should not have described himself as "comfortably well-off" to Mrs. B. Much of his wealth, clearly over half of it, was a result of Julie's death. *I am not comfortable with that. I wish you back in my arms, Julie, and the insurance money—well, forget it. I am certainly not comfortable with it.* Tears came to his eyes. *Oh, my Julie, why aren't you here? Why aren't we going together to Philadelphia to see our granddaughter? That would make me "comfortable."*

He thought then of little Julie, who, like the twins, had a future ripe with love and opportunity. He promised himself that, on Monday, he would find time to somehow check on baby Elena. He knew that she'd be crawling soon. *Maybe I can do something to help, something for Maria and Elena in your name, Julie. Perhaps that would make me feel more "comfortably well-off."*

AT THE CEMETERY

October 29, 1978

Dr. Glazer suggested that I write down a list of my blessings. She said it helps to see them in black and white. Here's the list:

Family *Julie, our children are constant. I get a letter from Miles every week no matter how busy he is. Joy calls each Wednesday and I drive to Pliladelphia every other weekend to see the baby. Little Julie is my dumpling.*

New Friends *Lori and Mrs. Bellington especially. And an outer circle: Stan, Mrs. Abernathy, Henry Glazer, Mr. Munchen, people I feel I could call on for help if I needed it.*

Work *At Reliance, I feel needed and worthwhile.*

Plans *I'm signing up to be an ESOL tutor.*

Memories *At first, memories upset me. But Mrs. Abernathy is right. I have a treasure trove of happy memories, a lifetime of wonderful memories of you.*

I should probably tell you that I thought about naming Vicki Glazer as a "new friend" but she's really my shrink. I pay her to listen to me so I thought maybe not. I look forward to Friday, seeing her and having her listen. I'll put this list under the paving stone where I put the "grief" poem.

Chapter 24

THE FIRST THING THAT HE DID the following Monday was stop at the reception desk. "Mrs. Abernathy, I decided on the Christmas gifts for our office party, and I went ahead and ordered them. You can cross that off your list."

"What are we getting?"

"It's a surprise."

"I won't tell."

"It's *my* surprise to all of you."

"Mr. Elsmore, I'm running this party—well, Carmie Rizzio and I are running this party for you—and we need to be aware of every detail."

"I thought you'd be relieved not to have this gift thing to worry about. Won't it be fun to be surprised?"

"I'm not all that big on surprises."

"But you're certainly curious, don't deny it."

"Will the gifts be wrapped?"

"Of course." He made a mental note to pick up wrapping paper.

"I just want the party to be well planned, to go smoothly. Let's say you ordered a lot of fully ripened fruit flown in from Hawaii. Then Carmie and I would have to be sure to have a supply of pretty bags on hand so everyone could easily carry their loot home. See?"

"Your logic is good, but it doesn't apply. It's not pineapples."

"Oh, hmmm." She slanted an innocent look at him. "Want to play twenty questions?"

"With you? Indeed not. You probably have some weird, secret system. But I hope you'll really like this surprise." He started down the corridor to his office then turned back. "Mrs. Abernathy, you know and I know Miss Rizzio handles all the purchase orders, but don't bother having her look it up. I'm writing my personal check for the gifts. I'll get reimbursed later." Her face fell, and he chuckled out loud. "Gotcha."

She stared after him in astonishment, not because he had outfoxed her, but because he had actually laughed, had sounded carefree. *That's a first. He laughed*, she thought.

The second thing that Julian did that Monday morning before he got down to business was check on Maria and Elena. A phone call to Social Services got him a transfer to Child Care Services. He explained briefly, "My name is Julian Elsmore. On Friday, several weeks ago, I found a baby abandoned on a ferryboat. The police picked the child up, and, a few days later, I was told that the baby and her mother were reunited and were in one of your programs. Can you tell me any more?"

"I need a name? Who you asking about?"

"The baby is Elena. I carried her up from the boat to the ferry office when her mother dumped her. I'm told her mother's name is Maria Montez."

"Are you a relative? You don't sound Mexican."

"No, not a relative, sort of a friend." *Ha, so Maria's from Mexico; Elena was probably born here, makes her a citizen.*

"A friend, huh, is that what you call it?" The voice was closed, caustic.

"Why, yes. Another friend, a woman, and I—we were together, see, when we found the baby abandoned—were wondering if there's anything Elena needs, or anything her mother needs, for that matter. We feel, well...connected."

"As far as I can tell from this file I'm looking at, both mother and child are in the program and doing just fine." The voice was still annoyed. "Visitors are not allowed."

"I understand. Probably a wise rule," he said heartily and tried another tack. "But I was wondering ..."

"The program provides everything that mother and child need: shelter, food, transportation, education, counseling, supplies. It's set up that way."

"I'm sure, but it was such a strange thing to have happen, finding a four-month-old infant like that. And we'd like to, well…well, I guess we keep thinking of that falling-apart basket she was in and the pitiful note written on a paper napkin and tucked in with her, and Elena, so cute in her little pink bonnet, not knowing she'd been dumped." He sighed a mournful sigh and cleared his throat. "Kind of sad, too…Don't you think?"

"I really don't know what to tell you." Julian thought there was a little softening in the voice.

"I was wondering, would it be appropriate, would it be permitted, to send a gift, maybe a sweater or a couple pairs of baby overalls, even a card? We want to help somehow; if you could perhaps suggest…?"

"Listen, we're not supposed to get personally involved with our clients, but I'm friends with the manager at the group home where Maria Montez is. If you want to send a card—encouraging Maria, you know—and put it in an envelope addressed to me at Child Care Services, I'll see it gets forwarded. That can't hurt." She gave him her name and address and hung up in a hurry.

Not great, but not bad either, he thought. He would slip a ten-dollar bill—no, two fives—in the card along with a cheerful note. He reminded himself to print the note so that it would be easier for Maria to read. *A little pocket money is always good for self-esteem. Not too much of course. The program might object. Maybe ten dollars now, ten each month.* He hoped that Maria would write back, but, remembering the note she had left with Elena, he reflected that writing in English was a struggle for Maria.

He wondered whether she could read and write in her original language. He assumed that she must have come to America when she was fifteen, maybe younger. *How long had she gone to school in Mexico? Did she go to school at all? Well, she's studying English now*, he thought. Maybe she could manage a brief thank-you note, even though it seemed to him a lot to ask. *It could be a class project*, he supposed, and he was glad he had signed up for the next session of ESOL training.

Chapter 25

Thinking about a gift for the Reliance employees, Julian remembered a neighbor back in Paducah, Sarah Gulley, who ran a little lending library out of her home. Julian and Julie had frequently rented one of her best sellers or chosen an old favorite from her shelves. She was a widow and lived alone in the home she inherited from her parents, so they usually took cookies or a slice of pie or even some macaroni salad when they went to make their selections. Julie said that Miss Sarah probably got tired of cooking just for herself and would enjoy a new taste now and then. Julian thought it was a great idea, though not something he would have thought of himself.

Last year they were browsing in the lending library, just before Thanksgiving, and saw a few kaleidoscopes displayed on a little table with a hand-painted sign that read "SHAKE GENTLY. LOOK. SMILE."

"I make them myself," Miss Sarah said proudly. "My little grandniece was visiting one day, and I got out a box of old toys for her. Down at the bottom was a cheap kaleidoscope I had as a kid. She loved it, and then I got the idea of making a more elegant version, a sort of grown-up model. Do take a peek."

The instrument that she handed them was a sturdy, twelve-inch-long tube covered in a handsome velour fabric. The material was a green and gold pattern of vines and butterflies. When Julie looked into the kaleidoscope, she saw bright shapes in beautiful patterns.

"Oh, Julian, look at this; it's lovely." Julie very carefully passed the tube to him, but, as it changed hands, it bumped slightly, and they knew that image was gone forever.

"Oh...I lost it."

"Not to fret," Miss Sarah said, laughing. "A kaleidoscope is a very forgiving instrument. A hopeful one. When a beautiful pattern is lost, it isn't a sad occasion because another beautiful pattern is just a tiny shake away. Come on, I'll show you my materials." She led them to her desk at the back of the enclosed front porch, where she had added a sturdy table and a cupboard.

"It took me six months to find out where to buy all the different supplies, but I have everything now, and everything is first rate." She showed them the three long mirror strips and how she had taped them together to form a perfect equilateral triangle. "These are front-surface mirrors. They're expensive but yield a much brighter image than ordinary mirrors or the shiny, tin strips from the old dime-store kaleidoscopes."

Miss Sarah opened a closet that held several compartmentalized boxes. Each little section within each box was padded and brimmed with a single color of tiny glass objects. There was ruby red, deep persimmon, royal blue, and light blue.

"Austrian crystal," she said, "to mix and match. Use just a few for an airy design or use a lot for a stained glass window." She picked up a little amber ball and then a glowing purple drop from a nearby bin. "I buy the tiny corkscrews and stars, but I'm learning flame work and I made these teardrops myself."

She indicated a shelf of equipment, several books, and several boxes of the cardboard tubes on the floor. "It's fun. And see here are the acrylic discs for the end you look through and for the end that holds the viewing objects."

"Miss Sarah, these are gorgeous; you are a true artist," Julie said. "Thank you for showing them to us. Are you in business? Will you sell me some?"

"Sugar, I'm certainly not in business. It's just a hobby, you know. Something to do that interests me. But people seem quite delighted with them—they're novel, you know—and I did have to buy supplies in quantity to get a decent price. So I've been making them ahead, and," she gave them a merry little wink and continued, "if a friend would like one, I figure with materials and incidentals, thirty dollars each."

"I'm a friend who would like this one." Julie looked at Julian, and he obligingly reached for his wallet.

As he counted out the money, Julian almost chuckled. *Incidentals such as profit*, he thought. He admired the spunky, little woman whose lending library had always been "just a neighborhood club." Now, equally genteel in a demure Southern tradition, her kaleidoscope business was to be "just a hobby." She had devised a way to add a bit of "fun" money to her social security check, to keep herself creative, and, even more importantly, to build a circle of friends. There was no need to bother with incorporation or taxes because she wasn't in business.

At any given time, there were about twenty-five "members" in her club: widows, retirees, and single women of a certain age. She catered to their tastes, and each one usually dropped in at least twice a month. When the rental dollars had paid for a book (about eight dollars with shipping), it was all clear profit. Miss Sarah operated out of her own home, so there was no overhead, no employees, no advertising.

Still thinking of Miss Sarah, Julian wondered if there were any lending libraries in New York City, in the little towns along the Hudson River, or in the lake communities farther north that didn't have a public library. *Life is come and go*, he thought. The bookmobiles were rolling in; the lending libraries were disappearing. *The world is constantly changing, even when we wish with all our heart that it stood still. Oh, Julie, my love, my love.*

The idea had been simple enough: The owner of a small yarn shop or gift store or tailoring and alterations business would add a "book nook" as a sideline. Every week a few new titles, usually popular fiction and biographies, appeared and were rented out for a dollar a week. People anxious to read a particular book signed a waiting list.

Julian wondered why people patronized Miss Sarah's lending library when there was a fine public library in Paducah that handled the same bestsellers, but he thought that there were two main reasons. First, he assumed that the Paducah library might have several copies of a title but that the waiting time was often longer. (The withdrawal period for the little lending library was two weeks, and people could phone in for a week's extension.) Second, there was a bit of snobbery about Miss Sarah's books. The group was exclusive. Members liked knowing that only genteel people like themselves had handled the books before them. In addition, Miss Sarah posted a comment sheet inside the back cover of every book. It was fun to express an opinion there (almost like being a paid critic) and to see what others had written.

Miss Sarah read every volume herself and offered her own advice, reader to reader. "You're sure to like this one, dear. A good read, and the sex is very delicately handled. Nothing raw," she would say.

Julian remembered that, as Miss Sarah closed the cupboard door on her kaleidoscope makings, the bell over the front door had rung. Hastily, careful not to use the forbidden word "buy," Julie had said, "I'd like to have four kaleidoscopes by, say, the middle of December, if that won't rush you."

"That will be fine. I'll phone you. Enjoy your books. Excuse me now." Miss Sarah hurried off, as any good hostess would, to meet the friend who had just dropped by.

"What will you do with four kaleidoscopes?" Julian asked.

"They'll make wonderful Christmas gifts. I already know we'll give one to Joy. And one to old Mr. Morris. He'll share it with everyone at the nursing home, I'm sure. And I'm already thinking of others. I'll probably be asking Miss Sarah to sell me a few more."

"Careful, sweetheart. Miss Sarah thinks 'sell' is a four-letter word."

But Julie wasn't listening. She had their kaleidoscope to her eye. She rotated the cylinder, murmured "ooh" and "aah," and stated once more, "A kaleidoscope will be a wonderful Christmas gift."

That was only a year ago. He and Julie had been safe in Paducah, making plans for Christmas. They could never have guessed that, in the year ahead, he would be promoted and they would move to New York. They could never have guessed that she would have a granddaughter whom she wouldn't ever hold in her arms because she would die in a horrendous accident a few months before the child was born. *Ah, Julie, my love. We never suspected. Yet, here I am alone, pouring out my grief to a psychiatrist named Victoria Glazer, having Friday dinner each week with Lori Seever and her grandmother, thinking of them as my new family.*

He reined his thoughts in and turned to the immediate matter: a present suitable for all the different personalities and ages in the New York City Reliance Insurance office.

"Kaleidoscopes make wonderful Christmas presents," Julie had said, and she had been right. "Julian, did you see how everyone smiled when they opened their gift and looked in?"

He remembered. He picked up the phone and called Sarah Gulley. "Yes," she said, "how many?"

"I absolutely need eighteen, Miss Sarah, and by the tenth of December. If you could send me twenty, that would be even better."

"People do seem to like them for presents, so I've been making them ahead. Yes, I can send you twenty. I'll mail them by the fifth. But no more before Christmas. I've quite a few requests to fill."

He gave her the address of his apartment. "Pack an invoice along with the kaleidoscopes, and I'll write you a check immediately."

"Oh, Mr. Elsmore, I don't do invoices. I'll just send along the kaleidoscopes, and I know you'll show your appreciation."

"Oh, of course. Sorry. Will thirty dollars each cover your cost?"

"And perhaps a bit more for postage. So high these days, you know."

"Yes, very high. I'll make it thirty-five, okay?" He smiled over the phone at the little businesswoman who wasn't in business.

"And, Mr. Elsmore, I want to tell you that I was so terribly sorry to hear about your wife. I'm sure I sent a card, but it's better to speak personally, isn't it? Such a dear woman, always so happy. Such a loss."

"Yes, a terrible loss, thank you." He hung up abruptly, choking as he tried to reply to words of sympathy from a person who had actually known Julie. Among the eight million people in New York, he thought, there had been no neighbor, church associate, or casual friend to say to him at the time of her death, "Such a dear woman."

Chapter 26

LORI AND JULIAN, FRESH from their "conversations" with Dr. Victoria Glazer, arrived at the Bellington mansion that Friday evening to find Dr. Henry Glazer already there and talking easily with Mrs. B. Greetings were exchanged, and, almost immediately, Victoria arrived. She wore a dark red wool suit with a notched, black velvet collar. The suit revealed curves that her dark office attire concealed, and Julian found himself staring.

Vicki went directly to Mrs. B, leaned down a bit to touch her hand, and said, "So nice of you to invite me." She tossed a smile and a casual, "Hi, Pops," to her father. Then, turning to Lori and Julian, she laughed. "You guys look familiar."

The laugh set the group at ease. Lori went to her at once and hugged her. "Vicki, I'm so glad you could come."

That's just what Julie would have done, he thought. *A warm hug, a first name says that this is a social get-together; the professional connection is on the shelf. Women seem to know instinctively how to manage these situations, and mostly they keep it simple. No involved explanations. Thank God for women and the things they know.* He cleared his throat and said, "A little nippy out there tonight. The weathergirl is calling for light snow."

"Good!" Mrs. B nodded. "Snow improves New York City."

"Indeed, it does, at least for those of us who are warm inside and looking out."

"That reminds me," Julian said, "I found out this week that our friends, Maria and Elena, are still settled in that group house. So we know they're warm. And it's a chance for Maria to get her act together."

"Where are they, Julian?"

"A halfway house that Child Care Services runs. It's a program for young women like Maria, who need to learn how to be good parents, need to learn English, and need to learn how to get and hold down a job." He looked around and realized that Henry had no clue what he was talking about, so he quickly filled him in on the story of the abandoned baby on the ferry.

"And you're trying to keep in touch, is that it?"

"Well, yes. It was an unusual event, you see, and somehow I feel I should. Keep in touch, that is. Help out."

"I feel the same way. I want to visit Elena. Can I, Julian? Where is the halfway house?" Lori asked.

"Child Care Services is pretty secretive about that."

"Well, can I at least send a present?"

"I have a contact at Child Care," Julian said. "I'll call her tomorrow and find out. We could go shopping. Let me see, Elena was four months old when we found her. She'll be five months old now, so maybe almost six months old by the time we can get anything to her. What does a six-month-old baby need?"

Lori frowned. "I'll ask Connie; she'll know."

"Good idea," said her grandmother. "Ask Connie. I'm too old and you're too young to know offhand."

Julian looked around. *Henry is also too old. Vicki's my age, but she's never had children, at least not that I know of. Of all of us here, I'm the one who knows. Why don't I want to say? Well, for one thing, it might be fun to go shopping with Lori.*

He decided that they'd go to one of those Tiny Tot stores. He supposed that they had them at any mall, though he hadn't really been shopping since he came to New York. *Maybe I'll ask Lori to help me pick out something for little Julie.* He realized that he hadn't told her about the baby, hadn't told her that he was a grandfather. He wondered why he hadn't. He supposed that he could ask Mrs. Abernathy what to buy for

Elena. She'd have ideas, he was sure, but, as soon as the thought crossed his mind, he discarded it. *Let Lori ask Connie, the mother of young twins.*

Cook appeared in the doorway. "Ah, I see that supper is served. Let us go into the dining room," Mrs. B said as she rose and put her hand on Henry's arm. Vicki and Lori followed, and Julian brought up the rear.

Lori turned to Julian. "I'll find out what Elena might need, and you find out where to send it. Then we'll go buy her some clothes and toys."

"Maybe next week. What night would be good for you?"

"How about Tuesday? By the way, Bill is coming right after Thanksgiving."

"Bill?"

Then Mrs. B was indicating where they each should sit, and he had to pay attention. In a moment, he remembered. *Bill was the boyfriend from back home.* Julian couldn't recall his last name. "Ah, yes, Bill…what's his name? Your boyfriend?"

She shot him a reproachful look. "Bill Letterson is my fiancé. He's coming the day after Thanksgiving for a long weekend."

"Glad to hear it."

"Grandmother," Lori said, turning to Mrs. B, "I just heard this morning that Bill Letterson, from back home, you remember, is coming to New York. Can he stay here with us? The Friday and Saturday nights after Thanksgiving? We have lots of spare rooms."

Mrs. B considered. "Lori, you agreed with your mother and father not to see Bill for a year. I can't stop him from coming to New York, but under the circumstances, out of respect for your parent's wishes, I don't think I should offer hospitality beyond dinner. Perhaps he can find lodging at the YMCA."

"Please, Gram. He doesn't have much money. Not to spend on a vacation. Anyway, he asked Mom and Dad about coming."

"We'll discuss it later, Lori."

Lori opened her mouth, ready to argue, but she thought better of it and subsided. And Mrs. B turned to Henry. "I asked Cook to make onion soup for tonight because I seemed to remember it was a favorite of yours. Was I correct?"

"Absolutely. I give my patients a list of comfort foods, and onion soup is right up there near the top."

"A list? Dad, do you really have a printed list?" Vicki asked.

"I do. People get interested, and it puts them at ease. They even add to it."

"What else is on it? I want a copy."

"Well, homemade chicken soup of course. And brownies. I ask for other favorites, and one man said his favorite was a grilled ham and cheese sandwich with a big side of fries. He is quite a bit overweight." They laughed and Henry continued the conversation. "What are *your* comfort foods?"

Lori spoke immediately, "Chocolate ice cream with chocolate sauce."

"Spaghetti and meatballs."

"Waffles with real butter and real maple syrup."

"Raw carrots," said Julian. "They have such a great crunch."

"Carrots?" The others looked at him in genuine amazement.

Then Henry chuckled and Lori giggled, and Julian admitted with a smile, "Well, maybe crunch and comfort aren't quite the same."

He liked these people, he thought, and he noticed the smooth way that they had steered the conversation away from what was apparently a sensitive matter: the pending arrival of Bill Letterson. He would bet that Mrs. B was going to check out the young man (dinner) but hang tough about sleeping arrangements. Later he would speak to Lori privately and make an offer that would lessen her anxiety.

Chapter 27

THEY BOUGHT FOUR PAIRS OF CORDUROY OVERALLS—pink, yellow, light blue, and navy blue—in sizes six months to a year, and four little white T-shirts with flowers embroidered across the front. They bought four knit sleepers, all pink and white, which the saleswoman called onesies and which zipped from ankle to right up under the chin.

"Don't they look cozy?" Lori smiled. "Wonder if they have them in my size?"

They also bought a music box and a rag baby doll. Julian said that the doll reminded him of one that Joy had had. Lori pointed out a display of Barbie dolls that she said were very popular, but Julian dismissed the creatures with a sharp shake of his head and said, "Not cuddly. Baby wants something soft."

"Oh, of course. I'm learning."

"Enough for now," he said then and, waving away Lori's money and wondering if it was babysitting money or if her parents sent her an allowance, produced a credit card. "Oh, I'd like another music box in a separate bag." When Lori looked at him in surprise, he explained, "I have a baby granddaughter. I'm driving up to Philadelphia to see her on Saturday." He was a bit embarrassed and watched closely for Lori's reaction. She was delighted of course. He thought again that she yearned for a baby of her own.

"Julian, you never told me. How old is she?"

"Nearly five months."

"About Elena's age."

"Yes, just about."

The clerk asked, "Would you like your purchases gift-wrapped?"

Julian turned to Lori as he would have turned to Julie. "What do you think?"

"I think yes. Unwrapping is part of the fun of getting a gift."

"Isn't an infant a little young for that kind of fun?"

She eyed him sternly. "Don't tease. It's Maria who'll have fun unwrapping the gifts."

"Oh. Well, I guess that's good, too."

She instructed the clerk. "Please put all the clothes in one box and wrap the doll and the music box each separately. Pink ribbons. Julian, do you want the other music box gift-wrapped?"

"Absolutely. I've just been informed that my daughter will get a kick out of opening it."

"You're making fun of me. But, believe me, a pretty package shows off a gift, builds excitement. That's why engagement rings come in satin-lined velvet boxes."

She's thinking of engagement rings, is she? "You sound like my wife."

"Well, presentation is important."

He said teasingly, "Are you saying you wouldn't like a two-carat diamond engagement ring if it were bubble-wrapped and packed in a scruffy, little, brown cardboard box?"

"Oh, Julian, I don't know how I'd react to that. I guess it would depend on the guy. I guess any ring or any box would be okay if the guy is right."

He supposed that she was thinking of Bill, her fiancé, who had not yet given her an engagement ring and who was soon coming to New York to see her. *Is she expecting a ring? I'll check him out. I'll check this Billy-boy out.*

Feeling a bit crafty while they were waiting for the gifts to be wrapped, he made his offer. "I have an extra bedroom at my apartment. Bill is welcome to stay there while he's in town."

Her face lit up. "Oh, Julian, really? That would be perfect. Thank you so much. I've been worried about where he'd stay. You'll like Bill. He's low maintenance. I don't know why Grandma's being so unreasonable. There are eight bedrooms on the second floor; did you know that? Why couldn't he stay in one of them? They're never used, even though Elsa comes in once a week to dust and vacuum them all. I'm the only one up there."

"Elsa? Oh yes, the maid."

"She's part-time help. Doesn't live-in. She polishes the furniture, washes the windows and windowsills, puts fresh scarves on the dressers, all that sort of stuff. I think she even keeps most of the beds made up with fresh linens. Grandma says a house never stands still. If you don't take care to keep it up, it goes downhill."

"Is Elsa Cook's helper too?"

"Always on Cook's day off, she comes to make and serve dinner. But she shows up other times, too. See, she used to be full-time, and everyone likes her, so I guess she just feels comfortable showing up whenever she feels like it. Mr. Munchen seems pleased when she drops by. She was here that night you told us about ESOL, remember?"

He remembered. "A tall, middle-aged woman with a long, blond braid wound around the top of her head?"

"That's Elsa. She's something, isn't she?"

"About Bill. When's he getting in?"

"About four on Friday afternoon after Thanksgiving. Less than nine days now. I can hardly wait! Dr. Glazer hasn't made any appointments for that Friday, I guess you know that, so can we come right from the station to your place? We'll leave his backpack, and then we can all go together and dine at Grandma's."

Julian cleared his throat. "Well, you see, that won't work. I'm going to spend Thanksgiving with my daughter and her husband and baby Julie in Philadelphia and stay over the next day. I'll give you the key to my apartment. You'll have to meet Bill at the bus station, get a cab to the apartment, and then take him to see your grandmother. She's never met him?"

Lori shook her head. "No, and *he's* never met anyone at all like Grandma. He'll be terrified. The house will terrify him too. He won't know what to say. Oh, Julian, I wish you were going to be there to make everything go smoothly."

"Well, you'll just have to give Bill some pointers before he meets your grandmother—what to say, what not to say. You did that for me."

"I guess." She sounded dubious. "I'll have to tell him not to eat so fast. He isn't used to polite conversation at the dinner table." She smiled as she remembered. "At his house, all the kids jibber-jabber all the time, and his mom raps with her fork and tells them not to talk with their mouths full."

"Another thing, Lori. Tell your grandmother—or I will, if you like—that Bill's staying at my place and that I'll be away most of the time. Your grandmother won't want you to be alone in my apartment with Bill. So don't be." *I don't want you alone there with him either. It's months since you saw him. No use asking for trouble.*

"Just give Bill the key and tell him he's welcome to use anything, eat anything he finds in the fridge—there'll be bread and butter and orange juice at least, peanut butter on the shelf—but don't you spend time alone with him there. Pretend he's at the YMCA. Will you promise me that?"

Silence hung between them. He knew that she would promise only because Bill really needed free accommodations.

"I thought Grandma would help out; there's plenty of room, like I said." She was silent for several seconds. "You sounded more like my father than a friend just now, Julian. Bill and I haven't seen each other in almost six months. We're not children, and *he is my fiancé*. We'd like to have some time alone together."

"Go to a movie, take a walk up Fifth Avenue, go on that boat ride we took. You'll be alone because no one in all of greater Manhattan will pay attention to you. But don't offend your grandmother and don't get me in trouble with her. She has her standards, and we both should respect them. Things were a lot different when she was a young lady, emphasis on *lady*. So, promise?"

She pouted. "Bill and I should have eloped as soon as we graduated. All this business of waiting, getting a fresh perspective, it's all bunk. We're wasting a year, and I'm not even having all that much fun in the big city. I don't know why I agreed. I don't know why Bill agreed."

He waited.

"All right. Okay, I promise."

He was unhappy that he had caused her distress, especially unhappy when she said that she wasn't having fun. He had really thought that some of the things they had done together had been fun, like the boat trip, the occasional stop for fast food, and this little shopping expedition.

"Lori, if you and Bill are right together, meant to be together for all your lives, this period of waiting won't matter." Even as he spoke, he knew that he and Julie wouldn't have paid attention to any such nonsense when they were eighteen and just out of high school. That wasn't so long ago, and he suddenly felt out of sorts with himself. Here he was, talking like a parent, which was okay with his own children, but he hated the way he must sound to Lori. And, to tell the miserable truth, he realized that, deep down, he hated Bill Letterson, the boyfriend. *No, the fiancé,* he thought.

"Did Bill really talk to your folks and get their blessing for this visit?"

"He talked to them. He's very honorable that way. They didn't exactly bless his trip. They think we should stick with the original agreement. Parents are so old. At least my parents are."

"Well, yes." *Older than I am. By how much?*

Their gift-wrapped packages were ready, and they took them and went to have pizza at one of those new food courts.

"How will you get these gifts to Elena?"

"I'll mail them to a go-between," he said mysteriously. "That's all I can reveal."

Her voice was snappish, probably left over from the promise that she had reluctantly made. "And if you hear from Elena's mom, will you let me know, or is that another of the secrets of New York City?"

"Oh, Lori, of course I'll let you know. I'm just trying to stay within the rules so we can keep in touch with Maria. The city is protecting her, and they don't know—they don't have time to know—that we're her friends."

She changed the subject. "You're going to spend Thanksgiving with your daughter, so you'll take the music box to the baby then?"

"Yes, or maybe this coming weekend. The baby's name is Julie, I think I told you. Named for her grandmother." He felt his throat constrict.

"What's your daughter's name?"

"Joy. And her husband is Brian. He's a CPA, an accountant, you know."

"Oh. Well, good for him, I guess."

"What does Bill Letterson do?"

"He drives a concrete truck; that's full-time. And he works a second job, two evenings a week and weekends, at Hillhigh Inn, which is a very fancy restaurant. The tips are good. He's saving money. It's just temporary of course, but he says he might as well have a second job since his girlfriend's in New York City." She smiled a bit grimly. "That's me, the girlfriend in the big city. He's saving for our wedding. I suppose that isn't very exciting, especially for a guy."

They put their luncheon trash in a can, gathered up their packages, and walked to the car. Not since their first meeting, when he drove her home from Vicki Glazer's office, had there been such constraint between them. He hated the stiffness and wasn't sure why it was there. *No wonder her parents want to separate them for a while, give Lori a chance to see the world, think things over, and have some other experiences before she gets married.*

When they were settled in the car, Lori said, "Bill's a good guy, Julian, really. In high school he was the star of the football team. I can't begin to tell you how much fun our crowd had. Senior year was a blast!"

And now he's a part-time waiter and drives a concrete truck full-time. Some blast. You're unfair, Julian. Maybe he has other goals. Sure, and maybe he doesn't. Grimly, he again promised himself, *I'll check out this Billy-boy.*

Chapter 28

IT WAS EXACTLY TWELVE NOON when Julian pulled into his underground parking space in his apartment building. He sat for a moment, a fond smile on his face as he thought of his baby granddaughter. It had been a wonderful Thanksgiving in Philadelphia. The first one without his Julie, and that was hard. But, when he had held the baby and had felt her heart beat against his chest, he knew it was Julie's heart pulsing anew, Julie's blood raced through the tiny body, and he gave fervent thanks.

As soon as Julian opened the door to his apartment, he smelled bacon and eggs and a drift of cinnamon. He stood at the opening to the living room area. The high-backed couch from Paducah sat in the middle of the room, facing the fake fireplace. As he watched, Lori's head came up into view, her mouth half-opened, her eyes alarmed.

He saw at once that she had been to the beauty parlor. *Do they still call it that? Maybe "Hair Today" or "Cut and Curl" or something modern. Julie would have known.* Lori's straight hair was cut short and uneven and fluffed out with gold-tipped curls, framing her face like a nimbus. She was wearing light make-up. *She certainly had fancied up for Bill Letterson.* The nimbus, he noticed sourly, was too mussed to look angelic.

"Julian," she squeaked.

"Well," he said and could think of nothing else.

Almost immediately, another head appeared over the back of the sofa. "Sir," said Bill Letterson. The young man got to his feet. He was wearing pajama shorts and an oversized T-shirt with "We Won, Guys" blazoned across the front. He knew that he was not at his best, and a blush spread across his freckled face. Nevertheless, he put out a hand to draw Lori up beside him, and he stood straight.

"Sir, I'm Bill Letterson."

"Julian Elsmore."

"I want to thank you for letting me stay here."

He was brought up with good manners.

"Julian, I just came over this morning to cook breakfast for Bill and me. It didn't seem such a terrible thing to do. We just..." Her voice trailed away.

"Well," he said again, and again his mind, despite Dale Carnegie, was empty of follow-up. Finally he said, "I suppose it didn't. Seem terrible, that is."

All three stood as if glued to the floor. Lori reached for Bill's hand, and together they looked so miserable that Julian finally turned away. He moved toward the little kitchen. "I believe I'll go make a fresh pot of coffee."

He was sitting at the cluttered table, drinking his coffee, when Lori came into the kitchen by herself. Silently, she picked up the dishes, scraped them, and put them in the dishwasher. As she bent over the table, Julian caught the scent of perfume, which mingled rather pleasantly with the smell of cinnamon. *Perfume. For Bill, she's wearing perfume.*

Lori poured herself a cup of coffee and came and sat down opposite him at the little table. With nervous fingers, she pushed a few crumbs on the tablecloth to one side. "Julian," she began, but he held up a hand to silence her. They sat and sipped their coffee, and neither knew what the other was thinking. Neither knew what to say.

After a few minutes, she began again. "When Bill got here late yesterday, I met the bus, and then we dropped his backpack here and went on to have Friday night dinner with Grandma. She was awful, just awful."

He raised his eyebrows. "Your grandmother was awful?"

"Well, yes. In her very nice way of course. She quizzed Bill, and all his answers came out wrong. He drives a truck. He's a waiter. He told my parents he was coming to see me, but he didn't really have their permission. And, worst of all, if he has any plans to better himself—that's what Grandma would call it—he couldn't explain them. Julian, it truly was awful. I found myself wishing he hadn't come."

"And then?"

"And then, after dessert, I excused us, and we went to see Mr. Dempsey. His bone is slow healing, so I drop in for a quick visit every day to try to cheer him up a bit. Grandma sees him almost every day, too. Anyhow, for Bill, it was the best part of the evening, talking to Mr. Dempsey about cars.

"You may not know this—I certainly didn't—but that limo in the garage is pretty special, a 'classic car.' It's a 1927 Lincoln L, in perfect condition, leather upholstery and all. Bet you weren't aware that the Lincoln Car Company introduced the greyhound radiator cap in 1927. That makes the one on Grandmother's limo a first edition. Mr. Dempsey called it, 'A wee sleek creature, a beauty, and a thousand times I've polished her 'til she shone.'

"He talked like a lover, no kidding, and he asked Bill, 'You want to see her?' So Bill handed Mr. Dempsey the walker, which he doesn't like to use, and they made a pilgrimage to the garage. I tagged along, and guess what I found out?" Lori made her eyes big and solemn to show the importance of her knowledge. "Very, very special. That car has *bullet headlights*, the spare tire *is on the running board*, and it was advertised as *designed to reach seventy miles per hour.*

"Well, Bill threw up the hood, and they started jabbering in a language I hardly understood, pistons and cylinders and torques and things like that. I went back to the house, and, about forty-five minutes later, Bill came in and said good night and that Munchkin had told him how to get to your place by public transportation. That was that. That was the evening I had looked forward to for months. I was almost crying."

"And this morning?"

"I wanted to make it up to him, to make things right, you know, so I called him and said I'd come over and we'd have breakfast together. Cook packed up some bacon and eggs for me, though she clearly didn't approve, but that's nothing new. Anyway, when I got here, things were better, almost normal, as if we were in high school again, and then, well, then you came home." She raised her head and, despite a flush of embarrassment, looked him in the eye. "Julian, I'm sorry I broke my promise to you. I know it looks bad. I'm very sorry."

He reached across the table to put a hand on her shoulder and squeezed gently. "Don't cry now, Lori. It's too bad it happened—I'm sorry too—but it's truly not the end of the world!"

Bill came into the kitchen. He was wearing worn jeans and a light blue sport shirt open at the neck and tucked in at the waist. Julian knew that he had made an effort. He stood awkwardly just inside the door, looking so young that Julian felt a moment's pity. *He's only a half-year out of high school.*

"Sir, Lori told me you didn't want us to be alone here in your apartment, that she promised you we wouldn't be. We'll go out for lunch now, take my backpack along, and maybe we'll go up the Empire State Building or something like that, and I'll catch the afternoon bus back home."

Julian wondered, *Did I push too hard for that promise from Lori? Was I unreasonable?* He suddenly took charge. "This is what *I* think you two should do. Right now, go on and do the tourist thing, see some of the sights. The Empire State Building is a good idea. Maybe Rockefeller Center or the Metropolitan Museum. Whatever. Get back here by six. I've made a seven o'clock reservation at a restaurant in Chinatown. I've not been there myself, so it will be an adventure for all of us. I'm told it's delicious and very authentic. My treat, but parking is a problem, so we'll take a cab."

It was worth it, he supposed, just to see Lori's face brighten and to hear her whisper, "Oh, Julian."

"I invited your grandmother, Lori, but the restaurant's on the second floor, no elevator. She said she wasn't up to it." He smiled inwardly at the little pun and saw a flash of appreciation in the girl's eyes.

It flew past Bill Letterson, however. He glanced at Lori. "I've never eaten Chinese food, but thank you, sir. I'm game, I guess."

"That's our plan then." *It would suffice for the present,* Julian thought, *smooth things over.* But Julian knew that Lori must soon face the facts that, although it was fun to pretend, she and Bill were no longer in high school, and never again would high school be a normal part of their lives.

Lori came around the tiny table and kissed him on the cheek. "Julian, thank you." She kissed him again. "Thank you for always rescuing me."

Chapter 29

LORI PHONED HIM ON WEDNESDAY afternoon at Reliance Insurance. "I need to talk to you, Julian."

"Sure, okay. What's up?"

"Not now. Face to face"

"When then?"

"I'm babysitting the twins now. It's the big, grey house just before you get to Grandma's. You remember where you left me off that night? Connie gets back at seven. Can you pick me up?"

"I'll be there."

"I'll watch for you."

Julian stayed at the office an extra hour, catching up on some paperwork. At six, he ate a candy bar, which had been in his desk for weeks, washed his face and hands, and changed into a fresh shirt. He was going to be early to meet Lori. But she might be early too, and he didn't want her standing at the curb waiting for him.

He parked across the street from the grey house and thought about Lori's call. Something was wrong. Lori's voice had been tight with strain. *Was she sick? Was her grandmother sick? Maybe Mr. Dempsey had taken a turn for the worse. Don't be an old maid,* he told himself. Then, just as he was wondering if he should go to the door and let Lori know that he was there, he saw a little Honda pull into the driveway and figured Connie was home.

Sure enough, in just a few moments, Lori came running out. She spotted the car immediately and ducked into the front seat.

"It's Bill," she said. "I need to talk to you about Bill."

Then she was silent for several blocks. "Bill," she said at last, "is dating another woman, a girl really, from our high school. She's a part-time waitress—just weekends—at Hillhigh. That's the restaurant where he works. Her name is Rusty. I asked Bill if that means she has red hair. He laughed and said, 'Oh yeah, Busty Rusty has a big bunch of red hair.'

"Julian, it was sort of nasty the way he said 'Busty Rusty,' but almost bragging too. What do you think?"

"Did he say how long this has been going on?"

"A couple of months at least. Julian, no one would ever call me 'busty.'"

He spoke carefully, "Well, no, but you have a lovely figure, Lori. Slim, willowy, graceful. Any man would be happy to be seen with you." He paused. "I know I am."

She hardly heard him. "Bill said I shouldn't think it meant anything, him going out with Rusty, just that he's lonesome, tired of watching TV until he falls asleep, and she's a lot of fun. And so, when they close Hillhigh on Saturday nights, Sunday mornings really, a whole bunch of them go out together and have a few drinks, and, since everyone else is paired up, he and Rusty just kind of paired up too." Lori stopped as if breathless. Her tone was indignant. "Rusty's still in high school. She's not old enough to drink."

"Maybe she drinks ginger ale or orange pop."

"Yeah, sure. There's more," she said after a sniffling pause. "She invited him to a couple of dances back at high school. Rusty even invited Bill to the Christmas Ball, and he had to rent a tux and buy her a corsage and spend a lot of money to take her to dinner and all that stuff, limo and everything. Almost as big a deal as a prom."

Julian realized that Lori was crying. "How could he do that to me? I haven't gone out with anyone since I've been in New York. A guy in my biology class asked me. I said, 'Thanks, but I'm engaged.' But...but Bill said it didn't mean anything going out with Rusty, that it was just to have some fun, that's what he said a couple of times. Julian, he's engaged to *me*."

"I know, I know," he said soothingly, but he really didn't know at all. He thought hard. "Lori, you told me your last year in high school was great. Think back to Thanksgiving. What were you and Bill doing last year at Thanksgiving?"

She seemed to calm down as she remembered. "Well...the Saturday after Thanksgiving was the football game with Belmont High. Big rivalry. The schools had played every year for thirty years. It was a tie. Each team had won fifteen games, so there was a lot of excitement. Last year we broke the tie, won by two touchdowns, and Bill made both of them in the last ten minutes. The stadium roared, and the band played double-time, and then everyone spilled into the field and tore the goalposts down. There was a celebration later at the school, a real bash; parents brought in food and sodas...and Bill was the hero!"

"And you were the hero's girlfriend. Pretty wonderful."

"Yes. And, when we came out of the school, it had been snowing for a couple of hours, so the night wasn't over yet. We rounded up some sleds and went coasting on Stickler Hill. Bill had a really long sled that he got out of his garage. He's a tall guy. He flopped down on that sled, and I knelt between his legs and hung on to the sides. We whizzed down that hill and almost went into the creek. Bill swerved in time, and, when we finally coasted to a stop, we rolled off and lay in a snow bank, kissing each other, with Bill coming up for air every so often to yell, 'Whoo-hoo! Superman!'"

Julian had to smile at her recital. And, since the telling seemed to comfort her, he encouraged her, saying, "Sounds like a great weekend."

"Yes, but we really didn't want it to end. It snowed all night, and, in the morning, it was still coming down hard, but we were psyched up. We were on the phone to each other, and Bill's parents said, 'If you can walk to our house, you can party here. Bring whatever you have around to eat, like popcorn or pretzels or cookies. You can roll up the rug and dance, but you have to promise to clean up before you go home.'"

"Pretty special."

"Yes, Bill's family is big and a lot of fun. His mother has a scrapbook of all the newspaper stories about Bill. There's all the football stuff. He's an Eagle Scout too, a counselor now. Last year he volunteered for a team that helped rebuild a little town in Mississippi after they got torn up by a hurricane. Bill's a good guy. I'm proud of him."

"Sounds like you should be."

"That Sunday afternoon, when it started to get dark, Bill's mom said, 'You kids need some real food before you walk home in the snow. How about pancakes?' So she made a big bowl of batter, and we sat on the floor in the kitchen and ate pancakes with syrup. Bill's mom told Bill to get apples from the bushel in the cellar, and she said we all had to eat an apple too, for balance.

"So that's what we had for supper. Pancakes and syrup and an apple. We told each other we'd never forget and we'd be friends forever. Then we washed the dishes and moved the rug and furniture back in place and thanked Bill's mom and dad. They asked each one of us to phone when we were safely home."

"You liked it at Bill's house, didn't you?"

"They liked me too. His brothers and his little sister Maureen liked me. I fit right in."

"Did Bill fit in at your house?"

"Bill didn't come to my house, not after the first time when he met my parents. They insisted on that, on meeting him, and it was okay. But, the times after that, he'd just come to the door, and I'd be waiting."

"Isn't that a little strange?"

"Not really, if you knew my mom and dad. I love them, but they aren't very sociable. I used to wonder if they were shy, but I think they're just sufficient unto themselves. They married late, and it's as if finding each other was a miracle, and they take the miracle very seriously. Anyway, it's quiet at my house. My mom's a sweet lady but she would be horrified at the thought of a dozen kids sitting on the kitchen floor eating pancakes. She's not really sick, the doctor says, but she's frail, almost afraid to talk to people. Dad is very protective of her."

"He's protective of you too, isn't he?" Julian felt that he was beginning to understand why Lori was at her grandmother's.

"In a different way, I guess. Mostly, I think he's scared because his little girl has grown up and is a woman. I think the actual word 'woman' scares him, except for Mom of course, and that's funny because he's a biology teacher."

"You never told me that. Where does he teach?"

"A small, private high school for boys. He's very comfortable there, with his little lab and his experiments, and everyone says he's a super teacher."

"After the party at the Letterson's, was that the end of the weekend?"

"Not quite. When we finished cleaning up, Bill walked me home. The snow was knee high, and we kept slipping around and holding each other up and hollering and wishing we had snowshoes. And, just when we got to my house and were digging out the front steps, Bill said, 'Lori, you're so great, and we have so much fun together. You're my girl forever, aren't you?'

"I said, 'Yes, forever.'

"And Bill said, 'Then we should get married. That would really be *forever*, wouldn't it? Is that a good idea, or what? We can get hitched next June, as soon as we graduate. Okay, Lori?'

"I said, 'Okay.'" Lori reached for a tissue, and Julian saw that she was crying again. She sniffled, and her nose started to turn pink. "It was the best weekend I ever had."

"Probably Bill's best weekend too. A real high point." He was silent for several long moments. "And now?"

"Now what?"

"Just a year ago, after he made those two touchdowns, people were slapping Bill on the back and telling him what a hero he was. I bet reporters interviewed him for the local paper. His mother pasted the write-ups in his scrapbook. He was a 'big man on campus,' and he had a foxy girlfriend, who was his regular date, and life was a blast."

"Pretty much."

"And now?"

"What?"

"Think, Lori. Is he a *big man* at the cement plant?"

"Of course not. He's driving a truck."

"How about the restaurant? Is he a *big man* at…What's the name? At the Inn? Does he have a girl who's fun to be with, who tells him he's wonderful?"

"Rusty takes care of that. Oh, Julian, I never thought this would happen."

He spoke slowly, "As far as you know, nothing *has* really happened."

"He went to the Christmas Ball with her, Julian. He didn't have to go. Nobody held a gun to his head. And those dances are a lot of fun, and sometimes a bunch of kids go to a motel afterward. I heard them talking about it last year, and Bill said we should go. He said it would be fun to just go with the gang, but I had a curfew. My dad would have been at the motel with the cops, and my mom would have fainted somewhere. And then they would have killed me." She had to laugh a little at her own jumbled outpouring.

"But, Lori, see, that's just it. Bill hasn't had much fun or been much of a hero since he finished school. I bet, at the Christmas Ball, all the fellows who were juniors last year gathered round, slapped him on the shoulder, and said how great it was to see him and how they'd always remember how he won the game at the last minute. 'Whoo-hoo.' And I bet all the girls wanted to dance with him."

"Yes. Bill likes to dance. He's good too. Other couples used to stop dancing to watch us."

"Exactly. And a cute girl asks him to a dance, notice that *she* asked *him*, and it's no surprise that he…Well, he goes because he's sick and tired of working two jobs, saving his money, never going dancing, and having his girlfriend—his fiancé, I mean—hundreds of miles away."

"Well, *he's* hundreds of miles away from *me*, and I'm not fooling around with some other guy. You know what he said?" she huffed. "He really was trying to pick a fight, I think, and he said why wasn't it okay for him to go out with Rusty because I was going out with you?"

Julian managed a laugh.

"That's what I did. I laughed. I said it was different because you weren't some brazen little hussy on the make. You're a reliable family friend."

"That's the funniest compliment I've ever had."

"What?"

"That I'm not a brazen hussy on the make." His chuckle, this time, was genuine. He would have to remember to tell Dr. Glazer, maybe get a little laugh from her.

"Oh, Julian, you know what I mean. But what should I do?"

"Nothing for a few days. Have you heard from him since he went home?"

"A short note. Well, Bill never writes much. It was a formula really. Sentence one: 'Thank you for (gift, dinner, check, recommendation).' Sentence two: 'It was very (generous, delicious, thoughtful, kind), and I (enjoyed, spent it on, will always remember).' And, third sentence: 'Your (gift, action, kindness) brightened my day.' 'Many thanks.' His mom taught all her kids to write thank-you notes, and she stood over them while they did it."

"Good woman. Bill was well brought up."

"Yeah, but she never taught Bill how to write to his fiancé."

"Lori, that formula for thank-you notes. Really, that's what he wrote?"

"Just about. He liked Mr. Dempsey and liked looking down from the top of the Empire State Building. He didn't say Grandmother was awful, but she was. I told you that. The art museum was a losing game for him, and do you know what he said about Chinese food?"

"What?"

"He said, 'Rice and little bitty shrimp and those water chestnut things, they turn me off. The men in my family eat meat and potatoes.'"

"So he didn't have fun in New York?"

"I guess he has his fun with Busty Rusty." She started to cry again. "I love Bill, Julian. I don't know what to do next."

"Why don't you just write to him, like always? Say you're sorry New York was a disappointment but don't go into a lot of details. Find something else to keep your mind occupied for a couple of weeks and see what develops."

"That's easy to say."

"I know, but I have an idea. Listen, I'm hungry. Have you had dinner?"

"A little bit. With the twins."

"Why don't we stop at a restaurant? I'll have dinner. You have a 'little bit' more, if you want. Then we'll have a super-sized chocolate dessert. Weren't you the one who said chocolate was a great comfort food?"

"That's your idea of what I should do to take my mind off Bill? Stuff myself with chocolate?"

"No, no. I'll tell you my idea while we eat. Okay?"

"Sure," she said. She sank lower in her seat, sniffled again, and blew her nose.

Chapter 30

LORI WAS SILENT AS THEY STOOD in line at the little neighborhood café. Julian ordered a sandwich, salad, and coffee, and she said listlessly, "Same, but no coffee. A Pepsi."

Julian looked around at the black and white tile floor and the maroon and blue faux-leather booths and thought that someday he would like to take Lori to a really elegant restaurant.

"Here's my idea," he told her. "I've signed up to be an ESOL tutor. A training course starts next Saturday, three Saturdays in a row, eight-thirty in the morning to two-thirty in the afternoon. If you want to go with me, I'll provide transportation. They supply lunch. Sound interesting?"

She cleared her throat and spit into a tissue. "I think I'd like that. Will we really be teachers then?"

"We'll be tutors, not teachers."

"What's the difference?"

"This program, by the way, is like the government program I told you about, but it's private, just a group of people from Trinity Methodist. They began it, some years ago, as a way to teach adults who couldn't read. It is based on the Laubach System of instruction, and their slogan is 'Each One Teach One.' That's how they do things. So, when a tutor is ESOL trained, for example, the program matches each one with a foreign student and they meet on a regular schedule—maybe three or four hours each week. The program wants them to meet at a neutral place, so they provide a couple of classrooms that are on the second floor of that building where we ate the Harvest Dinner."

"That's good. I was wondering how Grandma would feel about a foreigner in her house. She has some pretty strong prejudices."

"Some of the students are immigrants, some are just people who fell through the cracks in our school system. They dropped out as soon as they were sixteen because they never learned to read well enough to graduate. They get to be thirty or forty and they want to give reading another try."

"I didn't know there were people like that. But, Julian, we're going to be ESOL tutors, right? I'd like to tutor someone like Maria, maybe even Maria."

"No problem. The training I signed up for is exclusively ESOL, English for Speakers of Other Languages. It's been worked out carefully. Since we're volunteers, I guess we can stipulate that we want to tutor people whose original language is Spanish. And, when I tell them we travel together, they'll give us the same tutoring slots. They'll work it out, I'm sure. And your grandmother knows I'll take good care of you."

"Don't say that," she snapped in sudden irritation. "I can take care of myself. Everyone here in New York treats me like a baby or an idiot. I'm nineteen years old, and, no matter what Dad thinks, or what you and Grandma think, I'm quite competent. I can look after myself. I'd *like* to ride the subway, and, one day soon, I'm going to."

"Don't get on your high horse, Lori. I put that badly. It's just that I know you're considerate of your grandmother, and she will feel at ease if we're taking the course and tutoring together."

"Okay," she said. "Just remember, I don't need a chaperone or a protector, and, if you want to know something else, I don't need Bill Letterson either. If he wants to go out with Busty Rusty, let him go. I bet she's *Lusty* Busty Rusty who's just a ton of fun. I bet all the guys have found that out."

He soothed her with platitudes. "You're probably right, Lori. Time will tell. Right now, it's time for dessert."

They ordered what the menu bragged was a "Decadent Duo Plus: chocolate-frosted chocolate cake, a la mode with chocolate ice cream." Julian observed with relief that Lori wasn't too brokenhearted or angry to enjoy it.

He regarded her carefully and handed her a paper napkin. "You have a chocolate dribble on your chin." She snatched the napkin with an exasperated swipe and wiped her mouth and chin.

Does she think I'm treating her as a child who needs her face washed? Or maybe she's just furious with the whole world because of the vision in her head of Bill dancing with "Lusty, Busty Rusty." I'm glad to see her showing some spirit, some backbone. Good for you, girl!

"Grandma grew up when families practically imprisoned their daughters until they could hand them off to proper husbands."

"From what I've heard, your grandmother was a pretty independent young woman in her day and had some high old times."

"She's forgotten."

Or maybe she hasn't forgotten and just doesn't want you to repeat any of the stupid devilment she got into. Not on her watch.

Lori finished her dessert and suddenly asked, "How much does the ESOL training cost?"

"No charge. This program is run by good-hearted people who want to make the world a little better. If your grandmother has questions, she can call the pastor."

"Is there tuition? For the students, you know?"

"I believe that some students, who can afford it, leave a dollar after each class, and that pays for the extra time the janitor keeps the building open."

She had a sudden thought. "But, if the training is on Saturday, you'll miss visiting your daughter and granddaughter."

"I told Joy I'd be there next Sunday instead of Saturday."

"What about books and supplies. What do we need?"

"Not a lot. I'll get your stuff when I get mine."

"I'll pay you back."

"Okay." He wondered again if her parents sent her an allowance. Or maybe she had saved some babysitting money. *Who paid her tuition?* he wondered. Even at a community college and taking only two courses, that would add up. *Well, clearly she doesn't spend much money on clothes or cosmetics or getting her hair done.* He knew that she would be quite pretty if she made any effort, but she never wore any makeup and, except for the night of the Harvest Dinner, he had never seen her in a skirt.

AT THE CEMETERY

November 19, 1978

Julie, I know I told you I am seeing a shrink but not the one Stan recommended. It's a woman, I think I told you that. It's Dr. Victoria Glazer. I just tell her stories from our life together and about how much we loved each other. Does it help?

Maybe. I don't really know.

I had a sort of vague purpose. Since almost all of Dr. Glazer's patients are women, I thought maybe I'd meet...that she'd introduce me...well, I was thinking... don't really know what I'm thinking or wanting...but something because I'm empty. You left me empty.

I come here every Sunday just to visit. Sometimes I write down what I say to you. I don't know what helps.

The rumination was unfinished when he turned abruptly, strode down the hill, and drove back to his empty apartment.

Chapter 31

It was a somber little group, just Mrs. Bellington, Lori, and Julian, who sat down to Friday night supper at the Bellington mansion the day after the funeral. The huge, sparkling Christmas tree, which dominated the reception room and which Elsa and Mr. Munchen had loaded with antique ornaments and silver garlands, seemed sadly out of place.

Mr. Dempsey had died in his sleep on Tuesday night. A heart attack, the doctor said.

"He was just lying there, God rest him, when I went in with his morning coffee," Mr. Munchen had reported. "The light was on, the coverlet was smooth, and there was a copy of *Popular Mechanics* fallen by the bedside, so I guess his passing was easy. He was a good old boy. We worked together in this house for almost fifty years. We were friends. Got along just fine, you know. I'll miss him."

Cook was sure that Mr. Dempsey had a will. Years ago, he had hired a lawyer to draw up the will and then to come to the house, where Mr. Munchen and she had witnessed the document. Sure enough, she found the will in the bottom drawer of the little writing table in his room over the garage. He had left $3,000 each to Cook and Mr. Munchen. The rest, a modest amount, was divided between a church he had attended years ago and the American Legion. Apparently, there were no relatives.

Julian, alert to ripples from the sudden death, thought that Mr. Munchen moved somewhat more slowly than usual when he opened the big front door. *Of course that could be nothing but my imagination*, he thought. The butler's greeting was as courteous and sonorous as ever.

Lori had guessed once that Mr. Munchen was nearly eighty and should have long ago retired, but he seemed content. He was more than capable of handling his duties, which had dwindled significantly over the years. "Anyway," Lori had remarked, "this is his home. Where would he go?"

The days of the glorious, big parties with a multitude of distinguished guests were long past. The great house, polished and welcoming, blazing with candlelight, camellias, and laughter, was ancient history. Mr. Munchen had taken enormous pride in the Bellingtons' perfect hospitality, every detail of which he had supervised.

Now Julian wondered if Mrs. B was also recalling those luminous times, perhaps remembering the zeal with which a young Mr. Dempsey had polished the Lincoln.

She sat, poking listlessly at her food, and, as he watched, her fork slipped from her arthritic fingers. "Oh dear. My hands are quite twisted these days."

Lori jumped up to scoop the fork from the oriental carpet, waving both Cook and Mr. Munchen away. Without a word, she went to the sideboard and got another fork for her grandmother. "Here you go, Grandma, no problem."

Otherwise, Lori was downcast and, although she ate her dinner with the appetite of the young, she apparently had nothing to say. Cook looked dour, which made her the only one in customary mode.

Mrs. B glanced around, her voice almost tender, and observed, "Mr. Dempsey made a good death. Very tidy."

Julian's eyes went to Lori. He thought that she was about to giggle, probably a reaction to the strain of the past two days. While he loved her giggle, so like Julie's, he was aghast at the timing.

"A fine man," he said hastily. "We'll all miss him. He certainly was proud of the Lincoln."

Lori had gotten herself under control. Her face was solemn and respectful when she asked her grandmother, "What would be an untidy death, Grandma?"

"Well, you know, someone drunk, only half-dressed, has a fit of some sort, throws up all over the good rug, has to be hauled off to be cleaned and fumigated—the rug, I mean, of course—and sometimes not back in time for the wake. Mr. Dempsey was in love with me."

"Oh, Grandma…"

"Impossible. He knew it of course. I was older, married, his employer. Still, it was flattering." Her eyes were moist. "He was such a likable lad— cheeky, handsome."

Almost speechless, Julian was glad that he could find enough voice to break the sudden silence. "Well, I've some good news. I got a card from Maria Montez today."

Lori brightened. "What did she say?"

"A nice thank-you note." Julian reached into his jacket pocket. "And, best of all, she sent a snapshot of Elena. See?"

Lori reached for the picture and melted over it. "Ooooh, look at her. And she's wearing one of the outfits we sent, Julian. Look, Grandma."

Mrs. B's glasses hung around her neck on a gold chain. She fumbled as she lifted them and was slow getting them in place. But, when she finally inspected the snapshot, some of her natural vibrancy returned. "Life does go on. What a handsome child."

"May I see the note, Julian?"

"Of course. Read it to us, Lori."

Cook, who had been about to leave the room, lingered. Lori read:

Mr. Elsmore,
Thank you for your very pretty card and everything.
You made my day happy.
Elena is happy too, and loves new clothes.
                                        Maria Montez
P.S. A kind friend gave our house a camera. And gave
books to put pictures in. ?

Lori looked puzzled. "Maria put a big question mark after the last line. Why, do you suppose?"

"Maybe she just learned about the question mark and was trying it out. See how she used 'P.S.?' It's like she's having fun with the new things she learns in class."

"Let me see it," said Mrs. Bellington, and, after rereading the message carefully, she opined, "I think she's asking, Julian, if you're the 'kind friend' who sent the camera."

"Are you, Julian?"

"Well, yes, but I donated it to the house as a used item. I did use it first. My contact suggested I do it that way, so as not to embarrass Maria, as if, you know… Well, as if she has a protector, a 'sugar daddy.'" He coughed. "I think that's the term."

"And I bet you sent lots of film."

"Well, Lori, a camera wouldn't be much fun without film."

"And you sent scrapbooks too? One for each of the housemates?"

"Baby books. My wife and I kept a baby book for each of our kids right up to last year. I guess they turned into adult books as the children grew. They're still packed away, but, one of these days I'll get them out. I took some snapshots of my granddaughter—so the camera would be 'used,' you know—and I'll start a new book with them." He turned his attention to his meal. No need to mention that he had just set up a modest trust fund for Maria and Elena: The Julie Kaye Elsmore Trust.

Mrs. B spoke, "I should think it a very good thing for young women to start family records. Records give permanence. Remind whomever your contact is that Maria and the other mothers should put a date by every entry and maybe a line, something like 'Baby's first birthday' or 'Baby's first shoes' or 'Elena's first Christmas.' Good writing practice too."

She's making suggestions and expects me to see to it. Not quite orders, but close. He was glad to see her reviving.

"Furthermore, Julian," Mrs. B went on, looking carefully at the note again, "I notice that Maria named you a 'kind friend.' I was thinking the same thing, thinking how kind you were to stand with Lori and me at Mr. Dempsey's funeral. That must have brought back painful memories of your late wife's burial—such a short time ago—so it was doubly generous. Lori and I were in need of…" Her mouth twitched slightly. "'A strong protector.' I think that's the term. Thank you."

Julian blushed. To forestall more compliments, he glanced about, saw Cook leaving the room, and, knowing her to be somewhat deaf, boomed out, "This is the best chicken salad I've ever eaten. And the parmesan toast too."

Lori giggled. Her spirits brightening a bit, she tossed Julian a saucy glance that said, *Boy, oh boy, you're a top-drawer favorite with everybody in this household.*

He looked away but again thought that her giggle was cute.

Chapter 32

As THEY LEFT VICTORIA GLAZER'S OFFICE on the second Friday evening in December, when the Christmas decorations in the neighborhood were still relatively new and sparkling, Lori told Julian, "There's company coming for dinner tonight."

"Who?"

"Grandma's lawyer, Mr. Edward Carpenter, a very distinguished gentleman."

"Distinguished how?"

"Well, I met him once, and he certainly is distinguished-looking in a neat, lean, perfectly groomed way. Grandma says he has an impeccable background, both his heritage and because he attended Harvard Law School. She says he's on retainer, whatever that means. He's quite a bit younger than Grandma. Actually, she inherited him. She told me his father was her first attorney."

"Is he coming for a special reason, something to do with Mr. Dempsey, maybe?"

"Not that I know of. Why would you think that?"

"No, I guess not. It's just that, for a man who worked all his life and lived simply, Mr. Dempsey didn't leave much of anything when he died. Just wondering where the money he made in fifty years went. Did he have a secret family? A secret charity?"

"Mr. Munchen says he played the horses. It was his hobby. Never got himself in debt but never hit it big either. Could that be the answer?"

"Very easily. So, why is the distinguished lawyer calling on your grandmother?"

"He comes regularly, around the first of each month, and brings the report he gets from the estate manager, who is Mr. Metcalfe. Lawyer Carpenter and Grandma review the report together. Last month Grandmother asked me if I would be interested in joining them next time. She said it would be a good thing for me to learn about family affairs."

"Probably so. What about the estate manager?"

"Grandma calls him 'the factor,' though I don't know why. I thought 'factor' had to do with multiplying things together."

"I believe 'factor' was a term used for the estate manager in the days of the huge plantations, both here in America and in many of the English possessions around the world. It's pretty much an archaic usage."

"Mr. Carpenter always makes an appointment—no one just drops in on Grandma, you notice—and this month Grandma invited him to dine with us. That's the first time that's happened since I've lived here."

"Hmm. So Mr. Carpenter comes here to review the estate business. Was it always like that or just since your grandmother is less able to get around?"

"I don't know that. I used to visit here sometimes, when I was a little girl, but I've only lived here since last June, right after I graduated, remember? Sometimes I think this house is a little mysterious."

"If the attorney makes house calls, it sounds as if your *grand*mother may have quite a *grand* estate."

"I guess so."

"Lori, if tonight is a business dinner, maybe I shouldn't stay. It's not my business, you know. I can just drop you off."

"Oh, you mustn't do that. Grandma does business in the library, never at the dinner table, bad manners and bad for digestion, you know. Besides, she has this all arranged. She said she wanted you and Mr. Carpenter to meet."

"Why ever?"

"I'm not sure. Maybe just a whim."

"It seems to me that your grandmother is more apt to plan than to 'whim.'"

"I've noticed that too."

"Have you met Mr. Metcalfe, the factor?"

"Once. He's another distinguished-looking guy. Not like Mr. Carpenter, though, but sort of a jovial uncle type, affable and hearty. Mr. Metcalfe looks like pictures of Teddy Roosevelt, mustache and all. I asked Grandma—it was the night Henry Glazer was here—how come all the men she knows, including Munchkin, are so good-looking."

"And she said?"

"She said, 'Well, dear, why not?' After that, very seriously, she imparted some words of wisdom. 'Your grandfather, the Colonel, was a handsome man too, but, for a marriage partner, there must be other admirable qualities. I like good-looking men who are competent and who have a sense of humor, men who are intelligent, honest, generous.'"

"And rich?" I asked, just teasing.

"Not necessarily so but, in my experience, a man with those other fine qualities is often rich as well. Fall in love with such a man, my dear. He's a keeper."

"Keeper? What does that mean?" Julian asked.

"I took it to be Grandma's philosophy. When you meet a handsome man, get to know if there's more to him to admire, and, if there is, then keep him in your life. She did warn me. 'Some handsome men trade on their looks and charm. They spend all their time making themselves indispensable to rich women. Don't ever let yourself become dependent on such a man. Be wary.'

"Now, when Grandma met you, she knew you hadn't contrived the meeting. Point one. She decided you were a good-looking young fellow. Point two. And your offer of transportation for me was generous. Three stars right there. That's why you were invited to dine with us, so Grandma could check you out."

"Dr. Glazer said the same thing. I thought she meant table manners."

"That too, I suppose."

Julian said, "I see one flaw in your toot, toot train of thought, young Lori. I'm no movie star, just an ordinary, average-looking guy with a slightly receding hairline. Nothing objectionable, I suppose, but certainly not a hunk."

"Don't argue with Gram's approval. Grandma *knows*. She thinks you are, I quote directly, 'A very nice-looking man.'" She added, with that little giggle that he enjoyed hearing, "I think so too."

Chapter 33

THE CHRISTMAS PARTY, in Reliance Insurance's spacious conference room, was going well, Julian thought. There was lots of conversation and laughter, and the Christmas carols in the background were merely a whisper. He would be sure to compliment Mrs. Abernathy and pretty Carmie Rizzio on their arrangements before he left. He had thought about inviting Lori to the event. It would have saved time for them to have attended the party and then gone directly from Reliance Insurance to Dr. Glazer's, but he had discarded the idea almost immediately. *No point in stirring up talk*, he thought.

When Lori had said that she'd get herself to her appointment with Dr. Glazer, he had been relieved. "I can call a cab," she had said. "Afterwards, I'll wait like I usually do, and we'll go home for dinner with Grandma."

Julian stepped onto the little platform, which was almost filled already by a festive Christmas tree, and moved to the podium. Mrs. Abernathy clinked a knife against a glass, and the room quieted.

As Julian opened his mouth to speak, a loud, exasperated voice from the back of the room broke in, "Well, shit! I lost it." Carmen Rizzio glared in angry dismay at the kaleidoscope in her hand. "It was so beautiful!"

Glancing around, suddenly aware that her ill-chosen words had erupted just as her boss was starting to speak, seeing the startled faces of her coworkers, and realizing what had happened, her face crumpled as she stuttered, "Mr. Elsmore, excuse me…What I said…I apologize. It's just

…" Her voice became a nervous wail. "See, I had a beautiful view, and then I jiggled it, and I…oooooh…that's no excuse. I apologize everyone; I do apologize. I want to sink through the floor."

"Miss Rizzio." Julian's deep voice rang with authority. "Do not sink through the floor. Do *not*. That's an order. We need you here, and, besides …" He paused ominously. "You know yourself we've never completely gotten rid of the mice in the basement." A nervous titter swept the room, and he turned, with a slight smile, to the assembled Reliance family. "Mrs. Abernathy and Miss Rizzio arranged this party: decorations, food, music. Let's give them a hand."

The applause was relieved as well as heartfelt and Julian went on with words that he had not prepared but that he knew would divert the audience and give Miss Rizzio time to collect herself.

"I'd like to tell you a bit about your kaleidoscopes. Each is one of a kind, made by a friend of mine back home, back in Paducah, Kentucky. Miss Sarah Gulley is a genteel Southern lady, probably in her seventies, though she doesn't tell her age, and I, for one, wouldn't dare ask. She runs a lending library out of the old family home, not a business, understand, because Miss Sarah does not engage in business. She calls it 'The Friendly Library,' and one time when my wife and I were there, browsing, we noticed several kaleidoscopes on display.

"My wife picked one up and had the same experience Miss Rizzio had. She shook up a gorgeous view, and then, when she tried to pass it to me, it fell apart.

"Miss Sarah said, 'Oh, don't fret now, don't fret. A kaleidoscope is a very forgiving instrument. The next beautiful vision is just a tiny shake away.'

"My wife shook and looked and, sure enough, it *was* lovely. Miss Sarah agreed to make four for us to give as Christmas presents."

"Where can we buy these?" called out the wife of one of the agents.

Julian dodged sideways as if avoiding something unpleasant. His voice was lightly mocking. "You can't *buy* one because, as I said, Miss Sarah is not in business with all that fuss about income taxes and records, good heavens. A friend simply drops by, maybe to return a book. Miss Sarah serves tea and homemade molasses cookies. The friend asks Miss Sarah, if she pays for the materials, will Miss Sara make her a kaleidoscope? Miss

Sarah quotes a cost-of-materials price, at least double the wholesale price. When the kaleidoscope is ready, the friend pays in cash and adds ten or fifteen dollars 'to show appreciation.'

"I should add that Miss Sarah says, for this Christmas at least, she has topped out on friendly promises to make kaleidoscopes. For later transactions, inquire at my office next year.

"On a more sober note, many of you know that this past year has been a sorrowful one for me. I thank you for your consideration and kindness during a difficult time. Let's start right now to have a joyous Christmas season, and may we all receive many blessings in the New Year of 1979. On behalf of Reliance Insurance, and on my own behalf, I wish you a merry Christmas."

He stepped down from the podium and almost made it to the door amidst calls of, "Merry Christmas to you, Mr. Elsmore."

Mrs. Abernathy intercepted him. "It was great the way you handled that, Mr. Elsmore. You saved Carmie a lot of embarrassment."

"I hope so," he said, "and I'm glad you brought a friend to our party." He turned to the stocky man standing beside Mrs. Abernathy. "Good to have met you, Bernard." With a half salute to Mrs. Abernathy and a "See you Monday," he escaped.

Mrs. Abernathy stared after him, her glance a compliment. "He told that story because he wanted to help Carmie, to dig her out of that hole she was in, and that's why he talked about Miss Sarah and his wife. He never mentions his wife, but he knew we'd be interested, and about the kaleidoscopes too. We'd be interested and mostly forget about Carmie."

"Why doesn't he mention his wife?"

"Bern, my feet are killing me. Let's get some punch and we'll sit down while I tell you about my boss."

Chapter 34

JULIAN HURRIED INTO DR. GLAZER'S outer office, an unwrapped kaleidoscope tucked under his arm. Lori looked up from her reading, glanced at the wall clock, and said all in one breath, "You barely made it on time. How was the party? Vicki says to go right in."

"Great party. Listen, I can't give my doctor a Christmas present, so I want to give this kaleidoscope to the office. Should I put it on Mimi's desk?"

"Can I take a look? Then I'll think of a place to half hide it. You don't want Mimi to think it's her present. I'll see to it. Maybe back of the dish garden. Go on." She dismissed him as she raised the tube to her eye.

"Look toward the light," he reminded her, then stopped. "How did you get here, Lori? Call a cab?"

"Why, no," she said, casually self-satisfied. "I rode the subway. No problem."

"Ye gods, what did your grandmother say?"

"Nothing, because it's a secret and don't you tell."

He strode into the private office. Dr. Glazer glanced at her watch. "Must have been a good party. You stayed until the last minute."

"Meant to leave ten minutes earlier, but something came up and I couldn't get away then. I hope it didn't inconvenience you that I'm a few minutes late."

"Not really. I spent the time thinking about you."

"Really? Thinking what?"

"We've been having our conversations since August, about four months now. So, tell me, do you feel that you are working through your grief?"

"I think so. Yes, I think so. It's been hard for me to speak to anyone but you about Julie. But, at the party this afternoon, Miss Rizzio said something inappropriate and then was horribly embarrassed…well, I'm getting ahead of myself.

"See, I had ordered some handsome, upscale kaleidoscopes as Reliance's Christmas gift to the employees. Everyone loved them. Well, Carmen Rizzio is our bookkeeper; she helped plan the party too. And she was looking though her kaleidoscope at a beautiful pattern, but she jiggled it, and it fell apart. She was irritated at her own clumsiness, I guess, and it happened just when I was starting to speak. The room had quieted, and everyone heard her yell…Well, I won't tell you what she yelled, but she realized everyone had heard her. She was furious with herself, you see, and it was inappropriate what she had said and that she had interrupted me, and she turned terribly red and had tears in her eyes, and she said she wanted to sink through the floor. She's the excitable type, so…" He paused for breath. "Now I've blown it too."

She waited.

"I wanted to distract the crowd, give Carmie time to get hold of herself, so I launched into a story about how a similar thing happened to my wife and what Miss Sarah Gulley—she's the woman who makes the kaleidoscopes—said to Julie, and the story seemed to work because no one was staring at Miss Rizzio anymore, so I chatted along a few more minutes. And then I wished everyone a merry Christmas, and Mrs. Abernathy turned up the volume on the old record player—Bing Crosby's 'White Christmas'—and I got away. That's why I'm a few minutes late."

"Julian, are you making the point that you were able to speak naturally about your wife without going all emotional?"

"My throat didn't clog up. I didn't weep. Yes, it felt natural to tell a story about Julie."

"Then why did you say you blew it?"

"Oh that. Dr. Glazer, I brought you a kaleidoscope for Christmas. Only, I knew you wouldn't let me give you a present, so I told Lori to just tuck it away somewhere in the office, and I thought maybe you or Mimi wouldn't even find it until next week…and then just accept it as something that maybe an angel dropped off. But now I've spilled the beans about the kaleidoscope."

"So you've become an angel, a Christmas angel, I suppose. Very interesting. I'll take a look at the kaleidoscope, Julian."

"It's a good office accessory," he said earnestly. "You can nudge the top off and see what's inside. Just some odds and ends of colored glass, maybe a plastic-coated paper clip, a couple of uncooked alphabet noodles, maybe a dead ladybug. Fit the lid back on and all those ordinary things come together to form a beautiful pattern. Isn't that what we all want, to take the random pieces of our life and make something beautiful of them?"

"Hey, who's the psychiatrist here? Or the poet? Anyway, we need to talk about some other things while we still have some time. I'll think about the kaleidoscope, Julian. By the way, I'll see you and Lori shortly. I, too, have been invited to dine tonight at Mrs. Bellington's."

His face brightened with pleasure. "Wonderful," he said. And he thought, *Three special women.*

Yes, he was healing.

Chapter 35

AFTER THEY HAD EATEN DINNER, Mrs. Bellington, Lori, and their guests repaired to the smaller of the two parlors. Mrs. B sank into her armchair with a slight sigh and nodded to Mr. Munchen, who had followed them into the room.

He laid a writing board on her lap with the smooth, hard side down and the plush, tufted black velvet side up. He then stepped to one of the inner walls, which was covered by built-in bookcases, and swung out a section of shelves to reveal a small safe. Reaching in, he carefully turned the dial this way, that way, then back again a few degrees, and, when the safe opened, he drew out a rectangular box and respectfully laid it on the writing board.

Mrs. B nodded her thanks, and Mr. Munchen, with a grave inclination of his head, closed the bookshelf with precise care and left the room.

Julian watched curiously. He estimated that the box was about five by nine by three inches, and he supposed that it held jewelry. It was a jewel in itself—a slightly domed lid covered in what appeared to be tawny, hand-tooled Moroccan leather, the sides banded with narrow strips of gold, and the intricate catch, also gold, a work of art.

Mrs. B's hands rested lightly on the box, and she looked at Lori. "I picked out several pieces of jewelry for you, Lori, as an early Christmas present. Some come with family history and are quite valuable. Some, like the harlequin pin, are fanciful accessories that I chose for myself just because they appealed. I tried to select things suitable for a young woman to wear on special occasions. You are my heir, and it seems proper that you should have these."

She opened the jewelry box and lifted out a triple-strand faux pearl necklace. "These were very popular in the 60s because Jacqueline Kennedy favored them. They go with almost anything, dressy or sporty."

Next she laid a necklace of sapphires set in gold with matching earbobs on the velvet surface. "Your great-grandfather gave these to the wife he adored when he made his first million. He founded Rosen's Department Store in the mid-nineteenth century, you know, a small enterprise that he nurtured wisely. Incidentally, we still own a controlling interest in that store. He chose sapphires to match her eyes, and, in time, they matched my eyes and now will match yours. They look very handsome with evening wear. You'll find a matching bracelet underneath the top tray."

"Grandma, how beautiful!" Lori's eyes were misty. Vicki murmured, "Exquisite." Julian observed intently, as if he were watching a stage play.

Mrs. B drew forth a choker of onyx. Each stone was set in its own silver cradle, each cradle joined to the next by three small silver links. "I debated with myself about this. It seemed a bit mature for a very young woman, but then I thought with your fair skin and with the right outfit it would be quite suitable."

"Oh, Grandma!"

"There are a few other trinkets, a diamond sunburst pin, a pink crystal necklace, a lovely little rose-gold Lady Elgin wristwatch with gold hands on a black face. I hope you'll enjoy investigating this treasure box, yours now to do with as you wish." She shut the lid, made as if to hand the case to Lori, frowned vaguely, and put it back on her lap.

"I almost forgot." She opened the beautiful box again and pointed out a slit in the lining of the lid. It was so incorporated into the elaborate embroidery that it was scarcely noticeable as an opening. "In my day, when a man—a husband, a betrothed, a lover—gave jewelry to the object of his affection, he often wrote a tender note, sometimes for her eyes only. If she wished to keep the note, she could tuck it into this little hiding place." Her eyes softened with remembrance.

"Is that where you hid your notes, Grandmother?" teased Lori.

She was rebuked with a prim reply. "Only those from the Colonel. I did tuck something there for you, Lori. It's your personal no-limit charge card for Rosen's. As I mentioned, you are an heiress; and while I know you are comfortable in your faded blue jeans and sneakers, you will soon have occasion to need a proper wardrobe. It would please me enormously to see you dressed up, wearing jewels, some discreet make-up. What a lovely gift that would be. Maybe you'll give me a fashion show for Christmas?" She made the remark into a question and waited for Lori's reply.

Lori realized that she was being cozened into a plan that her generous grandmother had shaped, a plan with a time frame even. She couldn't think of a way out and didn't like being told what to do, but the shopping trip that her grandmother had proposed sounded rather exciting. And she suddenly realized, feeling intoxicated, that shopping with no need to check the price tag against her allowance would be especially delightful.

In high school, she had loved scoping out the dress stores with her girlfriends. "Let's go shopping" had been a rallying cry. Here, in New York, living a sort of exile for the past half year, she hadn't given her wardrobe much thought. *But...well, why not?* Her thoughts bubbled. *No need to seek out bargains.*

"Thank you, Grandma," she said. "What shall I buy?"

"Everything, my dear. What you would call 'the works.' Skirts, trousers, a camel's hair jacket, a tweed jacket too. Do you ride?"

"I've had lessons, but not my favorite sport."

"No jodhpurs then." Mrs. B looked regretful. "Maybe later. Jodhpurs would flatter you. For now lots of blouses and cashmere sweaters. Pretty undergarments. And a perfectly tailored black business suit, a must. A dressy black suit too. Well, the dressy suit could be charcoal grey. Oh, and shoes."

"Not high heels, Grandma. I can't walk in high heels."

"But not sneakers."

"We call them athletic shoes, Grandma."

"Not athletic shoes then. Something beautiful. Surely..." Mrs. B looked at Victoria Glazer for help.

"No problem. The classic pump comes in a flat version, beautifully trimmed, clever straps, toe decorations, many rich colors."

"That's what we want. And, Lori, Upper Level has a beauty parlor. They'll know what to do about your hair. They'll highlight your lovely cheekbones too."

"I thought I was going to shop at Rosen's. Where's Upper Level?"

"It's Rosen's seventh floor. My mother, your great-grandmother, who was a canny businesswoman underneath the feminine fluff, insisted on that part of the store. Today it would open as a boutique. Back then, it was Upper Level, very exclusive and very expensive. Wealthy women loved to shop there because they were assured of the latest exclusive styles and were catered to, bowed to, treated like royalty. Sometimes they *were* royalty or wives of high-ranking foreign diplomats. American society girls and brides too."

"Did my mom get her clothes there?"

"Occasionally. When she was married, I gave her a trousseau from Upper Level. Lovely garments, but she probably never wore even half of them. Why she was uninterested in her appearance, I'll never understand."

Lori thought of her mother's wardrobe, good quality clothes in mostly neutral shades. Seldom any jewelry, although Lori remembered that, over the years, Grandmother had given her only daughter, Alexis, some beautiful pieces. And Lexie had said, "How sweet of Mom. I remember that she often wore this ruby ring. How lovely." The gift would disappear into Lexie's jewelry box, never to be seen again.

And now, Lori thought, *what does Grandma want of me?*

"Mom always looks very neat and nice," she said loyally.

"Humff. She could look spectacular. Even now...*spectacular!* I gave her good bones, but about all she ever did with them was pass them on to you."

"I guess I should say thanks for that. Anyway, Grandma, are you going shopping with me to see I get the right things?"

"What a pleasure that would be—an expedition to Upper Level— but I'm afraid that trip is more than I can manage." She sighed, giving an impression of weakness. Looking at her with a doctor's eye, Victoria Glazer thought it might be more than an impression. Mrs. B could truly be running out of life's juices, her dominant energy simply drying up.

"I was hoping, perhaps…" Mrs. B glanced at Vicki. "Victoria, you have such good taste, an eye for line and color. I was wondering if you might accompany Lori. A second opinion is so important. Besides, it would, I think, be a pleasurable occasion." With a smile, she placed the jewelry box in Lori's hands.

Victoria had suspected that she had been invited to dinner that evening for some special reason. Now she knew what it was. "It does sound like fun. If you'd like me to, I'd be tickled to go shopping with you, Lori."

Mrs. B wasn't quite finished. She wanted to be sure the plans were finalized. "If you can set a time now, I'll call the manager and let him know. You reach Upper Level by a private elevator. He'll take you up."

Lori gave Vicki a questioning look. "What day is good for you?"

"What are the store hours?"

The question surprised Mrs. B. "It will be open for you whenever you want, day or evening."

"Well then," said Victoria, "the sooner the better, I suppose, if we're to put on a fashion show before Christmas. Lori, I have Saturday morning appointments tomorrow, but the afternoon would work for me. If it works for you, I can pick you up at about one-thirty."

Lori started to agree but then said, remembering, "Julian and I have ESOL training until two thirty. Is that too late?"

"Not for me."

Julian, careful not to irritate by sounding protective, offered casually, "If you want, Lori, I can drive you to Rosen's as soon as our class ends, and you can meet Vicki there."

It was so arranged, and Mrs. B, her mission accomplished, announced, "I shall retire now. Good night to you all, my dears, and thank you for dining with me this evening. Lori?"

Lori, as she did every night now, stood in front of her grandmother, and they grasped each other's wrists. Lori braced herself and pulled gently. Carefully, slowly, and with immense dignity, the old woman rose. To catch her breath after the effort and to be sure of her balance, Mrs. B stood still for a regal minute and beamed on her guests.

"Julian," she said with a gracious nod, "I hope you will attend the fashion show. If all goes well, shall we say after dinner on the Friday before

Christmas? That's December 22." Having driven in the last nail to secure her plan, and without waiting for a reply, she took Lori's arm, and they walked slowly from the room.

Vicki turned to Julian. "A riveting performance."

"Worthy of applause. Vicki, will you really go shopping with Lori? I thought there was some sort of rule, a professional restriction or something...you know..."

"No problem. For women, shopping is *therapy*. Just wait 'til you see what this new wardrobe is going to do for Lori's self-esteem because, I promise you, it is going to promote her from high school kid to womanhood. She will look as her grandmother would like her to look: *spectacular*. She does have great bones."

Julian thought that when he made his regular visit to Julie's grave on Sunday, he would have a great story to tell. *Maybe Julie's tired of my grieving.*

As Mrs. B and Lori made their way to the downstairs bedroom that Mrs. B had recently established for herself, she advised Lori, "While you're at Upper Level, if you hear Vicki admire something in particular—a scarf, a scent, a handbag—do take note. That item will be her Christmas present."

"You think of everything, don't you, Grandma?" The only answer was a small, complacent smile.

"Is there anything else I can help you with, Grandma?"

"I can manage, thank you. Just turn down the bed covers. Is the electric sheet on?"

"Munchkin would never forget, Grandma. It's toasty." Mrs. B closed her eyes for a moment and then reached up to pat her granddaughter's face.

"Grandma, I love you," said Lori. "I'm excited about the jewelry and the shopping trip, thank you. Sweet dreams." She bent and kissed her grandmother's cheek.

"Good enough," said the old lady. "That's certainly good enough."

AT THE CEMETERY

December 17, 1978

It's almost Christmas, Julie.

Remember how when we were little kids we had a ritual? On Christmas Eve, we'd go out into the back yard when the stars were just coming out and the day was fading into the darkness. You'd say, "Look over there by that cloud, Julian. I see an angel."

I'd say, "I see another one, right over the roof. They'll start their glad tidings soon."

You and I would hold hands in the twilight and sing "Oh Little Town of Bethlehem" or "Silent Night." We took turns picking the carol. Then quick we'd duck back into our houses because it was cold and anyway we needed to get to bed early so we could get up early.

Remember how Joy and Miles loved it when we tested the Christmas tree lights? And when you unpacked the snow globe and let them shake it? When they were old enough, we took them to church to the midnight services and one of them always fell asleep.

Julie, I'm forty-three years old now and it will be the first time in my life that I've celebrated Christmas without you.

Well, the office party went well. Thank you for telling me last year that kaleidoscopes make wonderful gifts.

A lot going on. After our conversation, next Friday, Vicki and I are invited to a fashion show at Bellington's. Lori is the model.

And on the next day Lori and I finish our ESOL training course. There will be a little celebration for that. Lori says she is going to bake some cookies to take, even if Cook scolds, and I've unpacked our 30-cup coffee machine. I never use it so I think I'll just donate it to the church kitchen. That okay with you, Julie?

Then the day before Christmas, I'm driving to Philadelphia to spend the holidays with Joy and Brian and little Julie. I've a few more presents to buy so I need to get cracking. Miles will be there, too, so that will be great. But Julie, we will miss you terribly, so terribly.

Dr. Glazer says all the activity is good. I guess so.

He sat and had to wipe his eyes before he could start the car. He drove away, wretchedly lonesome for her.

Chapter 36

Lori called Julian at work. "I need some help. I have a Christmas gift for Maria—a white wool hat and scarf set—and four more of those onesies in the next size up for Elena, but I don't know how to send them."

"I can take care of that. Get them wrapped and I'll pick them up at your house after work tomorrow. My contact can pass them along to Maria with my gifts."

"What are you sending Maria?"

"I'm sending my gifts to the whole house. Six dozen decorated sugar cookies—cut-outs, you know—stars and bells, Christmas trees, and gingerbread men. And a dozen rolls of film. All from an anonymous donor."

"That sounds good. Can I put my name and address on my gifts to Maria?"

"You can try. If they object, they'll cut them off, I suppose."

"Well then, I've a few more cards to write and I'll be ready for Christmas. Grandma's present was delivered today."

"What did you get her?"

"The neatest thing. See, whenever I walk her to her bedroom at night, her hands are always cold, really cold. Her heart is running down—I talked to her doctor—and can't pump her blood as fast as it should. I noticed there's an electric sheet on her bed. Munchkin turns it on each evening so the bed is cozy for her.

"I said, 'There must be a heating pad somewhere in this house. I'll ask Munchkin, and, if we move your chair against the opposite wall, there's an outlet we can plug it into, and you can be nice and warm in your chair.' You know what she said?"

"What?" Julian asked.

"Very pleasantly—have you noticed that Grandma is always pleasant?—she said, 'I like my chair where it is, where it has always been, and I really don't like dangling cords.'

"I asked, 'Maybe a lap robe then? A light, wooly lap robe?'

"'Lori,' she said, 'a lap robe looks sporty when one is at the race track on a chilly day. Other times it makes one look old and feeble.'

"Well, Gram thought she had scratched my suggestion, but she always says I'm her heir, and one thing I inherited was her strong will. I said, 'Okay, Grandma, bummer idea.' But I said to myself, *We'll see about that.*"

"So you got her an electric heating pad, anyway?"

"Oh, Julian, I'd never do that. She would smile and say, 'How thoughtful. Thank you, dear,' and hand it to Mr. Munchen to be donated to the next rummage sale at church.

"About her present. Mr. Munchen gave me the name of the company that has taken care of all the furniture in this house for simply decades, and I told them what I needed. Grandma's Christmas present is a liner for her chair, same upholstery fabric, hardly noticeable at all, heated by batteries. The upholstery people were very clever. They made long panels that drop over the sides of the chair. They look fashionable, and they warm the arms of the chair and her arms at the same time. If Grandma wants, she can discreetly pull one panel up over her lap."

"This liner was custom made? Sounds expensive." Not for the first time, he wondered if she had a substantial allowance or maybe some private source of income.

"It *was* expensive. When they quoted a price, it blew me away. I simply couldn't afford it. But I called my mom and dad and asked if they wanted to go in on the gift, and, you know, they were delighted. Mom said, 'We never send gifts because we never have any idea of what would please her. She has everything.' Dad said, 'You did all the research, made all the arrangements, Lori. It's only fair that that we pay for it. Tell them to send the bill to us.' And that's what I did. That's how I had enough Christmas money to send four onesies to Elena, instead of two as I had planned."

"And what did you send your parents?"

"That's pretty neat too. When we were at Upper Level, after the beauty shop had done its magic, Vicki asked them to take a photo of me in my tailored black suit. They set up a mirror, so there's a side view in the picture too. It came out okay, and that's what Vicki is giving Grandma for Christmas. She had an extra print made for me, and I had it put in a very nice frame for my parents. I think they'll like it. I hope so."

"You aren't going home for Christmas then? Or for a New Year's visit?"

"I hardly thought about that. See, not only did I say I'd stay with Grandma for a year, but I really think she wants me here. She's been sort of fixated on this heiress business."

"But families usually get together at the holidays."

"Julian, this is simply how it is. If I were home for Christmas, my parents would be pleased. If I'm not there, they'll be happy together. As for me, I like being with my grandmother, even if she is a bit eccentric at times."

The whole set-up is a bit eccentric, he thought, but he didn't push it any further. Instead he told her of his own Christmas plans. "I'm driving up to Philadelphia on Saturday to spend Christmas and the day after with Joy and her family. Miles will be there, too."

"But you'll be here for the fashion show after dinner next Friday?"

"I wouldn't miss it."

Chapter 37

On the day after Christmas, Julian sat at the kitchen table in Joy and Brian's little apartment and watched his granddaughter bounce in the jump seat that he had given her.

"Look how strong her legs are," he observed to Joy as she poured him a freshly brewed cup of coffee. "Look how beautiful she is."

Joy pretended to assess her child critically. "Needs a hair bow." She drew from her pocket a length of narrow red ribbon, which only yesterday had adorned a Christmas present. "I saved this."

"She doesn't have enough hair."

"Watch." Joy blew along the baby's head, and, sure enough, Joy's breeze lifted a few strands of pale blond hair that she caught together and twisted slightly. "Hold them for me," she told her father, and then she deftly tied the ribbon into a tiny bow around the wisp of hair. When Julian let go, the hair fell into a little topknot and he laughed.

"She's a kewpie doll."

The baby, for no reason at all, chortled with delight, and tiny dimples flashed in her chubby cheeks.

Julian caught his breath. "She has her grandmother's dimples, did you see that?"

"I've seen them. I think she takes after Mom in lots of ways."

"The dimples. When your mom's smile had dimples in it, it was a sign to me that all was right in the world."

"You miss Mom terribly, I know, but Christmas was okay, wasn't it?"

He nodded. "Better than I expected, the first Christmas without her and all. A baby makes a family happy."

"And the stories. That was a good idea." She picked little Julie up. "It's time for her nap. I'll change her, and then, if you want to, you can rock her to sleep. You have a special talent for settling her down."

Maybe it was just flattery. Whatever it was, he loved hearing it. "Just bring her to me. She'll be asleep in no time."

A few minutes later, with the baby nestled over his heart, he began to pat her back and hum, the lullaby a deep, steady sound in his chest. He watched with almost unbearable tenderness as little Julie's eyes drifted shut.

The Stories

Yesterday, Christmas Day, after dinner, acting on a suggestion from Vicki Glazer, Julian had proposed that they each tell a favorite story of their mother.

Joy went first:

"When I was seven years old and a Brownie, it was my turn to bring the treat for our troop meeting. Mom sent cupcakes, and each one had a face. The colors were the most vivid she could make from her drops of pure food coloring—the eyes were the bluest of blues, the cheeks and lips the reddest of reds. Mom liked more delicate shades herself, but she knew that kids would go for the strong colors.

"Each cupcake's face had hair—toasted coconut curls, a shock of candy corn with points toward the center, little black spit curls made with the thinnest of licorice strings. And every face was different. Some had laughing lips and happy eyebrows. Others had worried eyebrows and upside down mouths. Some noses were slices of pink gumdrops.

"My friends actually drooled over their choices, and my troop leader laughed and said, 'Your mother is very creative, Joy.' I was proud."

Brian went next:

"My story is a thanksgiving story." He looked at Julian. "I don't mean Thanksgiving Day. I mean I give thanks. It was actually the Fourth of July picnic when Joy and I told you and Mom that we wanted to get married. I had been invited to dinner a couple of times before, and Mom had asked me about my work and been quite cordial. Now she regarded me speculatively and said not one word about our announcement for several minutes. I was getting nervous. Surely our plans weren't a total surprise to her.

"Suddenly, she turned to me and said, 'Brian?' And, when I looked up, she frowned and then, amazingly, crossed her eyes for a moment. That alarmed me. I didn't know then that it was her signal to *pay attention.*

"'Brian, if you marry Joy, you get our whole family, Julian and Miles and me and Julian's father. We are not an exciting family, like some who enjoy loud music, lots of fights with lots of cursing, firecrackers going off all over the place, big, emotional binges. But we're normal, I think. We love one another quietly, and we solve our problems as best we can. If there is trouble or sorrow, we draw closer, we love each other harder. Sometimes we scold each other a bit, but we don't yell, we don't throw china, we don't punch our fist into a plate of spaghetti to make a point. If that sounds dull to you, well…talk it over with Joy before you get married.

"'Each family has its own way of living. It's the little day-to-day differences, the fact that she *never* throws anything out, the fact that he *never* puts the toilet seat down, that blow up into fights and resentment. Different points of view can ruin a marriage. You have to work at being compatible. Your family too. Tell Joy how your family lives, how they celebrate, how they mourn, even if they live way up there in Montana. Do you understand me, Brian?'

"I said, 'Yes, ma'am.'

"She went on. 'You know it's against my religion for a couple to live together before marriage, as so many do these days, but it does have a few advantages. Maybe you could take a cross-country trip in Joy's VW. See how it goes when you're stuck together in a little car for four days. Anyway, Brian, you and Joy make sure you figure out, *before* you marry, how you are going to solve differences.'

"It was the best of advice. As an old married man, I realize now that engaged couples need to do more than kiss and hold hands and teeter on the verge of sex." He gave Joy a fond glance. "Not to denigrate that kind of fun, but they also need to talk about each one's lifestyle and how they will blend those lifestyles into a strong marriage, how they will compromise.

"Today, when I looked at that snapshot you brought of Julie's gravestone, I changed the inscription a little. In my heart it says 'Beloved wife and mother and wise mother-in-law.'"

After a tender moment of silence, Miles spoke, starting slowly:

"Even as a little kid, I was fascinated by numbers, and, when I was about five years old, I learned the most amazing thing. I went to Mom and told her I could count to a hundred by twos. 'Want to hear me?' It was a bad time. She was getting dinner and teaching Joy to set the table, where the silverware goes and that stuff, and she replied, 'Not right now.'

"I coaxed her. 'I could count to one hundred by even twos or odd twos.'

"That caught her interest. 'Okay then. By odd twos.'

"I thought it over and realized I had made a mistake. 'Well, you see, I can't do that, but I could count to ninety-nine or one hundred and one by odd twos.'

"She gave me a surprised, 'Okay, Miles, you do that. Count to one hundred and one.'

"I had just finished counting when you walked in the door from work."

"I remember," said Julian. "She was kneeling on the floor, hugging you, and she looked up and told me, 'Our son is ever so smart. He can count to one hundred and one by odd twos.'

"While I was sorting that out, she suddenly wrinkled her nose, jumped up, and ran to the stove. 'Oh dear, I'm serving scorched potatoes tonight,' she said. 'Wash your hands for dinner.'"

"Great story," said Joy.

"Great mom," finished Miles and turned to his father. "You going to tell a story, Dad?"

Julian could hardly speak. "Next year I will. I can't right now. I thank you for this year's stories. I'll always remember. They help." Feeling that he had perhaps let them down by not contributing, he added, "I will tell you now, though, there was a song that described your mother. The title was 'You Are My Everything.' All my life, that's what she was—my playmate, my schoolmate, my best teen-age friend, my challenge, my wife, and my soul mate." Although embarrassed by his own emotion, he managed to finish what he wanted to say. It was important. In a broken voice, he told his grown-up kids, "Always remember that you were born the children of love. Your mom was my everything."

Sitting relaxed in a big, overstuffed chair, holding little Julie warmly, Julian realized that he was getting sleepy himself, and he looked around for Joy. She came and lifted the limp baby from his arms. "Let's all take a nap, Dad, and later we'll go out for a walk."

He nodded, thinking that he must remember to tell Vicki that the stories had been a very good idea. He slept peacefully then, leaning back in the chair. He dreamed—a precise recall it was—of Lori and the fashion show.

Chapter 38

JULIAN DREAMED:

Lori had worn three different outfits at the pre-Christmas fashion show. First, she walked across the parlor looking confident in well-tailored slacks and a camel hair sports jacket, the harlequin pin dancing on the lapel. At Rosen's, they had indeed known what to do with her hair (mousey brown was now honey colored), had highlighted her cheekbones, and had taught her to use subtle eye make-up. She walked like royalty, her head held high and a faint smile on her face.

Her second outfit was more girlish but still impressive. She wore a pleated, plaid skirt of blue, brown, and white; a creamy Irish fisherman's sweater; cable knee socks; and moccasins of soft, brown leather. Her only jewelry was a gold bracelet that she had found when she explored the little treasure chest.

Lori's skirt was cut just a bit longer than mid-thigh length, and, when she stood in front of her grandmother, she asked, "Is the skirt too short, Grandmother? They said at Rosen's it's what all the young people are wearing. And that's what I am, a young person."

"Then it's fine. Some girls are too heavy or too thin to look good in that length, but you have the legs for it."

Vicki, who had worried that the skirt might offend Mrs. B, let go of a breath that she hadn't known she was holding.

Grandmother added, "I've seen some young women—I won't call them 'ladies'—on the TV whose skirts aren't much more than ruffles around their waists. When they sit down, they sit on their panties because the skirt is too short to tuck under. That's *too* short." She added complacently, "You walk very gracefully, Lori."

"Thank you, Grandmother. The grand finale of this little fashion show is the black business suit you said was a 'must.' It's a wool and silk blend, feels good as soon as I put it on. I'll be back in five or six minutes." She winked triumphantly at Vicki as she left the room.

When she returned, she posed for a long moment in the archway to the parlor. Then, like a model, she pivoted on the balls of her feet so that her audience could appreciate the rear view, pivoted back, gave them all a haughty look, and, as if she were on a runway, promenaded across the room. Another flirty turn and she came to stand for her grandmother's inspection.

Mrs. B nodded. The suit draped perfectly. Tiny black satin piping finished the collar and lapels, and there was a froth of white lace at Lori's throat. The slim skirt was two inches longer than the plaid one that she had worn earlier. It was not dowdy at all, indeed high style, but there was plenty of skirt to tuck under. Mrs. B smiled with approval as she took in the charcoal grey panty hose and the black flats with intricately embroidered toes. For jewelry, Lori had chosen the sapphire earrings and bracelet that had belonged to her great-grandmother.

The old woman beamed. "What a treat for me. I'm pleased with your new wardrobe, Lori."

"Great show," said Vicki, satisfied with her own role in the transformation. "You look lovely." As Lori left the room, she added, "Mrs. B, she's a princess. Beautiful!"

"A fairy-tale princess," confirmed Julian, and then he blushed, ashamed of his sudden, nasty thought. *She's too good, too special, for Bill Letterson, that muscle-bound klutz.*

Mrs. B expressed her own view, "A princess, yes, I suppose. To me, she looks the way my granddaughter should. She looks like my heiress. By the way, Vicki, the next time you and Lori go to Upper Level, be sure Lori gets a ball gown. Something young but elegant. With her coloring, I think jade green would be very becoming. That's just a suggestion of course. It should be whatever she wants."

"Of course, whatever she wants. Jade green would be perfect." Both Vicki and Julian had hidden a smile. End of fashion show.

Julian woke easily in his daughter's living room. He stood up, stretched, and heard that little Julie was also awake. "Let's go for that walk," he said.

Despite the anguish of the past year, they were enjoying Christmas. It was because they had celebrated the birth of Christ together, they had happy memories of the dear woman they had lost from their family circle, and they had a baby just learning to sit up and play patty-cake.

Chapter 39

TRINITY METHODIST CHURCH held a prayer service on New Year's Day. It was announced as "Petitions and Promises for 1979." Contemplating the new year, Julian struggled between his heartfelt need to keep Julie's memory forever a brightly lit votive light and his equally strong need to remake himself.

As Julian left the church, Pastor Wellington called him aside. "Julian, the church council has voted to set up a new committee to help our young people grow in fellowship. We've been thinking maybe a drop-in center, a Saturday night coffeehouse, what we used to call a teenage hangout, I guess. Maybe some trips, perhaps a choir or band. Nothing definite yet, lots of ideas, another planning meeting set for early this month. Your name came up, and I was asked to ask you if you would be interested in serving on that committee."

"What's involved?"

"The basic aim is two-fold. We want to bind our youth to the Church socially and spiritually, and we'll encourage group projects where they work together to help the disadvantaged in our own area. Get our young people to stop thinking about themselves and experience the satisfactions and disappointments of doing good."

"Sounds worthwhile, but I don't have any training or particular skill in that kind of work, none at all."

"I believe you have two children who have grown to be responsible adults, right?" Julian nodded. "That's pretty good on-the-job training. Will you think about it?"

"Give me some more details. What sort of time would I be committing to?"

"Well, don't think it would be an honorary position where you would go to a meeting once a month and review a proposal to buy a pool table or vote to approve the financial report and dull stuff like that. We hope the committee members will be role models. Active ones who will chaperone trips, show up at the Saturday night coffeehouse, which is one of the things I'm pretty sure will happen, and be advisors for do-good projects."

"Let me think about it."

"Of course."

He immediately thought about Lori. *A chance for her to meet some local young people without feeling she's cheating on Bill. She'll be working with a group and doing good. Sounds perfect. I can transport her since I'll be going there too, to keep an eye on things.*

He said to Pastor Wellington, "How about I go to the next meeting and see for myself if it's something I'm comfortable with?"

"Good idea. Have you met Melissa Stoner? She's head of the planning committee. She's having a little dinner party meeting week after next, just a sociable gathering of movers and shakers on this project. Eight or ten people. Heads of other committees that will have to be involved. My wife and I will be there. Shall I call Melissa and tell her to invite you?"

"Be sure she understands I'm just there as a *possible* member."

"Thank you, Julian. I really think you'd be a strong addition to the committee, but, if nothing else, it is a chance to get acquainted with others in our fellowship." The pastor paused and then, following his own train of thought, added, "Melissa Stoner is a widow."

Oddly enough, when he told Vicki about the dinner party later, she said immediately, "Melissa is a widow, Julian. Very energetic."

Because he knew how interested Mrs. B was in the activities of her church, he also told her about the new committee that would sponsor youth activities. "It would be a chance for Lori to get involved. A suitable chance, I think, if you approve."

"I would approve." Mrs. B eyed him carefully then and spoke bluntly, "You do know that Melissa has been a widow for almost three years, do you not, Julian? She's on the prowl. At dinner, it will turn out that you two are a couple."

Julian wasn't surprised when that was exactly how it turned out. Nevertheless, because of Lori, he signed up to serve on the committee.

Chapter 40

EARLY IN JANUARY, LORI AND JULIAN were assigned students by the ESOL program and began tutoring every Tuesday and Thursday evening from five-thirty to seven o'clock.

"My student," Lori said proudly, "came to this country from south of the border to be an *au pair* but realized right away that she needed to improve her English because parents don't want their children to grow up speaking some garbled language. She wants to get a green card and then eventually become a citizen. Her name is Rosita, and I'll bet, by next year, it will be Rose or even Roz. She's very eager to be American."

"I have a couple in their thirties. He has a job bussing tables in an upscale American restaurant, makes pretty good money, and she stays home with their three young children. The two oldest are in school and in ESOL programs there. Juan says he gets along fine at work because he doesn't have to talk to customers and there is a bilingual worker in the kitchen. But he's ambitious. His goal, he tells me, is to sell real estate in the many neighborhoods of the city that are turning Hispanic."

"A realtor? Is that likely to happen?"

"Why not? He's smart, motivated. As soon as his English is good enough, he can work in a realty office as an interpreter, certainly there's a growing need for that, and get familiar with the business while he's working. Then he can get more formal training and a license."

"You make it sound easy, Julian."

"I don't mean it that way, but it's possible, even probable, if he works hard and sticks to his dream..Juan doesn't want to be a busboy when he's fifty years old. He and his wife are studying to become citizens. Just the type of newcomers this country needs."

"Rosita works in a restaurant too, but it's Hispanic."

"I know it's only our second week, but do you enjoy tutoring?"

"I'm hooked. I feel like I'm doing something worthwhile. I feel it goes back somehow to finding Elena and that it all makes a kind of wonderful pattern. Maybe it's destiny." She spoke so solemnly that he knew better than to laugh. He just nodded seriously when she added, "I suppose I'll be an ESOL tutor all my life."

"With Bill?"

"Bill?" She looked surprised at the thought. "I don't think so. I picture Bill running a little business—installing carpet or detailing cars, something like that. I'll help with the business, taking care of the phone, banking, taxes. Then I'll be off to my tutoring, and he'll go coach the high school football team. He'd like that." She giggled. "You understand, Julian, that's twenty years from now, when Bill and I are a settled married couple with children almost as old as I am now."

He shuddered inwardly at that vision and pushed it from his mind. To cover his sudden anger, he picked up a business card that had been posted on the bulletin board in the entry hall. "Some family in our parish runs a restaurant nearby—Reuben's Old Time Home Cooking. Let's try it. I'm hungry for home-made mashed potatoes and gravy."

"Let's go then. I'm starved for most anything."

Julian told Dr. Glazer that he was now tutoring two evenings each week.

She said, "Good."

He told her that he had resumed his regular exercise program and taken membership in a local gym. "Don't want to go soft around the middle."

She said, "Good."

He mentioned that the get-acquainted meeting for the youth committee at Melissa Stoner's home had been amiable—good food and easy conversation.

"How did you feel about that?" Her question was cool.

"Why, it was fine. She has a very lovely home. Don't you like Melissa?"

"I went to school with her," Dr. Glazer said cryptically. "She can be bossy once she gets a bee in her bonnet." *What an unprofessional remark! I shouldn't have said that,* Vicki scolded herself.

"Well, she is very upbeat about this youth project, very enthusiastic. I said I'd join the committee. The target is to make it a club of sorts with prayer sessions and service projects but mainly a place where the kids can hang out. It's to open in April, downstairs in the parish center, maybe the Saturday after Easter. It will be a soft-drink version of a coffeehouse night. We need a catchy name. Live music and a planning session. Don't you think it will be good for Lori to get to know some other young people and have fun?"

"Of course. You've met her fiancé, haven't you? What do you think of him?"

He tried to be fair. "Bill's a good-looking jock. Well brought up. High school football was the apex of his life. And Lori was part of that. That's what he feeds on."

"Is he right for her?"

"Who knows?"

"I'm asking your opinion."

He gave up. "No. He's an okay guy, I guess, but sort of aimless. No plans, not much ambition. She's too good for him. I'm glad about this youth group. It's perfect for Lori because she'll meet other young people but not be dating anyone in particular. She's so engaged to Bill Letterson, so true to him, she feels guilty about having fun without him."

"But she feels safe doing things with you, doesn't she? Let's see, you tutor together two nights a week, you transport Lori here on Fridays and then take her home and stay for dinner at Mrs. Bellington's. Coffeehouse on Saturday nights will be coming up in a few months. You'll both be there. And of course you also have those committee meetings with Melissa, let's not forget them. You drive to Philadelphia every other weekend to see the darling granddaughter. My, you are busy, Julian. Does it help?"

"Well, I guess." He thought the conversation had taken a strange turn. His shrink was talking as if she knew something that he didn't. "Yes, Doctor, I guess it helps to be busy."

Chapter 41

AFTER TUTORING ON THURSDAYS, Lori and Julian usually ate at Reuben's.

"Eating late but eating homemade," Julian commented as he lifted a forkful of beef potpie. "Worth waiting for."

"It's funny. I never feel hungry while I'm working with Roz. Then, all of a sudden, the tutoring ends, and I'm starved. Like now. I'm glad that Reuben's is only two blocks away. I don't think I'd survive three." She giggled and he smiled.

"How's it going with Rosita?"

"Good. She's making progress. I just wish we could meet more often."

"Mr. and Mrs. Umberto want to know if they can bring their three children to class."

"Can they? I mean, is it allowed?"

"Why not? We're volunteers. If I choose to add three little kids to my tutoring family, who's to say I shouldn't?"

"How old are they?"

"The baby's two, a very cute age. The older children are in first and third grades. Probably they all—even little Joey, who's just starting to talk—speak English better than their parents. They'll grow up to be perfectly bilingual."

"I remember that. If you learn a second language after age fourteen, you'll probably always speak it with an accent. But not the Umberto children. They'll speak English perfectly, and Spanish perfectly, and they'll help their parents. Will you ask?"

"About including the children? No, indeed. See, Lori, suppose I ask a council member. He says he really doesn't have an answer but will put it on the agenda for the next regular meeting. Bad move because, at the meeting, it's easy for some fusty, self-important member to say, 'We established that program to teach *adults*. If we let kids in, we'll soon have them running all over the hall. The janitor won't like it. We'd have to look into whether we need more insurance. Anyway, it's not needed. The public school has ESOL classes for their students.'

"I can see other heads nodding gravely. It won't matter that the Umbertos sometimes have trouble finding a babysitter, that babysitters are expensive, that the family that learns together learns faster. The council members are good stewards, and they feel safe when they say no."

"What if the kids *do* run all over the hall? What if the baby falls down the stairs?"

"Trust me. We insurance men know about safety. Besides, I got a lot of practical experience protecting my own children. The baby won't fall down stairs or off a table or eat an eraser. I'll childproof the room. Then I'll close the door and put one of those fake doorknobs over the real doorknob. Kid or adult, you can turn that gadget forever and the door won't open."

"What if the janitor snitches?"

"Are you playing devil's advocate? If anyone objects, I'll apologize. 'Oh, sorry, I didn't know…' See?"

She changed the subject abruptly. "Julian, do you think I could drive the Lincoln?"

"The Lincoln? Now I'm the fusty bureaucrat who says that's something you should ask your grandmother."

"I don't mean permission. I mean, is a limousine hard to handle? It seems so bulky, so long, and I don't have a lot of experience."

"Lori," he asked, "where do you want to go?"

"No place in particular. It's just the idea. I depend on you all the time. Shouldn't I depend on myself? I tried the subway and Grandma is right. It is damp and dark. I don't think the platforms have been washed in a million years. And the subway cars are covered in graffiti, and the whole place stinks a little. Meanwhile, that limo just sits there useless. Since it was repaired after the accident, it hasn't moved out of the garage."

"Can you drive a stick shift?"

"A what?"

"Oh boy," he said and hit his forehead with his hand. "What did you drive back home?"

"Well, my dad has a sporty little Chevy, but he only took me out to practice in it once. You wouldn't believe how nervous he was. Made me nervous too. I ran up on a curb."

"You didn't have a car you drove regularly?"

"We had a driver's ed class at school. I drove the student-driver car."

"Lori," he said firmly, falling too easily into parental mode, "if you don't know what a stick shift is and you don't have much experience, then, no, you can't drive the limo. Don't even think about it. I'll take you where you want to go."

"Thank you," she said politely, but under her breath she said something that sounded like "Bummer."

He ignored it and beckoned to the waitress. "Am I right that you bake apple pies on Thursday?"

"Just out of the oven four hours ago."

"I'll have a piece."

Lori, perhaps to show her independence, chose devil's food cake for dessert.

Chapter 42

Mr. Metcalfe had been invited to Friday night dinner. He and Julian were introduced, shook hands, and settled down to one of Cook's good meals.

Mrs. B looked around the table with approval. "I am pleased that you are all here, and," she added with her signature firmness, "so is Cook. She has complained for over ten years now, ever since the Colonel died, that it is dreary to make meals for just one old lady. Cook presumes on her long years of service, but, still, I sometimes eat more than I really want just so I won't hurt her feelings."

Rotund Mr. Metcalfe spoke, "Not to worry tonight. I volunteer to eat for two. Always a delight when I'm here."

Julian smiled, thinking that the factor carried pleasantness with him into any situation. *Some people are blessed with that kind of personality.* Cook entered the room just then, frowning as usual. *She's his opposite,* Julian mused, *and who's to say why?*

Lori pulled an envelope from her pocket. "Today I got a note from our Maria. She says thank you for the Christmas gifts, and she sent a picture of Elena."

Julian realized that Mr. Metcalfe had never heard the story of the baby abandoned on the ferry, so he quickly sketched the event.

"What a pleasure to hear from Maria. What did you send her, Lori?" Mrs. B smiled. "Please read us the note and pass around the snapshot."

"I sent onesies for Elena, six to twelve months, and a winter hat and scarf set for Maria. I'll read the note, and you'll see how Maria has improved. She dates her letter; she didn't date that note to you, Julian. She uses new words and even a compound sentence." Pleased to hear Lori's comment, Julian nodded to himself. *Spoken like an ESOL tutor.*

Lori read what Maria had written:

Dear Lori,
I am glad to know your name. Thank you for the lovely Christmas presents. Elena was growing more than the sleepers you sent earlier. The picture shows she is beautiful. The scarf and hat made me gratified. We have good clothes here but it is very nice to have something new.
A kind friend sent cookies from a bakery. And Christmas plants. And more film. Name of anonymous. Do you know the kind friend? I thank that person too.
I learn many things.

Maria

January 10, 1979

Mrs. B approved the snapshot. "That baby has a bright look in her eyes. I think she's a quick one. And she *is* beautiful, but babies usually are. God made them adorable so we'd go to all the bother of bringing them up. It's a full-time job. And sometimes they don't turn out as we expect." She sighed as if in memory.

Julian almost laughed at all the effort Mrs. B must have poured into bringing up her only child. No doubt she had had a nursery maid for Alexis, a laundress to wash the diapers and the delicate little sweaters, and, later on, a nanny. He kept his mouth tightly shut so that his smile wouldn't show.

"Well, I think Elena is *especially* beautiful," said Lori, looking at Julian with a sigh. "I wish I could visit her. That would be fun."

He shook his head slightly, not wishing to interrupt Mrs. B, who had just introduced a change of subject. "About the Lincoln, Mr. Metcalfe?"

The factor pulled a little leather notebook from his pocket. "I stopped in the garage to look at it before dinner. Mr. Munchen was kind enough to…Well, that car is a beauty, a genuine antique. No question, you can dispose of it at a handsome price. There are several options." Mrs. B, Lori, and Julian gave him their full attention. "To be brief—private sale, classic car auction, donation to a museum. The last would produce quite a significant tax advantage."

"Grandma, you're thinking of selling the Lincoln?"

"As you pointed out, Lori, it just sits there doing nothing but taking up space. I have been remiss, let it slide. One should not hold on to assets that produce no profit."

"As to your second question, Mrs. Bellington, yes, the proceeds from disposing of the Lincoln should more than pay for a new runabout car."

Lori's eyes grew bigger as she listened. She leaned forward when her grandmother asked her, "I suppose, Lori, that you would like something smart, like a roadster?"

Although Lori had never before heard the term "roadster," she made a good guess. "You're going to buy a car that I can drive, Grandma? Maybe a convertible? Maybe a red convertible? When?"

Her grandmother's frail hand patted the air. "In due time."

Lori rushed on. "Of course we want a car that's easy for you to get in and out of, nothing too low-slung, maybe not bucket seats. What color will you choose, Gram? I'll drive you anywhere you want to go."

"Lori, I am buying this car for you, so the color is for you to say. The car will be in your ownership."

"You mean it? Oh, Grandma, thank you, thank you. I'm blown away! I'm fractured. I can't believe it! Red, that's the color I choose. Red."

Mr. Metcalfe cleared his throat with a pleasant little cough. "It will take time to further investigate the options I've mentioned, but, assuming all goes smoothly, I believe I can promise, little lady, that you will have your little red car in a month to a month-and-a-half."

Julian added, "In the meantime, you can get your driver's license switched from Ohio to New York. If you want to brush up on your driving, we could probably find a place—maybe a school yard on the weekend— and use my car for that. Before I moved to New York last year, I got a book from the Department of Motor Vehicles and read up on local laws and regulations. You can borrow it if you wish. Or send for your own."

There was an awkward pause. "Actually," Lori said, her voice subdued, "there's a tiny problem. I don't have a driver's license."

"What?" Julian was floored. "Every teen-ager gets a license the day she's sixteen. I know my kids did. You never got your license back in Ohio? Never took the test? You wanted to drive the limo, and you don't even have a license?"

"That was only an inquiry about the Lincoln," Lori said, pulling her dignity around her. "If you remember, I just wondered if I could *handle* it." She hesitated. "There was a good reason I didn't get my license when I was sixteen. I didn't want it then, but now I do."

Suddenly sensitive to the pain in Lori's eyes, Julian asked gently, "What reason, Lori?"

"My best friend, Anda—her name was Miranda—was sixteen about two months before I was, and her mother took her to take the driving test. She passed and she was so thrilled, so out of her head with pride, that she took off from the testing site, pressing down hard on the gas pedal, singing, yelling, 'It's my birthday! I got my license, first try, parked perfectly. Oh hurray and jubilee!'

"She was speeding, almost drunk on all that horsepower, and, when she went around a sharp curve, she couldn't straighten up fast enough, and she plunged down an embankment. She went flying out of the car and …" Lori swallowed painfully. "She cracked her head against a big tree. So, she was dead. Life is very fragile."

"She wasn't wearing her seat belt? She had just passed her driver's test, and she wasn't wearing her seat belt?" Mr. Metcalfe was unbelieving. Mrs. B shook her head in dismay; Julian's heart cracked.

"Oh, Lori, how sad, how sad." All the natural concern that adults feel for new, inexperienced drivers on the highway coalesced for him around this one young girl and her cruel memories. He wanted to comfort her somehow, erase the anguish, and take her in his arms. At the same time, his own pain surfaced abruptly. He suddenly stood again in the New York City morgue gazing down at his beloved wife—her broken body, her quenched breath. *Yes, life is fragile, temporary, so easily gone. Let us weep together.*

"Oh, Lori," he said again, "no wonder…However did you manage?"

"I didn't really manage very well. At the funeral, I overheard one of the high school jocks say, 'Of course it's a closed casket. She cracked her head wide open, and her brain spilled out. Who wants to look at brain drain?'

"It was such an awful thing for him to say, for me to hear—so cruel— even if it was true. I hated that boy. And, when I dropped my flower on the casket—the casket that had been lowered into the hole, that held Anda, my best friend who would not laugh ever again—I told myself I'd never drive, I'd walk. I had finished the classroom part of driver's ed and had had one behind-the-wheel session. That was it. I dropped the class."

There was a moment of helpless silence. What could anyone say? Julian thought, *We will bow our heads and remember our loved ones, forever gone from us...yes, we who are stricken, we who are brokenhearted...*

Mrs. B was the first to recover. "Your reaction was understandable, Lori, completely so. Are you sure you are ready to drive now?"

"Yes, everyone drives. It's the normal thing to do. The way I am now, I'm always counting on someone else to take me places. At home, I lived three blocks from the school, so it wasn't a problem. When I got here, Mr. Dempsey drove. Then Julian. Julian, you've been wonderful, but I need to be able to drive myself places."

Julian recognized the desolate truth. He thought, *Although I would happily drive Lori wherever she wishes to go for the rest of her life, she needs to be independent, to grow up.* He would not rob her. Fiercely, his voice strained, feeling helpless, he turned to her. "Promise. Promise me you'll always wear your seat belt."

With her mind on the red convertible, with a lilt in her voice, she promised carelessly, "Oh sure, always. I'll always wear my seat belt."

He had had to ask her. She was terribly young. He felt old, old and foolish.

Chapter 43

―――――――――

Melissa Stoner flattered Julian Elsmore. She would ask his advice, would praise his "insights," and, after The Downstairs Club opened in April, she would come to his table, bringing a cup of coffee fixed just the way he liked it. Sometimes he didn't want coffee at all, but, gentleman that he was, he would take a few sips so as not to offend. She was never bossy, but Vicki's cryptic remark lingered in the back of Julian's mind.

Early in March, Melissa had phoned Julian with an emergency request. "I've been invited to this banquet, a United Way thing, and my older brother was to be my escort. It's this coming Saturday night, but now he's in the hospital with a bad case of the flu. I was wondering, Julian, would you be free to be my companion?"

"I'm free," he said. "But is it formal? I don't have a tux."

"Well, we must get you one." She laughed. "But, for this occasion, only the head table will be formal. The women will wear long gowns because we love to get dressed up. Most of the men will wear business suits. It would really help me out if…"

"Good then, and thank you for the invitation. Just tell me when to pick you up."

Because he was unfamiliar still with the big city, he also got the name of the hotel where the banquet would take place. "I like to trace out my route," he told Melissa, "know where I'm going to park, especially for driving in the early evening rush hour. Seems to me that New York is one giant rush hour; the whole city is always in a hurry, while I'm just a slow bumpkin from Paducah, Kentucky."

"Did you trace the route when you came to my house for dinner the first time?" There had been two more of those dinner/committee meetings.

"Yes, I did. Didn't want to be late, you know."

"Oh, Julian," she said with a little laugh. "you're funny."

I'm just careful. Is it funny to be careful?

The banquet room was quite large and filled with movers and shakers from Manhattan. When Melissa and Julian entered, an alert hostess welcomed Melissa with an air kiss, a congratulatory murmur, and a corsage of red roses. The woman smiled curiously at Julian and led them to their places, which were close to the speakers' table. They were the first ones to arrive at that table, and, when they had been seated, Julian picked up his program.

"You didn't tell me you were a guest of honor," he began, but then another very important person arrived with his party. Melissa knew the man, his wife, and their two adult children, so she made introductions. Julian was surprised when the last couple at their table for eight turned out to be Pastor Wellington and his wife. The Wellingtons, on the other hand, were clearly unsurprised to find him there. Mrs. Wellington asked if Melissa's brother was recovering, and, as sophisticated people do, the group then fell into easy chatter about mutual interests.

Pastor Wellington was called upon to ask the blessing, and, while he spoke, Julian reflected that the evening had been well-planned, with no detail neglected, and that the arranging of it all pleased him. He liked things to be orderly. He also liked the fact that he was the escort of a striking, well-regarded woman. Melissa wore a lovely gray and black evening gown that fit her sleek body faultlessly. The red corsage—he supposed that had been arranged too—was perfect. He relaxed.

After dinner, the mayor spoke first, thanking the whole city for contributing to the outstanding success of the United Way campaign. He trumpeted what everyone already knew, that they had gone 16% over their goal. "Think of that, folks; think of the great generosity our citizens have displayed to help the less fortunate. I'm proud to be the mayor of this noble city." Applause rolled through the hall.

"We are gathered this festive evening to extend heartfelt thanks to all of you who were in any way involved in the campaign. We honor our wonderful volunteers, and, especially, we want to recognize the five magnificent team leaders who led this tremendous effort. People have asked me where they get their energy. I'll tell you folks, they get it from their generous hearts, God bless them all.

"Right now, I'm proud to introduce Gip Luccano, chair of the United Way Campaign, who will present plaques," he said as he held one aloft, "and certificates of honor to five wonderful people, all of whom, I'm happy to say, are with us here in this hall tonight. Let's put our hands together for Gip, folks, a round of applause for his magnificent leadership and dedication."

It was an unusually short speech for the mayor. *Flowery*, Julian thought, *but not too flowery*. He settled back.

Gip was a successful businessman, jovial, efficient, and at ease. He cautioned his audience to hold their applause until all the team leaders had been called to the stage. As the honorees walked forward, two women and three men, he paid each of them a tribute.

Of Melissa, he said, "A daughter of one of Manhattan's founding families, Melissa Stoner is the mother of two fine young people now away at college, the widow of the late Lucas Stoner, who served for many years as a city commissioner. She is a remarkable woman whose own loyalty and endeavor inspire others to serve our city. The greatest compliment I can pay her is to say that, for years, she has been a pillar of the United Way, supporting it with time, treasure, and remarkable talent."

Melissa received the praise and her handsome plaque with a becoming blush and a breathless "thank you" to Gip. His Honor the Mayor kissed her on the cheek and whispered something in her ear that made her laugh. With the other special guests, she floated from the stage on a tremendous wave of applause and went to Julian, who rose to seat her. She flung her arms around him and kissed him smack on the mouth.

"Oh, Julian, dear Julian, I'm so excited ...so humbled and excited," she burbled as she slipped into her chair.

He sat down too, astonished at what had just happened. His face felt hot, but he managed to lean forward and congratulate her weakly. "Well, good for you, Melissa."

He heard a camera click and wondered if that, too, had been arranged.

AT THE CEMETERY

April 8, 1979

Ah, Julie.

Tuesday next is the first anniversary of your death. I have tried to mend my heart. I have followed the suggestions—kept busy, made new friends, started projects. Some of it has worked but there are still times when I am as desolate for you as I was the first day.

Twelve months ago today you were alive.

You kissed me, loved me.

He rested a few more minutes. Then he coughed to clear his throat, strode down the slope, and drove away from there.

Chapter 44

ONE FRIDAY EVENING IN MARCH, Lori had brought a big, bumpy manila envelope to the dinner table. As soon as the plates were cleared, she said, "I made some visual aids for our students, Julian." She spilled the contents of her envelope out for her grandmother and Julian to see. "Look." She had cut, from heavy, white cardboard, the sole of a shoe, had outlined toes, and in red marker had labeled it "a foot."

Then she had pasted a red, plastic twelve-inch ruler down the middle of the cutout. The "foot" was exactly a foot long.

"And I've written the equations here along the edge, see—'twelve inches equals one foot or 12" = 1'.' What do you think? I got the idea from a book and added some things of my own. There's a second red ruler and a tape measure. We can measure things, like the desk and how tall the children are. Your rulers are green, Julian; mine are red. Don't you just love color-coding?"

"A good visual," Julian said approvingly. "Easy to remember. Thanks."

"I have more ideas, more things I'll make to help our students learn faster."

Mrs. B was intrigued. "I think such tricks are very useful. I remember—after eighty years, I still remember—when I was in school, our teacher taught us horizontal and vertical and how to remember which is which. She drew a level line on the blackboard and then drew a stick-figure horse standing on the line. 'This,' she said, pronouncing 'horse' as if it was two syllables, 'This is a hor-us on a line. Say it quickly. Horizontal line, see? The straight up and down line, the vertical line, is the one the horse *can't* stand on.'"

Lori's eyes crinkled with approval. "Far out, Grandma."

"I know one too," Julian spoke up. "If you eat a piece of chocolate cake with chocolate frosting..." He raised a quirky eyebrow in Lori's direction and said, "that's *dessert* with an S for each hip. The one-S desert is the one the children of Israel wandered in for forty years."

"I bet there's a book of tricks like that, of memory aids. English spelling is so crazy. I'll ask the Literacy Council librarian. Like, in fifth grade, I misspelled 'separate,' spelled it 'seperate.' My teacher said, 'Always be sep-*a-rat*-e from *a rat*.' And, Julian, is it okay with you if I invite Roz— she's asked me to call her 'Roz,' how about that?—to eat dinner with us at Reuben's next Thursday after the tutoring? I'll pay for her meal. The way it is, she works in a Hispanic restaurant. Everyone talks Spanish, and the food is Mexican, even the menu is Mexican. Not a good learning environment."

"Reuben's sounds like a good idea. We can teach Rosita, excuse me, Roz, how to read an American menu."

"And how to order in English. We'll tell her what we want and let her order for us."

"Lori," said Mrs. B, her voice tinged with disapproval, "if you try to pay for Roz's meal, both she and Julian will be embarrassed. And think what that would teach her about gracious dining in America."

"I just mean I don't want to impose on Julian..."

"Relax. If I take two young ladies out for dinner, I'll pay for two young ladies. You can't run everything, Lori."

"I'm not trying to. How about this—I was thinking I could bring Roz into your classroom one evening and introduce her to the Umbertos. And them to her. Don't you think that would be a good lesson? And I was thinking, when we are teaching measurements, I could bring in a dinner plate, and we can use the measuring tape to teach circumference."

Mrs. B looked dubious. "Isn't 'circumference' an awfully big word for your students?"

"When we were training," said Lori, self-important with her knowledge, "we learned that it's the little words that are confusing to ESOL students, words like 'on' and 'in.' They say, 'I put the book in the shelf,' instead of 'on'. But when it comes to a word like 'kangaroo,' well, how could you possibly get 'kangaroo' mixed up with any other word? Anyway, after the circumference lesson, we'll put cookies on the plate and let the kids pass them around."

Julian smiled. "The kids'll love that."

"Everyone will love the cookies because I'll make chocolate chip. Let Cook fuss, okay Grandma? Julian, why don't we combine our students into one class, maybe every Tuesday, and I'll write some dialogues that they can practice with each other? Would the Umbertos like that? Would you? And what about Roz? Shall I ask her to eat with us, excuse me, to *dine* with us, next Thursday? Another thought I had is…"

"Slow down, Lori. Yes, it's okay about Roz. Tell her we'll drive her home afterwards. Yes, the Umbertos would enjoy the dialogues. Please, Lori, please, do not have any more bright ideas right now. You've overwhelmed me."

A little flushed, she subsided. "Julian, it's just that I keep getting brainstorms how we can help our students. Roz wants to be a data processor; did you know that? I'll talk to the Literacy Council and see if there are any programs she might fit into. If you hear of any scholarships… Well, she's a quick study."

Mrs. B patted the air. "Settle down, Lori. Leave something to do the day after tomorrow. Tell Cook I said I want you to make the cookies. Give her a day to vent; she'll enjoy steaming."

Mr. Munchen appeared to tell Lori that she had a phone call from Connie, and, while Julian was wondering what the twins' mother wanted, Mrs. B murmured, "Lori's very enthusiastic about tutoring, isn't she?"

"I'll say. Born to it. Makes me feel like a slacker."

Mrs. B spoke carefully, "It's a worthwhile hobby, very worthwhile. I was wondering if she plans to get a teaching degree."

"She's never said anything to me about that, but she is certainly charged up by the tutoring. And her ideas are good. She'll find out what works right in the classroom."

"After her first visit to Upper Level, she made several lively suggestions too. Ways, as she said, to update a bit, to attract a younger crowd. She's a clever girl. Merchandising is in her blood, you know, and while tutoring is a very worthwhile avocation, I hope she does not choose teaching as a career."

He started to ask, "Why not?" but bit his tongue and said diplomatically, "I suppose that is a decision Lori will be making later on. After all, she's barely started college; she has lots of time to think about it."

"Perhaps the Rosen Trust will fund some ESOL projects next year; another way for Lori to get involved. She mentioned a few needs—scholarships, job training, employment counseling, even proper wardrobes for job interviews...Well, we'll see."

As if musing, Mrs. B changed the subject. "I've a favor to ask of you, Julian. At the moment, I'm revising my will. When I die, Lori will be my prime heir, be enormously wealthy, with all the responsibility that entails. For the will, I wish to name two executors, and I would be pleased if you would be willing to serve as one of them."

Julian's heart thumped. This old lady constantly surprised him. "Mrs. B, I am honored, but I have no particular qualification for that role."

"Julian, do not insult me. Do you think I would choose an incompetent?"

"I didn't mean that at all. Of course not."

"Well then, I have considered this request carefully, and, as you must know, I do not have a lot of time left for making arrangements."

She raised her bejeweled hand against his protest. "I arranged for you to meet Lawyer Carpenter and Mr. Metcalfe. They manage the estate most competently. Your role will be oversight, as mine has been for several years now. They agree that your opinions carry weight with Lori and that you are a careful, practical businessman. So, good enough."

In other words, they've checked me out. Of course. They too are careful businessmen. The matter is important.

"In addition," her benign voice continued, "my instinct tells me you have the most important qualification of all."

"What is that?"

"I have observed that you love my granddaughter. You will always have her welfare at heart."

He was flabbergasted to hear it spoken. *I love Lori.* It was true, but it was a shock to hear it uttered so matter-of-factly. *I love Lori. Yes, but how?* It was more than he could explore at the moment, so he said, "Yes, I will always have her welfare at heart. I will always do my very best for Lori. Thank you for asking me to be an executor of your will. I accept."

Mrs. B nodded in satisfaction. "Good enough. Lawyer Carpenter will send you a copy of the document shortly. You'll notice," she said, "that Victoria Glazer is your co-executor. I have great confidence in her also. She's a thoughtful, splendid woman. You can always count on her. Good looking too, don't you think? As a team, you'll complement each other nicely."

He looked up sharply, wondering if the wily old lady had just said something special. Her silver head was erect, her hands at rest, and her eyes calm as she turned a bland smile on him.

How could anyone suspect her of manipulating people?...Hah, he thought, just as Lori came back into the room, explaining that Connie needed her to baby-sit on Tuesday afternoon.

"But she'll be back in time for me to get to tutoring. Will you pick me up at her house, Julian, at five sharp? I told her I couldn't miss tutoring, and she understands. She promised to be back." She looked at them seriously and reflected, "A few months ago, I didn't know anything about ESOL until what you told us that night at dinner, Julian. Now I'm a trained tutor, and I think about it all the time, about how I can be a better teacher, how I can help Roz. Life's a surprise, isn't it?"

"Indeed, it is," Julian said. Mrs. B nodded in agreement.

Chapter 45

IT WAS THE SECOND WEEKEND FOR THE DOWNSTAIRS CLUB. Julian had arrived early to turn up the thermostat, make the coffee, and see that the sodas were chilling. Very soon, these chores and others, such as ordering supplies and cleaning up afterwards, would be taken over by committees that the young people would elect. It was their club.

There would be live music later this evening—a local group—but for now he was at a round table playing Scrabble with Lori and some other teenagers. He was pretty good at Scrabble and was trying to decide whether it was better for the chaperone to win or lose when Melissa arrived, a gift-wrapped package in her hand.

"It's a thank-you gift for being such a wonderful escort at the United Way banquet, Julian. What an evening! What a memory!"

"Well, thank you, thank you very much. I'll open it later, okay, after this game?"

"Oh, no, no. Open it now, Julian dear. I want to see your face."

He glanced around, saw the avid looks. He said, "Break time, kids."

No one moved. From the shape of the box, he guessed it was a tie, which was safe enough. "All right then." He tore off the pretty paper, lifted the lid, and reared back. "It's...Ye gods, it's *pink*."

"Isn't that the coolest thing? High fashion, Julian. Just coming on the market this spring. In a year or two, every well-dressed man will have a pink tie. You're among the first, a trendsetter." Melissa was delighted with herself.

The Scrabble players craned their necks to see. "Pink!" one of the boys said, grinning, "with red and green stripes."

"With rose and apple-green stripes," a girl amended.

"What I said."

"Not." Otherwise, she ignored him, bent on teasing Julian, "Hold it up, Mr. Elsmore, so we can all see."

He put the lid firmly on the box and said to Melissa, "I'll save it for a special occasion." *Halloween maybe.*

Melissa squeezed his shoulder, laughing a bit to show that she wasn't offended, and bent towards him to say in a soft voice, "See you later then." She drifted off.

"Is she your girlfriend, Mr. Elsmore?" The asker was a bright-eyed young girl."

"What?"

"Well, people say—a lot of people say—that you and Ms. Stoner are dating."

"I don't have a girlfriend. I'm not dating anyone."

"I didn't mean…"

Lori looked up from the other side of the table. "It's a bunch of silly gossip, Gen— garbage. Drop it. He doesn't have a girlfriend."

And if I did, it wouldn't be someone who buys me a pink tie. He needed to redirect the conversation. "Whose turn is it, anyway? Mine? Okay then, let's see." He put the gift box on the floor under his chair, lifted a tile, and forced his mind to the game.

AT THE CEMETERY

End of April, 1979

Julie, all the people in my new life are upset.

Melissa is upset because she gave me a pink tie and I don't like it. Pink! Ye gods! Doesn't she know I'm not a pink-tie-kind-of-guy?

Lori is irritated because there is a lot of gossip about Mel and me—garbage, she says—and she scowls at me as if it's my fault.

Dr. Glazer—well, if I try to talk to Vicki, she'll ask me one of those dumb questions psychiatrists ask: "How do <u>you</u> feel about it?"

I'll tell you how I feel. I feel like leaving the office early on Friday, driving straight to Philadelphia and playing with little Julie all weekend. Lori wants to be independent, she can get herself to her appointment. I'll cancel Dr. Glazer and dinner at Bellington's.

Baby Julie is the only female I know who isn't upset.

Julie, Melissa squeezed my shoulder, all chummy-like, and said 'see you later then' as if we had a date. I didn't see her later. I feel pretty darn mad. I'm blowing steam.

Even as he said it, he knew he would never cancel his shrink or dinner with Mrs. B. They were bright spots in his week. He took ten slow breaths, ten more, and drove home.

🍀   🍀   🍀

Chapter 46

Mrs. Bellington celebrated her ninetieth birthday by inviting a little circle of friends to dine with her on the first Friday in May.

She stipulated no gifts, but Julian brought her a nosegay of wild violets, and she beamed on him. Lori filled a shallow silver bowl with the last of the daffodils that had bloomed along the paths around the house.

"A beautiful centerpiece for the dining table," approved the old lady. "Spring is here, thank the dear Lord. April and May are months of grace and good beginnings."

Mrs. B had asked the ladies, Vicki and Lori, to wear evening dresses, and Lori knew it was because her grandmother wanted to see her in her new jade green ball gown.

"Okay, so another fashion show, another appointment at Upper Level." Like any normal young girl, Lori was pleased to get her hair done, to get dressed up, and to strut her stuff.

Mrs. B herself wore a long-sleeved gown of silver lamé. At the hemline, purple irises had been woven into the fabric. They swayed gracefully as she moved. It was a timeless style. Strands of perfectly matched pearls eased the wrinkles in her neck.

Mr. Metcalfe arrived with demure corsages of white rosebuds for the ladies and matching boutonnieres for the men.

"We are quite festive,' Mrs. B observed when they were seated around the table. "And ninety is a fine, round number."

When Cook brought in the beautiful angel food birthday cake, there was polite clapping. Mrs. B knew that, when it was cut, it would be so airy, so delicate, that you would think Cook had somehow baked it from snowflakes. *Perfect for an old lady with high cholesterol,* she thought.

Just before presenting it on an antique crystal plate, Cook had frosted it with great dollops of whipped cream; had put a fat, rosy candle in the center hole; and had surrounded it all with sliced strawberries.

"Oh, Cook, thank you," Mrs. B said. "It's truly a work of art. And strawberries so early!"

"Hard to get 'em with much flavor this time of year, but they'll do." Mrs. B ignored the grumpy remark. She was used to Cook.

Mr. Munchen lit the candle, and they all sang, Julian's strong bass lending resonance and Henry Glazer's baritone connecting nicely to the soprano tones of Vicki and Lori.

"Happy Birthday to you," they sang. "May the dear Lord bless you," they sang.

Mrs. B blew out the single candle, her breath so faint that it took two tries. The Drs. Glazer eyed her with concern.

"Cook," said Mrs. B, "we are retiring to the small parlor. Please serve the cake there." She coughed on a gasp of breath, and Lori saw that a fine sheen of sweat had formed on her upper lip. "And demitasse."

Mrs. B put her hands on the arms of her chair and carefully lifted herself upright. The others rose also, and Henry moved to assist his hostess. That was fortunate because her left leg buckled suddenly, and she tilted into him. Instantly, his strong arm circled her waist.

"Steady, girl." He held her, as she fought for balance, and was glad to see that Julian had come to stand at her other side and now said quietly, "Take my arm, Mrs. B."

She drew herself erect. "Those ninety fine, round years haven't been kind to my knees," she said tartly.

Reassured by her little jest, they all proceeded to the parlor where the old lady sank gladly into her favorite chair, warmed now by her granddaughter's thoughtfulness. She raised her hand. "Lori, go back. Make an entrance."

"Oh, Grandma." It was a light protest. This was her grandmother's ninetieth birthday celebration, and Lori would please her any way that she could. She left the room and returned only when she knew that everyone was watching. She swirled into the archway, lovely in her ball gown of jade chiffon, posed, pirouetted. The cleverly cut skirt frothed about her ankles. Then, with a smile for her grandmother only, blowing a kiss from her fingertips, she dropped into a deep and graceful curtsey.

Julian watched with delight. It was a performance. He supposed that Lori had taken dancing lessons. He caught Mrs. B's fond look and knew that she saw her own young blood coursing merrily through her granddaughter's body.

Mrs. B spoke, "I knew it; I knew it." She gasped again but, buoyed by the importance of what she wanted to say, managed to add, "See her. *That's* my child."

Then she seemed to shrink into the chair, coughed once, and again struggled for breath. Her face blanched; her hands trembled. Vicki suggested softly that she lie down.

"There are pills…" she gasped.

Mr. Munchen stepped forward, pulling a tiny enameled box from his vest pocket. He handed it to Lori. "Nitroglycerin. I'll get water and a spoon."

He and Lori stood together in front of Mrs. B's chair, forming a privacy screen. They managed to get the tiny pill well back on her tongue and helped her take a few spoonfuls of water. "It usually acts quickly," said Mr. Munchen gravely. Lori drew up a footstool, sat down, and held her grandmother's hand.

And indeed, almost at once, Mrs. B resumed her role as hostess. "Thank you all for coming…to celebrate…tonight,… to celebrate Lori,… very kind…about Lori, oh, I knew it…" Her body spasmed once; her blue eyes stared straight ahead, fixed on a distant scene, dulled, then closed. She spoke her last words in a whisper, "Do not resuscitate."

Lori felt her grandmother's hand go lax. "Do something!" she cried to Henry Glazer, pleading. "You're a doctor. Vicki, do something!"

Henry Glazer felt for a pulse, found none, and bowed his head. "Dear, old friend," he said gruffly, and he laid a compassionate hand on Lori's shoulder. "Lori, if only I could do something, but sometimes… Her heart just ran down, stopped pumping, just stopped. She was happy tonight, very happy. Her soul rests in peace."

Vicki stepped forward and traced a cross on Mrs. B's forehead. Her voice was tender,

"'May flights of angels sing you to your rest.'" There were murmured "amens," expressions of shock, and glances of sympathy for Lori.

"She was the last of her generation, a remarkable old lady."

"So sudden."

"I can't believe it."

"Never expected the party to end this way."

"Is there anything we should do?"

"Why did she say, 'Do not resuscitate'?"

Mr. Munchen, who seldom spoke out of turn, answered, "It was a standing order. She told me once that when her time was up it would be undignified for some young medic to pound on her chest to revive her. Her dignity was important to her."

They all understood that. They wandered around, stunned, wondering what to say.

Henry beckoned to Mr. Munchen. "Call Dr. Riley to come right away. We'll wait."

At that moment, Cook, all unaware, pushed a tea cart laden with slices of angel food cake into the room. Julian went to her at once, speaking rapidly. Cook's mouth dropped into an O of shock. She backed out of the room, with her cart, and fled to the kitchen.

"Coffee," Julian called after her. "Strong."

Vicki bent to embrace Lori. "You must grieve, of course, but please remember that your grandmother was delighted this past year to have found you, the heiress she so desired. She loved watching you, had faith in your character, your energy, your ability. And she was so proud because you are beautiful."

Still holding Mrs. B's hand, Lori reached to pat a 'thank you' on Vicki's comforting arm. Otherwise, she sat as if unhearing. Tears streamed down her face, down her slender throat, flowed over her great-grandmother's sapphire necklace, and drenched the bodice of her jade ball gown.

Chapter 47

Mrs. Bellington died Friday evening. The obituary, which she had written herself to ensure accuracy, appeared in the Sunday papers. Early Monday afternoon, family and friends followed the casket to Heavenly Rest Cemetery. A reception followed at the Bellington mansion.

After the mourners, a much larger group than Lori had expected, had been thanked and had departed, the new heiress and a small group designated in the will followed the instructions that Mrs. B had left.

Lori, Julian, Vicki, Mr. Munchen, and Cook went into the library with Mr. Carpenter and Mr. Metcalfe. (Lori's mom, included on the list, had not attended the funeral. Her dad had been present but had already headed out.) In solemn tones, Mr. Carpenter read the last will and testament of Clarissa Bellington. She left $50,000 to Trinity Methodist Church, $30,000 each to Munchen and to Cook. Her beloved granddaughter, Lori Seever, inherited everything else—stocks, bonds, investment property, part ownership of the department store, jewelry in a safe deposit box, and the Bellington mansion and everything in it. It was an enormous total. And it was an agreeable surprise to Lori that Vicki and Julian were named executors of the will.

When the others had left the library, Julian said to Lori in his most serious voice, "You are a very rich young woman. Wealth is a responsibility. You may want to learn how to handle it yourself. It could become your life's work, being chairperson of a charitable foundation or an educational trust…whatever. Or you can just keep your grandmother's lawyer and her estate manager, and they will take care of everything for you. Above all, don't feel rushed into making any decision. We'll discuss this all in good time."

"When an event like this happens," Vicki cautioned, "it's unsettling of course. Julian is right. Do nothing in haste, Lori."

"Like what?"

"Anything impulsive. If this gets into the papers, as it probably will because it's such an enormous inheritance, you'll be bombarded by people who want money to get their secret invention launched, people with incredible investment opportunities that will make you a second fortune in just weeks. Charities will woo you. Also kooks will come out of the woodwork. Some will be very distant and dubious cousins."

"Sounds scary."

"Don't give any interviews. Especially not to the sympathetic young woman from a grocery store tabloid, who will seem like your sister. I don't know who she is, but someone like that is bound to show up, and she'll have a way of making you want to confide in her. Don't talk to her. Just say, 'No comment.' to anyone you don't know.

"Sit tight. Things will go along all right here while you think over your moves and decide what to do. Your grandmother expected you to be sensible, else she wouldn't have put so much power in your hands. Look, I have to go now, but I put a sleeping pill in this little envelope. Take it with a glass of water. It'll help you settle down."

Julian knew that was good advice, knew that Lori would heed Vicki's counsel.

"Money is powerful, isn't it?" Lori's voice quavered. "I suppose I could do a lot of good with some of this money. And, once I get used to being rich, I can have a lot of fun, can't I? I'll call Bill tonight. I haven't heard from him in a few days. Maybe there's a letter among all those cards. Would you look, Julian? Oh dear, I'm dreadful. I should be mourning, not thinking about my wedding."

"Your grandmother was an old lady. She was ready to leave this life, and she went as she wished, with style and dignity. It is a terrible shock of course, and of course you have to mourn for her," Vicki spoke softly. "You were a credit to her at the reception. You looked just right, and you acted just right. No crumpling or bawling. She would have been proud. Take comfort in that, Lori."

Julian added, "So much has happened. The full impact will take time to sink in. Right now, you're exhausted but still on an emotional high. What I think you should do right now is take Vicki's pill and get some rest."

"Grandma was very good to me. I suppose I thought she'd leave her money to Mom. I truly didn't think about it at all or how much it was, you know, even when she said I'd be her heiress. She seemed indestructible, like she'd go on and on forever. You know, Julian, I never even dreamed of how I'd spend her money."

"Lori, calm down. You're all over the place. I'm going to get a glass of water and see that pill down the hatch. You need it."

"Yes, but I'll call Bill first. I'll tell him we can afford a big wedding. A big white wedding, a big, beautiful white wedding. I'll pay for it. Julian, I'm independently rich, isn't that what you said? I'll tell Bill to go ahead and buy that electric guitar he wants from the money he's been saving. And he should take lessons too. He'll like that. Having money makes things easier."

When she finally picked up the phone and reached Bill, bubbling with her news, she realized at once that he sounded strained. "Lori? Hi, I've been intending to call you. Or write. I've something important to tell you."

She was alarmed. Maybe it was because she was so high-wired, but she seemed especially tuned to his tight voice. She put her own news on hold. "What is it, Bill?"

"Well, you see…" She could hear him take a deep breath and then speak all in a rush. "The way it is, Lori, well, something came up, all of a sudden, and I'm sorry, Lori; this is hard to say, but, see, I have to break our engagement. I'm getting married next week."

After a stunned moment, her heart beat again. "To?"

"To Rusty, the girl I told you about, remember?"

"I remember." *Oh yes, Busty Rusty.*

"It'll be a quiet little justice-of-the-peace, out-of-town ceremony. We're keeping it a secret until Rusty graduates. Then we'll announce it.

Lori, I'm so sorry. I do love you, and I never wanted to hurt you. It's just that…well, see, Rusty…is…"

The inescapable truth hit her. "Rusty is pregnant. Rusty is going to have a baby. Am I right?"

"I feel like such a jerk, but things just happened somehow. I've been trying to figure out how to tell you."

"You could have written a 'Dear Lori' note, perhaps? I think there's a handy-dandy model for that, based on the 'Dear John' letters." Utterly shocked and miserably injured, she babbled along, her voice caustic, "Did you think of that, Bill? You're good at writing short, little notes. I should know. 'Dear Lori, I love you, but I'm marrying Rusty.' That wouldn't have taken too much time."

She was being nasty, fighting the hurt by hurting back. *Try for dignity, Lori. Don't flatter him with your grief.* "Bill," she held the receiver over her heart a moment while she tried to think of a crushing phrase that would devastate a groom, somebody else's groom. *Congratulations? Good wishes? Hardly.*

"Lori, I wish it hadn't happened. I wanted to marry you, but…"

She couldn't bear to hear another word. "Bill," she interrupted, "listen carefully. I wanted to marry you too. We could have had a good life, but that won't happen now and understand that it's *your* loss." Her voice rose. "You've lost *me*, you Daddy, you!" And then, muttering, "Loser, loser, loser…you dumb loser," she hung up without even a goodbye, absolutely sure that she had cradled the receiver before she murmured, "Bill, I love you so." Then she let the tears fall.

She turned to Julian. "Julian, Bill is getting married."

"I heard."

"He's getting married to Rusty. He just dumped me."

Julian saw the naked shock in her face, the disbelief and hurt. He opened his arms and accepted her shaking body. He thought of many things to say: *It's not the end of the world. It was just puppy love. You'll see, you'll survive. You're right, he's a loser. He never deserved you. Don't cry, he's not worth it. Rusty trapped him. She got pregnant on purpose. Hush now, the sun will rise again.* He discarded all those platitudes and just held her, rubbing little circles of love between her shoulder blades, murmuring sounds of sympathy to mingle with her sounds of woe.

Holding her, comforting her as best he could, he remembered Fats, the football player whom Julie had dated so long ago, and remembered telling Vicki that he had wanted to rip the guy's face off. Same feelings now for Bill.

When Lori finally lifted her head from his shoulder, she said, her voice hoarse from crying, "First, we lost Mr. Dempsey. Then Grandma died. Bill is marrying Rusty. Ooooh..." She reached for a handful of tissues and put her head down again. The new bout of weeping was short. When she spoke, it was as if she had caught her breath and was picking up an earlier conversation. "Bill said they'd announce it after Rusty graduates. Announce their marriage. My mom and dad will read it in the paper, and they'll be glad, I suppose, never mind that my heart's broken. It's their fault for making us wait. Did you meet my dad, Julian?"

"Yes, I did, briefly, just before the service. He said your mom was too frail to make the trip. He seemed quite concerned that he couldn't stay longer."

"But he had to hurry back to her. I've heard that a thousand times or more—school plays, recitals, basketball games, birthday parties; I heard it every time."

"He said he'd call in a day or two."

"He didn't even stay for the reading of Gram's will. He doesn't know I'm rich. When he finds out, it will probably be a relief."

"He'll know soon enough. Will it matter to him that your mom didn't inherit?"

"I don't think so. He's probably the least materialistic man in the world. He never had to scrabble for money, never seems to think about it. Just expects it to be there. There's income from his family, from investments, and he wrote a textbook that's very popular. And my mom has her own money, a trust fund that her dad established for her when she got married.

"Anyway, as I was growing up, there never seemed to be money worries. They gave me all the advantages their child should have: I had tennis lessons, dancing lessons, gymnastics, went to good summer camps, had my teeth straightened But they didn't care about keeping up with the Joneses, giving fancy parties, or going on expensive vacations. There always just seemed to be plenty of money. I guess I don't really know. My parents seemed different..."

He thought that she might start crying again, but instead she sat on the sofa, folded her hands precisely in her lap, and fell into a reverie. Her sudden calm made him almost as anxious as her tears had. *This girl has had it for today. She's breaking apart. She needs down time.*

Her face was flushed, but it didn't seem to him to be a healthy flush. He guessed that her mind was still going at high speed because she suddenly roused herself and made a pronouncement. "Julian, I was wrong about money. It doesn't make everything easier. Some things—things like death and like Bill—well, nothing makes them easier. Money doesn't help at all."

"I know. Things like death, money doesn't help."

"Listen, Julian, I should go to the kitchen and talk to Munchkin and Cook. To reassure them, you know."

"I could do that, if you want me to. They'll understand that you're wrung out and need some rest."

"No, it's my job, so I should do it. Grandma would expect it. But maybe I'll wait and do it tomorrow. Right now I am just about bushed, but it was a nice funeral, wasn't it? Julian, could you just go tell them thank you? Tell Cook the buffet was perfect. Tell Munchkin that Grandma would have been pleased with the way the house looked, the way the flowers and candleholders were arranged. You always know what to say. I'll see them tomorrow morning; well, I'll see them sometime tomorrow. Anyway, tell them they shouldn't worry. Nothing will change. Where's that pill?"

He gave it to her with the glass of water and a pat on the shoulder and said, "Now go along and get in bed. A good rest will help you calm down, help better than money. Think how much your grandmother loved you. She was very proud of you, you know. Think that and fall asleep. I'll stay the night."

Lori downed the sleeping pill, blessed him with a tiny smile, and disappeared up the stairs and out of sight.

Weary himself, he reflected that things had changed already and would change even more in the weeks ahead. He would help her cope with the changes as he had promised Mrs. B. He would do his best. For the moment, he simply wondered if Lori would manage to brush her teeth before she conked out. As Julian went on his mission to the kitchen, he wished that Vicki had been able to stay longer. She was like a rock, a soft, sweet rock. *What a crazy idea.*

He found Munchen and Cook and, surprisingly, Elsa, the maid who came "as needed," having a cup of tea at the kitchen table.

"Miss Lori," Julian said, and at once wished he had not used the old-fashioned designation. Too tired to think of a less aristocratic term, he plowed on, "Miss Lori is resting. She asked me to give you a message." He passed along Lori's compliments on the funeral reception and added his own. "Mostly, she doesn't want you to worry. For the time being, everything will go along as usual. She'll see you in the morning,...well, probably later than that. Dr. Glazer left her a sleeping pill. Anyway, sometime tomorrow."

As he turned away, he was stayed by Cook's cracked voice. "Tell Lori, no need to worry about me. I own a condo in Florida with my older sister. She's retired and now I'll be retired too, and we're going to live together and watch the soaps and play bingo the rest of our lives. I plan to be packed and out of here before the end of the week."

Julian was too exhausted to be astonished. *Would Lori welcome that news or not? And who will cook?* Lori had intended to make cookies, he remembered. *Maybe she can cook.* He had never asked. *That can surely wait.*

"Mr. Munchen, I'm going to stay the night. Which bedroom should I use?"

It was Elsa who answered. "The very last one at the end of the upstairs hallway. It's made up and has a bathroom. You'll find shaving supplies and such in the medicine cabinet."

He nodded to the three of them, conscious that they watched him closely. "Good night, and thank you again from Lori."

Chapter 48

JULIAN ROSE EARLY THE NEXT MORNING. The house was completely silent, so he drove to his apartment, showered, breakfasted on toast and coffee, and arrived at Reliance Insurance at the usual time.

He phoned Lori at noontime. Mr. Munchen said, "Not yet, sir. I believe I hear her stirring, but I've not seen her today."

"When you do see her, please tell her I'll come by around three o'clock this afternoon in case she needs anything."

"Very well, sir."

Julian reflected that Munchkin was, like Vicki, a rock, and he was glad that Lori had such stalwart people around her. It was unapparent from the old butler's demeanor that big changes were underway and indeed inevitable at Bellington mansion. Julian wondered if Munchkin, like Cook, had made plans.

When he saw Lori later that afternoon, he was surprised to find that she had forsaken her jeans and was wearing the black tailored suit, black flats, and grey pantyhose that she had modeled at Christmastime and had worn publicly for the first time at her grandmother's funeral. She had not worn the lace blouse then, though, just jewelry. Today the outfit was completed by a simple yet expensive-looking, light blue, cowl-neck sweater.

After her brief fling with modeling, Lori had, except for Fridays, reverted to her usual uninspired clothing and had combed her hair straight back because it was too short for a ponytail. But today her hair, newly shampooed, hung free. *A little limp but at least an improvement. Needs a cut and styling,* Julian thought. *Well, I'm not making any suggestions, not me.* He would leave that job to Vicki.

"I waited for you, Julian. How did Munchkin and Cook react last night? And, Julian, Cook must have a real name. Do you know what it is?"

"Your grandmother told me. It's Mrs. Weston."

"Mrs.?"

"I believe so."

"Well, maybe she has family to go to."

"I don't know about children, but she said she and her sister own a condo in Florida, and they plan to enjoy retirement together. She said you shouldn't worry about her."

"That's a surprise, but good, I guess," said Lori. "But who will cook?"

"I can't. Can you?"

"Of course. Well, at least a couple of things, nothing fancy. Grandma said it irritated Cook if anyone else used her kitchen, but, at home, I made quite a few of our meals. Especially Hamburger Helper with fresh fruit or a green salad. Instant pudding too. What about Mr. Munchen?"

"He didn't say anything last night, so who knows?"

"Let's go and find out."

When they entered the kitchen, Julian was again surprised to find Elsa there.

Cook spoke immediately. It was clear that she had prepared a few words and wanted to give her little speech. "I suppose Mr. Elsmore told you, Lori, I'm leaving as soon as I can make arrangements. I just want to say that your grandmother was a good employer. She knew exactly what she wanted, and she let me know. So that's what I did, and we got on well. Never a question about the bills either; not that there was ever any reason to question, you understand, but some employers are tightfisted and always suspect that the bills are being padded. Your grandmother wasn't like that, and I was glad enough to work for her all these years." Cook closed her mouth firmly, as if to say, "Take that. I'm finished."

Julian thought wryly that Cook had just recklessly overspent her daily quota of graciousness. *Not an easy woman. A very good cook, though.*

He was pleased that Lori, who had just lost both her grandmother and her fiancé and who had been desolate the night before, seemed almost miraculously mature.

She replied with a simple, "Thank you, Mrs. Weston. And I'm sure Grandma would thank you for all the excellent meals you've prepared. Also, I was wondering if there is anything in this house that you would like to take with you as a keepsake. Maybe a vase or a pair of candlesticks or something from the kitchen?"

Cook's grey head snapped up. "I'd like to take the eggbeater."

"The eggbeater. That's not much."

"Your grandmother bought one of those appliances that chop and puree and whip cream in almost an instant, and it's fine enough in its newfangled way, but I'm sentimental, I guess, about the old eggbeater. And, if it suits…" Cook was warming to the possibilities, "I'd like to have the rocking chair from my bedroom."

"Of course."

"It's pretty old, maybe an antique, but sturdy enough. Pennsylvania Dutch. The decorations are a bit faded, but so am I. We suit each other." She almost smiled, but managed not to go overboard.

"I'll have it crated up and shipped to you in the next few days."

"Thank you, Lori. I wasn't looking forward to breaking in a new rocking chair. Not at my age."

"Be sure to leave your new address," Julian reminded Cook, "and also your sister's name just so we can add 'in care of,' you know."

Cook ignored him. "Now that I think on it, Lori, there's one more thing I'd like and that's a letter of recommendation." Even the unflappable Mr. Munchen was surprised. Cook grouched at their reaction, her face settling into its usual harsh lines. "It's not that I'm going to be looking for another job, you bet not. But it would be something to show. If it's a trouble to you, Lori, no matter."

"No trouble at all. I'll do it right away so you can take it with you."

"Well then, I've packing to do. I'll prepare meals as usual, including breakfast on Thursday. Then I'll leave mid-morning after the dishes are done. I won't be ordering groceries or planning meals for the weekend." The old woman huffed off to her bedroom, turned in the doorway, clenched her teeth, lest an emotion or a compliment escape, and said almost inaudibly, "Miss Lori, I believe you are like your grandmother after all."

The door closed, and Lori said, "Poor woman. I do hope she has a happy retirement."

Mr. Munchen said, "It is my observation that Cook is happiest when she has something to be unhappy about. It's her way. As for me, Miss Lori, I will also be leaving shortly." With a disapproving glance at Cook's door, he added, "I shall of course give proper notice."

Lori had not expected his announcement. Julian saw that she was taken aback. She sat down at the kitchen table, as if her backbone had melted within her, as if her newfound maturity had just flown away and out of sight. "But what will this house do without you, Mr. Munchen?" she wailed. "How will we manage? Where are you going?"

Mr. Munchen cleared his throat and glanced at Elsa. "Miss Lori, I've a partnership in a small business that is growing rapidly. It requires more attention than I'm able to give to it while working here full-time. So I would now like to give two weeks' notice. That means my service here would end two weeks from today. If that suits."

"You have a business? Why, Mr. Munchen, I didn't know. Did Grandma know?"

"Wealthy people hire servants to serve them, Miss Lori. As long as the service is satisfactory, they aren't interested in what those servants do on their days off, unless of course they somehow bring scandal to the house. I never discussed my outside life with Mrs. Bellington. That is not a reproach to her. She was a very proper employer indeed. I was very fond of her. It's just the way things are."

"What kind of a business?"

Mr. Munchen reached across the table and took Elsa's hand. "Elsa and I—and, by the way, we are married—Elsa and I run a school that trains people for employment in wealthy homes, to be butlers, maids, cooks, our fields of expertise. Our classes are small. We're selective about our students. No broken English; no broken dishes. No one clumsy, you understand. In ten years, we've built quite an exclusive reputation. All the realtors and factors know us."

"You're married? But when? Why doesn't Elsa live here?"

"She did. This house was her first job when she came from Denmark. I trained her, helped her with English. She's a fast learner, and we got on well. We've been married for eighteen years."

"Wow! And you started a business together?"

"Yes. Ten years ago, we bought a big, old house much like this, something of a white elephant, but perfect for our purposes. We invested our savings, you know, renovated the place. Downstairs, we've a couple of small classrooms and a modern kitchen. We kept the dining room intact, bought all the dishes, linens, candle holders, vases, everything like that, as part of the purchase, in order to train for proper table setting and serving.

"Our apartment—quite spacious, I might even say lovely—is up. That's where I've been on my days off and several late evenings each week, writing lessons, setting things up, a lot of decisions, a lot of details. I'll be there with Elsa full-time from now on." As he spoke, Mr. Munchen seemed younger than they had thought.

Lori reviewed in her mind what she had just heard and added, "And Elsa was here one day a week to do the upstairs. And to cook for Grandmother on Cook's day off. So it all went smoothly."

"Yes, quite satisfactorily."

"But you must have been working nonstop, constantly on the go."

"If I may say so, Miss Lori, I see myself as a vigorous seventy-two. Elsa is twelve years younger, just coming up on sixty, and when one is working for oneself, is one's own boss, as it were, well, that's a pleasure."

Elsa nodded. "If you decide to continue to live here, Miss Seever, I'm sure we can supply your need for household help. For us, it would be a priority placement." She pulled a business card from her pocket and slid it across the table. "We'd be pleased to have you call on us." Her accent was slight, pleasing. It didn't interfere.

Lori studied the business card. It read "Upscale Household Help" and, underneath that, "Full-Time or Part-Time" with the business numbers to call.

"Did Cook know?"

"Certainly. She supervised the foods program for us in fact. She doesn't really have a teaching personality, didn't want to teach anyway, but she's a whiz at organizing, knows how to present menus, draw up shopping lists, how to keep food palatable when dinner guests are an hour late, how to use leftovers so that no one suspects they're leftovers, knows which leftovers are hopeless and should be discarded. Things like that.

"Cook sold us her secret recipes too, wrote them up in great detail. We have packaged them in a recipe box that we call 'The Weston Way.' Each of our students gets a box upon graduation. Cook gets a royalty. We plan to go national with the recipes soon. It's hard to be sure, but I think Cook is pleased."

"Mr. Munchen," said Lori, "you heard Cook say she thought I was like my grandmother 'after all.' What did she mean by that?"

"Well, Miss Lori, the first few weeks you were here, you were very quiet. If I may say it, you moped around and dressed in those dreadful, dull clothes, and we decided you were like your mother. She's a nice enough lady, but meek, a trifle vague, no…uh…no sparkle. We hardly knew when she was here or missed her when she wasn't here. Such a contrast, her personality and your grandmother's. If I may say so." Munchen stopped. He was unaccustomed to speaking so freely. Julian thought that Mrs. B's death, the change in all their lives, had loosened his tongue.

"And then?" Lori prompted.

"Then it seemed you took hold. You gave your grandmother some bright moments, in this last year, with your stories of the twins and the classes you were taking, and finding that infant on the ferry, bringing Mr. Elsmore home. She was pleased to have you in residence.

"All of us took note how you visited Mr. Dempsey after the accident and made him laugh. You took an interest in the grounds. Everyone mostly thought of Dempsey as the chauffeur, but that was little enough to do. He was the groundskeeper too and proud of it. You cared enough to find that out. And you brought him a couple of gardening catalogs, so he was looking forward to spring. We decided maybe you are more like your grandmother than we first thought." He wrapped it up with a final statement of candor. "As for our business, Elsa's and mine, servants have a life of their own, Miss Lori. A separate life that the employer doesn't pay for and has no right even to know about."

"Well, yes, of course. I just never thought about…" Suddenly in a panic, Lori glanced at her watch. "Julian, we've got to get going or we'll be late for tutoring."

"Lori, maybe I should go solo tonight, be glad to. I'll explain to Roz, bring her into my classroom, do that introduction lesson with the Umbertos that we talked about. You rest."

"Julian, I need to go. There's no reason to tell our students of Grandma's death. I don't need any more condolences. Come on. It'll be like an oasis. We'll pretend, for just this evening, that everything is normal, nothing has changed."

"Okay, if that's what you want. Get your stuff."

He knew that denial wouldn't help in the long run, but it was a help for the moment. He thought, *I need it too.*

AT THE CEMETERY

May 13, 1979

Julie, I don't know how or if you tell time in Heaven but maybe you noticed that I didn't come to visit you last weekend. First of all, Mrs. Bellington gave a small dinner party on Friday night to celebrate her ninetieth birthday. Our little group was quite festive even though Mrs. B seemed a bit at low ebb. From time to time, she would gasp for breath but in general she was her usual gracious self. We moved to the small parlor after dinner and then she sat down in her chair and died.

Well, I guess it's not really a surprise when a ninety-year-old person dies (not like when you died), but upright in her chair, wearing a gorgeous gown, practically in the middle of a sentence? We were all stunned, shocked, and Lori just sat on a hassock by her grandmother's chair, clinging to her hand and crying, crying, crying.

The next few days were busy with funeral arrangements. According to Mrs. B's will, Lori is a very rich young woman and Vicki and I are the executors of the will. Since we're co-executors, I'll call her 'Vicki' when I talk to her from now on.

All that money! A heavy responsibility.

As he drove home, he pondered how best to care for Lori.

🌸   🌸   🌸

Chapter 49

It was Mr. Munchen's last day. When he came to say goodbye to Lori, he told her, "If you wish to hire a temporary cook and housekeeper, Miss Lori, we have a rather unusual woman on our roster who would, I believe, be just right for the opening. Mrs. Barnes is a retired librarian—been retired five years—who likes to travel. She's just back from an Alaskan tour and available right now."

"How is she unusual?" asked Lori.

"Oh, nothing objectionable. Quite the contrary. A very smart lady. Very refined. She just wants it known that she is a temporary hire until she saves enough money for her next trip. But she's accommodating. If she's ready to leave your employ but you say you need her for an extra month or two, she'll stay. Much longer than that, she asks us to make other arrangements."

"She sounds resourceful. I'd like to talk to her."

"I'll ask her to phone then, and you can arrange an interview."

"I've hired a housekeeper," Lori told Julian as they drove to their tutoring session. "A Mrs. Barnes, formerly a librarian. She starts next week."

"Can she cook?"

"She belongs to a gourmet club. She says she can do plain or fancy. Thing is, she's temporary because she also belongs to a travel club. She only works at a place until she's made enough money to take her next trip. I also talked to Maria yesterday."

"Our Maria? Elena's mom?"

"That's the one."

"How did you manage that?"

"Lawyer Carpenter. I told him what I'm thinking about, and he arranged it."

"What is it that you are thinking about, Lori?" He was a trifle miffed that Lori had turned to someone else for help. *I guess I'd better get used to it.*

"First, let me tell you what I found out and then what I'm thinking. See, I wanted to get an opinion from the program Maria is in about her progress. Mr. Carpenter reports that they have only good things to say. Maria is an excellent student, very committed to the opportunity she's been given, gets on well with the others, is a wonderful mother."

Julian nodded but said nothing. His own inquiries before he set up the Julie Kaye Elsmore Trust for Maria and Elena had led to the same conclusion.

"And then I visited where Maria and Elena are living—did you know they call it 'Take Heart House?' And, oh, Julian, Elena is so darling, just learning to walk, climbing everywhere, a sunny disposition, black curls. I love her."

"You didn't try to drive there?" The red Corvette had been delivered two weeks earlier, and Julian had gone with Lori for several practice runs. She was still an apprehensive driver, uncertain at times whether to step on the gas or the brake and not ready by any measure to navigate in traffic.

"Of course not. I took the bus. Just one transfer."

He glanced at her fondly, wondering how long it would take her to realize that she was rich and could afford a taxi. "So what are you planning?"

"Maria says the program she's in is for one year, and, after that, she can apply to stay three more months at Take Heart. They are urging her to look for a job at a day care center where she can enroll Elena as part of her salary. The problem with that is most centers don't take children until they are at least two years old. Elena's first birthday is coming up in a few weeks."

"So there's a serious gap there. I begin to see where you're heading."

"So I'll ask Maria if she would like to work for me after she finishes her program. That will be just about when Mrs. Barnes wants to leave, so it works out perfectly. Maria can be the new Mr. Munchen and the new Cook too."

"Do you know, can Maria cook?"

"About as much as I can, I think. I'll send her to Mr. Munchen's school if she wants to go, and that will give her another job skill beyond child care. She can teach me what she learns about buying food and cooking and all that—it'll be fun—and I'll help her practice English every day. It'll be like immersion, you know. She'll learn fast."

"And who will take care of Elena when Maria is at school?" *As if I didn't know.*

Lori's face softened, her eyes dreamy. "My pleasure."

He thought, not for the first time, that Lori had been looking forward to marrying Bill and having a baby of her own, probably a lot of babies, and loving them immensely, extravagantly, exuberantly, as she herself had never felt loved.

Darn that Bill Letterson, he thought, though he was just as happy that Bill was no longer in the picture. *Lori will recover from the guy's betrayal if she has a baby to watch over. Yes, Elena will bring joy to the house, just as little Julie has brought me a measure of peace.*

After a moment, as if he had been considering the plan, he said, "Sounds like a good idea. Here we are. What about Roz?"

"I'll invite her to dine with us at Reuben's next Thursday, if that's okay with you. And I'll tell her she won't have to wait for the bus. We'll drive her home, okay?"

Julian smiled at Lori's use of the word "dine" and thought fondly of Mrs. B. "Good. Another time when we invite Roz, let's invite the Umbertos, the children too. Probably be a treat for Juan to have someone else bussing *his* table."

Chapter 50

LORI AND JULIAN HAD DECIDED to continue their custom of eating at the Bellington mansion after their Friday conversations with Dr. Glazer, just as they had done when Mrs. B was alive.

"Once we get a good menu going, let's invite Vicki," said Lori, "for a simple meal. But we do need to practice." She eyed the hamburger that she was browning. "I bought sour cream to top off this skillet casserole—that'll jazz it up—and earlier today I made lime Jello for dessert. That's 'dessert with an S for each hip.'" She smiled at him, pleased with the memory that they shared.

"You slice up the raw vegetables, Julian—they're in the fridge—and put them in a silver bowl from the china cabinet in the dining room. I'll set the table." They decided to use the good china and the linen napkins but to eat in the kitchen. "Right now I can't bear to see Grandma's empty chair at the big table."

Julian felt the same way. "But what about Mrs. Barnes? When she starts—is that next Monday?—she'll expect to serve you in the dining room."

"Mrs. Barnes lives a short bus ride away, and, half the nights, when we're at Reuben's or cooking for ourselves, like now, she'll just leave mid-afternoon. I'll figure out the rest somehow."

He was surprised. "I thought you hired a housekeeper so you wouldn't be all alone here, especially nights."

"I've thought about it. Mrs. Barnes will stay Saturday, Sunday, Monday, and Wednesday nights. She's okay with that. Would you stay on Friday nights, just until Maria comes?"

"That would hardly be proper, Lori. Think about wagging tongues. How would it look for my car to be parked in your driveway overnight?"

"How does it look for poor Lori to be all alone?" she pleaded. "Grandma asked you to watch out for me, remember? And you promised you would. There's plenty of room in the garage for both our cars. Anyway, who's looking, that reporter from *Lives of the Rich?* She's been hanging around, by the way. I even ran into her in the grocery store, so I told her politely to get lost. I said I'd never give her an interview."

"Lori, yes, I told your grandmother I would always look after you because I…" He stopped short, suddenly floundering. "And that's what I'm trying to do. Just ask Mrs. Barnes to be a full-time live-in. Be firm. That will solve your silly little problem."

"I wish you were my uncle or my big brother." She made a face at him. "Then *you* could move right in. What if I told you I'm scared to death to be here alone? I'll have nightmares; Grandma will haunt me because I didn't listen to some advice you gave me or maybe didn't listen to Lawyer Carpenter's advice. I'll wake up screaming with no one to comfort me but me."

"Why you poor little rich girl," he drawled the rebuke. "I repeat, just tell Mrs. Barnes you need her here full-time. Simple."

A comfortable silence fell as they started to eat. Julian was glad that he could compliment the casserole. "This is really quite good, Lori. Maybe next time, add a side dish of slaw."

"Julian, I want to ask you about something. I think I'm turning into a VIP. Yesterday I had eleven letters and three serious phone calls. Is that part of being rich?"

"Did they all want money?"

"Mostly. One letter was from my mom, though. She invited me to come home."

"Invited?" He almost choked on the word. "Do you need an invitation before you can go home?"

"Not really. Of course not. It's just that my parents are somewhat formal. They never get enthusiastic about things."

Not even about you, their only child, their lovely child?

"Mom said that they heard, she didn't say how or where, that Bill had married Alice Sheehan—I didn't even know that was her name— and so our agreement about a year's separation was really moot. Now that Grandma is dead and Munchen is gone, she said they worry that I am alone in this big, old house. If I come home, I can day-hop to the community college or I could just base at home and go to any college I wished as a resident student. She didn't say a word about my inheriting from Grandma."

Did they say they missed you or to please come home or that they would love to have you home again? That was what he wanted to ask and probably what Vicki would ask. Instead, mindful of Lori's growing independence, he said, "Have you decided what to do?"

"It's an awkward time. I definitely want to finish up my college courses; final exams are in just two weeks. After that, if I took a Wednesday morning flight and came back here the following Tuesday, I'd only miss one session with Roz. You'll take care of her, won't you? I'll leave my lesson plans."

"I'll take care of her."

"And I'll just park the Corvette at the airport, so I won't be any trouble to anyone."

Again, he sensed her need to grow up. It was a big triumph that she finally had her driver's license, could drive herself places and manage her own life, so he did not protest that he would be glad to ferry her to the airport, that she was never any "trouble" to him.

"Another thing. Mr. Carpenter called. He says that coming up next week is the regular quarterly meeting of the trustees who managed Grandma's affairs, and he thinks I should be present at it because now they're *my* affairs. He said, until very recent years, Grandma always attended. So I will too."

"Ask Vicki what to wear. You shouldn't appear to be a teenager, even if you are. No jeans. You want to look like a sophisticated young woman who is also a powerful heiress. I think your Grandma anticipated this. That's why she sent you to Upper Level: to get the right outfits for your new roles and to know where to go for more. And, Lori, just listen at the first meeting."

"That's what Mr. Carpenter said. That's my plan. I'll just say, 'How do you do?' And, when the meeting ends, I'll say, 'A pleasure to meet you. I'll study these handouts.'"

"That last bit makes you sound like a student. Think about it and be prepared to sound like an heiress. For example, you might say something like, 'I'm glad to have attended this meeting and to have met the members of the Rosen Trust. I'll review these reports.' Slip the papers into a slim, handsome briefcase. No three-ring binder. That's schoolgirl. Then take a long, slow look at each person around the table, nod your head graciously, and give them a pretty smile. Leave."

"I'll practice that. There's another problem, Julian. You say I'm rich and maybe I am rich, but I don't have any money."

"Ye gods, Lori! Whatever do you mean?"

"I can't reach into my pocketbook and pull out even a dollar. My mom asked on the phone if they should continue my allowance, and I told her no. They've been sending me thirty dollars a month, but now they've stopped, and so I don't have any spending money. Just a few dimes. That's why I took the bus to see Maria. I didn't have money for a cab."

"Ye gods!" he said again and started to laugh. "I should have thought of that. You *are* a poor little rich girl. Ask Mr. Carpenter. What a fine pair of executors Vicki and I are, never thinking…Well, there's probably a checking account at some bank with a lot of money in it, maybe even an account in your name. Your grandma was a great one for thinking ahead. You just need to write a check to cash to get some real money." A thought occurred to him, and he asked cautiously, "You do know how to write a check?"

"I never needed a checking account, but I'm sure I can learn."

"I'm sure you can too. After we dine, let's look in your grandmother's desk. Who knows what we'll find. If there's a checkbook there, I believe all you need to do is get new checks with your name and of course change the signature card on file at the bank. Talk to Mr. Carpenter."

"Another question, very important." She giggled and rose to clear the dinner plates. "I've got Rediwhip in a spray can. Want some on your green Jello?"

Chapter 51

AFTER SHE TOOK HER EXAMS (an A in History of England and a B+ in Biology), Lori went home to Ohio for six days. As planned, she returned in time for her ESOL tutoring on Tuesday evening. Julian picked her up at the mansion, and, frankly curious, he immediately asked how the visit had gone.

"Cool," she said. "I had a good time, saw a few old friends. Mom made a lovely dinner the first night and had flowers and candles on the table, like it was a special occasion. The next night, she ordered in some of that Italian wedding soup, and we had that and sandwiches from the leftover roast pork. Mom and Dad have a quiet, little restaurant—quite elegant—where they often eat, so we went there on Friday and..."

"Lori," he interrupted, "I'm really asking what you talked about. Did you make any plans?"

"Oh, that. We talked some about Grandma. Mom said she used to watch from the upstairs window when her mother and father went out at night to parties or to high-toned restaurants, and, when her mother swept down the path and stepped into the limousine, she thought her mom was a queen.

"Sometimes, when they would give a ball at the mansion, Mom would crouch on the stairs and peek to see her parents lead out the dancing or the Conga line. They did it with such a flair! She said she grew up liking the smell of cigarette smoke because it meant her mother was home."

"That's sad. Poor little girl. I didn't know Mrs. B ever smoked."

"I guess she was smart enough to quit in the sixties after the Surgeon General had that warning put on all the packs of cigarettes. I learned about that in my high school social studies class."

"Lots of people knew even before that warning that they should quit smoking. My parents taught me that cigarettes were 'coffin nails.' But some folks kept right on smoking because they didn't have enough backbone to stop. Your grandmother had plenty of backbone."

"Yes, and Mom said Grandma was always beautiful and full of life and pranks, always dressed to the hilt in beautiful, bright clothes but quite often was also autocratic, a bit sharp-tongued. My mom knew from her earliest days that she was a disappointment to her mother because she was such a timid child. Once she overheard her mom tell someone, 'I have a lackluster daughter.'"

"Ouch! That must have hurt."

"Grandma didn't know Mom was anywhere in earshot, or she wouldn't have said it. Mom said she was mostly the shy little girl in the background, but she didn't think her mom ever hurt her intentionally, which is sad in its own way." Lori paused to reflect. "When I have kids, well, believe me, they'll never wonder if they're loved.

"Mom said she tried to make herself over and be like Grandma, but she just couldn't do it. She flopped. It wasn't until she was thirty-two that my dad came along and, thank goodness, loved Mom just the way she is—dreamy, slow to make friends, somehow a little dowdy even in her expensive suits. Mom said that's when her life really began.

"Listen, Julian, I've been thinking about our students. Roz loved going to Reuben's, and don't you think she learned a lot? Can we take her again and take the Umbertos too?"

"Sure," he said. "While you were home, did you think you might move back there?"

"They did ask me if I intended to live by myself in the Bellington mansion. My mom said she always thought it was a scary place, sort of big and sort of overwhelming. They were relieved when I told them that I had hired Mrs. Barnes and planned on getting more help. I didn't tell them that Mrs. Barnes was a temp or that the new maid wouldn't be coming for almost four months."

Julian parked in the church lot. As they entered the building, Lori continued, "Next Thursday the Umbertos can follow us to Reuben's in their car. We'll take Roz. See you after class."

Yep, she's like her grandmother, getting more so every day as she realizes the power of her money. She just organized Roz, the Umbertos, and me for next Thursday, and it didn't occur to her that any of us might have different plans. Well, I know I don't. He was happy that she had apparently decided to continue living in New York.

He greeted his students with his usual enthusiasm, showing them a booklet that he had ordered on how to become a naturalized citizen of the United States. Tonight he would start on that and use part of the period to teach that the government consists of three main branches: legislative, executive, and judiciary.

AT THE CEMETERY

June 10, 1979

Lori went home for a week, so there was no dinner for me at the Bellington mansion last Friday. That sounds selfish, but, after my conversation with Vicki, which ends at six o'clock, I was feeling abandoned, nowhere to go but back to the apartment. I was feeling lonely, I guess, and I wanted to ask Vicki to dine with me but, of course, there are those patient/doctor rules.

Maybe she wouldn't have accepted anyway.

Julie, I think Lori's parents are strange. Lori said her mother invited her to come for a visit. Can you imagine? Can you imagine Joy or Miles waiting for an invitation? Our children came home because it was home, and, whenever they came, they knew our arms would be open. I'm glad I can say that.

Lori says she loves her mom and dad and they love her back, but from what I hear, they're a stiff pair, almost as if they are afraid of each other or afraid to show emotion. Maybe that's why Lori was so happy with Bill's family.

I took care of Roz, Lori's ESOL student, while she was away.

Chapter 52

WHEN DR. GLAZER ASKED LORI how her visit home had gone, Lori was far more forthcoming than she had been with Julian. She told how she had not wanted to talk to Bill, not even get a glimpse of him, but had phoned his mother before she unpacked her suitcase.

"I felt I really needed to talk to Mom Ellen, that's what I called Bill's mom. I had written to her every week while I was away, kept her up to date, because, to me, she was already my mother-in-law. Then I stopped writing because what was there to say?

"But I knew I had to call. What if she heard I was home and hadn't visited her? See, I didn't want her to think for a minute that I was mad at her or blamed her at all. I still love her, and I wanted to hear from her just what happened and how Bill is. I guess I needed to tie off that portion of my life."

"Closure." Vicki gave a name to Lori's feelings.

"She was glad, a little surprised, I thought, when she picked up the phone. She said, 'Can you come tomorrow, Lori? It will be so good to see you. We'll have a cup of tea. All the kids, except Maureen, have summer jobs, so we can be fairly private. Three o'clock work for you?'

"She sounded perfectly normal, her usual brisk self, but, the next day, when I knocked on the back door (when Bill was a kid, he got in the habit of using the back porch door because his mom said his shoes were always muddy, even when it hadn't rained for days), she gathered me into a big hug and started to cry. I cried too.

"'Oh, that foolish, foolish boy,' she said. 'Sit down. I have the kettle on. I'll make tea and we'll talk. Lori, you look different. You're not a high school kid any longer, are you? Is it the hairdo, the clothes? New York? What?' She surveyed me with approval and continued, 'I guess you're just more grown up, grown more sophisticated, more beautiful. Bill's still a clumsy teenager. Doesn't seem to have caught on yet that he's an adult, or supposed to be. Oh, I'm happy to see you—and sad too. These past months…' She ran out of words then and shook her head as if she found the entire situation utterly inexplicable. 'Oh, that foolish, foolish boy!' she repeated. 'And not even a grandchild to show for it.'

"'What?' I exclaimed.

"'Oh. Sorry, Lori. Of course you wouldn't have heard, all that distance away in New York City, but, right after Rusty and Bill married, Rusty miscarried. She never even showed.'

"'She's not pregnant?'

"'She's not.' Ellen shut her mouth and did not say about her daughter-in-law what she and I were both thinking: *Rusty tricked Bill.*

"At that moment, Maureen Letterson, six years old, was dropped off from a playdate down the street. She appeared in the doorway arch, her eyes wide. 'Law-wie, Law-wie,' she squealed, 'you come home!' She launched herself across the room and onto my lap, her little arms hugging tight around my neck. 'I'm lots happy.'

"'Me too.' And I thought how good the small body, still a bit roly-poly from babyhood chubbiness, felt in my arms. I hugged longer, hoping to hide how stunned I was at Ellen's news. 'And how you've grown!' I said.

"'I'm finished kindergarten,' the child said proudly. 'Yesterday I finished kindergarten. I'm on vacation.'

"It was a milestone of course. It was the first time Maureen had had anything to be on vacation from. 'Oh, I love you,' I said.

"'I'll show you my report card,' Maureen said, and, as suddenly as she had appeared, she raced out of the room. Ellen and I smiled at each other, glad to have been distracted from the wretched turn our conversation had taken.

"'She's an energetic one,' said Ellen fondly.

"'She's a darling.'

"'Lori, I'm embarrassed for that darn Bill. He's my son, and, in many ways, I'm proud of him, but he did a very stupid thing. I can't tell you how sorry I am. You were already part of our family circle, and it felt as if a daughter had died...'

"Moisture filled Ellen's eyes. 'We had all welcomed you, welcomed the engagement. Rusty was a terrible shock to us.' She dabbed at her tears with a tissue.

"I told her, 'When Bill told me about, you know, about marrying Rusty, it was the day of my grandma's funeral. I had called him to say I had inherited some money and we could have a big bash of a wedding. Yes, I was bummed out when...' I couldn't finish.

"Ellen said, 'I didn't know your grandmother died, Lori. It wasn't in the paper. I guess your mom and dad thought no one here knew her. My sympathy. But does that mean you're home for good?'

"Not exactly. I inherited her house in New York, a big old mansion. I'm going to live there for a while," I said.

"She asked if I was there by myself, and I said, 'I've hired a live-in housekeeper.'

"Ellen's eyes widened in amazement. 'Your grandmother left you a house and enough money to have a housekeeper too?' she asked. 'You must have grown close. Or are your parents...oh, I shouldn't pry.'

"I answered her, 'No, the money's my own now. Grandma left enough for me to live there and to see me through college. I've already earned six credits. I'll be busy, make new friends. That will help, help me get over Bill.' To Mom Ellen, I didn't add that Julian had said it was just puppy love. Maybe so.

"Ellen said, 'Good. I read in your letters that you've already made some new friends in New York. Connie and Vicki and—what's his name?—Julian and that woman who abandoned her baby. How old is Julian, by the way?'

"'He's forty-three. Kind of an uncle, a friend. But my grandmother was my best friend. We were kindred spirits. Then, all at once, she died, and Bill got married to Rusty, to Rusty who was pregnant.' Then I asked, 'Where do they live?'

"Ellen told me, 'Bill still lives at home. Rusty comes for Sunday dinner. She'll graduate next week, and they're looking for an apartment. They usually go to a movie on Wednesday night. That's her day off.'

"Does she still work at that Hilltop restaurant?" I asked.

"Ellen didn't correct the name of the eatery. 'Yes, and so does he. They're saving money to set up housekeeping. It's pretty grim between them.'

"Maureen had returned and was perched on the arm of her mother's chair, the forgotten report card lying on the carpet. She said, 'Mom says we have to be nice to Rusty, but she's no fun. Talks about dopey things like matching sheets and towels and lamps that will go with any … with any *décor.*' After she got the word out, Maureen made a face.

"Mentally, I made a face too. Because, in a way, it serves Bill right. Whether Rusty had been pregnant or not, the rotten cheat believed she could be. But I sipped my tea, took a cookie from the platter and handed it to the little girl, took another for myself.

"Then Ellen said, 'I know it's a lot to ask, Lori, but I hope you're able to forgive Bill. He lost *you*, and he'll probably regret that all his life. The wife sets the tone for the family. You are a class act.'

"'Thank you, Mom Ellen,' I said. 'I'm going back to the city in a few days, and I may never see you again, but I'll always remember how the Letterson family was such a great part of my teen years. That includes Bill. I hope he has a good life.' I put my hand, for a moment, on Maureen's cheek, then stood to leave.

"Ellen gave me a straight look. 'I'll hold you in my prayers, Lori. Be happy. I love you.'

"'Me too. I love you,' Maureen said, wanting to be part of the conversation.

"'Me, three. I love *you*,' I choked out. I walked down the back steps thinking that Bill's mom is strong. I hope I brought her a little comfort. She and Maureen helped me too, gave me courage, because they love me and they don't even know how rich I am."

Chapter 53

LAWYER CARPENTER, NEATLY TRIMMED AND SHAVEN, well-tailored in a gray, summer-weight wool suit, picked Lori up to escort her to and introduce her to the five movers and shakers who were assembling, even at that moment, for the quarterly meeting of the Rosen Trust.

When she was settled in the car, he remarked, "That's an attractive outfit you're wearing. You look just right."

"I know. Thank you. Dr. Glazer helped me choose." She clapped her hand over her mouth to stifle a giggle. "I know, I know, I'm not supposed to giggle. Julian says not to say *anything*, but that I shouldn't look bored either, or haughty. Vicki says to remember I'm not a high school kid. She says not to fidget or glance at the clock or pick my nose."

He glanced at her sharply.

"Just kidding about that last bit. Do you have any further advice, Mr. Carpenter? I'm thinking this must be a very important meeting. Julian says I should just glance quietly around the conference table from time to time, as if I'm committing everyone and everything to memory."

"Well, first impressions count. As your lawyer, I suggest that if you are asked any questions, refer them to me."

"There's something I've been wondering about, Mr. Carpenter."

"What is that?"

"I've gotten so much good advice about this meeting. I'm wondering if the members of the Board have also been getting advice on how to impress *me*."

"They are all businessmen, Lori, chosen by your grandmother for their diverse experience. Dr. Glazer and Mr. Elsmore and I just want to make sure you start off on the right foot with them."

"No boo-boos, huh? Keep my mouth shut. No giddy remarks or slang. Smile prettily. Okay, that's a plan."

He nodded and spoke smoothly, "I have your best interests at heart, Lori. I'm dedicated to your welfare and the growth of your holdings."

"I'm sure you are." She smiled at him quite prettily. Then, seeming to change the subject, she mentioned, "You know, I've just taken a college course in English history. King Edward VI was the son of Henry VIII and Jane Seymour, and he was crowned king when he was only nine years old, poor little boy."

"Interesting, I'm sure."

"Yes. His uncle got himself declared Lord Protector and tried to run the show in the young king's name. I suppose Edward needed someone to look out for him."

"Sounds like it."

"I'm almost twenty, Mr. Carpenter, do you know that? In just a few weeks."

"I am well aware of that. Here we are." Mr. Carpenter wheeled the car expertly into the underground garage and, courteous to the point of gallantry, ushered Lori to the elevator. "The conference room is on the tenth floor. Do not shake hands, just nod."

"Mr. Carpenter," she said as they rode swiftly upward, "I'd like to take some business courses next semester. As well as another class in English History. I'm on a roll there. Could you check out a good place nearby to take business courses?"

"Glad to," he said, "if that's what you want." His voice was a bit frosty. "By the way, Lori, you own this building."

She swallowed. "I didn't know."

Two hours later, back in the car, Lawyer Carpenter was beaming. "Went very well, I thought. Your performance was perfect."

"That's a relief, I guess, but what I want to know, Mr. Carpenter, is how do I get things done?"

"What things?"

"I've some ideas. I don't expect to sit around at meetings forever, being ornamental and keeping my mouth shut."

Mr. Carpenter spoke thoughtfully, "You don't have to attend the quarterly meetings at all, Lori. That's not necessary. I just wanted the trustees to meet you. In a few years, if you wish to be more active, just let me know."

That's probably what the little king heard from his Uncle Ed Seymour. "In a few years, little prince, perhaps...In the meantime, leave it all to us; we'll handle everything." Aloud, she said, "I know I have a lot to learn, but there is a project I want to hop on right away. I need you to tell me how to get things done, to guide me."

"Could you summarize your thoughts in writing—a paragraph or two, no more? That will give me a starting point."

He knew that putting an idea, no matter how good, into a nutshell is hard work. He wondered whether Lori would be up to it or if she would take a stab at it and then drop it all on his desk. *Will she be a figurehead?* he wondered. *That would probably make my job easier. Or will she want to run things, her grandmother's child?*

Aloud, he said, "Don't worry about it, Lori. One thing I can assure you is that nothing Colonel Bellington or your grandmother proposed was ever turned down by the Trust. Of course, they leaned conservative. Anyway, just give me a precise idea of what you wish to do, and I'll put it into proposal form."

"Thank you, Mr. Carpenter," she said. "Please do it at least a month before the next meeting. I'll want to look it over." She folded her hands in her lap and smiled prettily.

He thought, *I should see that she meets more young people, becomes part of a younger crowd.*

Chapter 54

Mr. Metcalfe phoned on a Wednesday in mid-June to ask if he could come by to introduce a new gardener he had hired.

"Can you come before two?" Lori asked. "I have a babysitting job at three, the twins, you know."

"Is nine a.m. too early?"

"I'll be here." She hung up, relieved that Mr. Metcalfe could find a gardener in New York City. She didn't have a clue how to go about it, but she knew that the grounds were looking scraggly and needed attention. She thought of Mr. Dempsey and hoped that he was in a happy place where the gardens were glorious and the paths properly edged. She hoped that he was able to be down on his knees, thinning seedlings, his hands dark with the good brown soil.

Lori wondered if it was up to her to approve the new employee. *No, Mr. Metcalfe said he had already hired him. Maybe Mr. Metcalfe had thought I'd be alarmed if I found a stranger on the property without having met him first. Got to protect dumb, little Lori, huh?* Then she realized that she didn't know, didn't have a clue, how much a gardener makes. She was glad that she could turn to Mr. Metcalfe. *There's a lot I don't know…yet.*

She herself made two dollars an hour when she babysat Martha and Matthew, but she knew that Connie paid higher than usual rates because, as Connie said, "They're twins and they're fast little imps."

Lori knew that gardeners must make more than babysitters. She had heard vaguely of a minimum wage. She reflected that she hadn't even asked how, or how much, Mrs. Barnes was paid. Mr. Munchen and Mr. Metcalfe had arranged it all. Lori wondered if Mr. Carpenter had to put his stamp on it. She knew that they'd taken care of her.

It's easy to let yourself be taken care of, she thought. *But I'm not Edward VI, and I'm not nine years old. They think they'll be my Lord Protectors, and I am grateful for their know-how, up to a point. I wonder, can they sign stuff in my name? I'll find out. They must have some sort of power like that. That's scary, even if Grandma handpicked those men herself. I don't think she intended that I rely on them forever. I'm glad I can ask Julian about stuff.*

She said aloud to no one, "Hear this, O Lord Protectors, I won't be coddled all my life." She resolved to get on the stick and to learn all that she could as fast as she could. She smiled to herself. "I'm Lori One."

Some of the very first things that she learned were taught by Mrs. Barnes. The retired librarian, although always dignified, apparently had no aim in life except to please Lori.

It was to her advantage, of course. Lori well knew that Mrs. Barnes's clearly defined goal was to save enough money to go on another jaunt with her travel club. Because Lori's wealth would make that trip to Italy possible, Mrs. Barnes sought to please. *Lesson 1: Have a goal.*

When Lori said, "Let's eat together in the kitchen tonight," Mrs. Barnes replied, "I'd be delighted. What shall I cook?" It turned out she was a good conversationalist.

When Lori said, "I don't like cucumbers," cucumbers were immediately banished from salads, sandwiches, and grocery lists.

When Lori said, "Mr. Elsmore will be here for dinner tomorrow evening. I'd like a small pork roast, gravy, mashed potatoes, a green vegetable, some kind of fruit pie for dessert, that's dessert with two S's," Mrs. Barnes just nodded approvingly. The meal was wonderfully prepared and beautifully served in the dining room. *Lesson 2: Give clear orders.*

When Lori said, "I'd like you to sleep here every night, Mrs. Barnes. I don't like being all alone in this big house," Mrs. Barnes, toting a large suitcase, moved into Cook's old room.

This business of being rich is remarkable. Mrs. Barnes didn't even know me ten days ago, and now she can't do too much to please me. I mustn't think it's my due. It's the money that does it. I wonder if rich people ever get fed-up with being rich? There are some disadvantages. I'd better not say that to anyone but Julian. No poor person would believe it, anyway. Most people want to be rich, dream of it. I sound ungrateful.

I'll ask Julian. He knows a lot of things, and he knew me before I was rich.

She heard Mr. Metcalfe knocking at the back door, and she called, "Come in!"

It was something that Mr. Metcalfe later reproved her for. "Keep the doors locked, Lori, keep safe even when Mrs. Barnes is here. Know who's knocking before you open. That's what those little peepholes are for."

At the moment, though, he said, "Miss Seever, this is Jack Salvo. We've just been looking the grounds over, checking the tools and machinery. I'll need to order some supplies—mulch, lime, things like that. Salvo will make me a list."

"How do you do, Jack?" She wondered what had happened to his birth name. He certainly looked Hispanic.

"Miss Seever." He nodded. "You have a beautiful place here. Needs attention, which I will be happy to supply." There was no hint of an accent or subservience. "The apartment too. Very nice. I noticed a hot plate, so I'll be fine."

"Where have you worked before, Jack?"

"The New York Botanical Gardens. Government workers have a good retirement plan, so I retired early. If you're interested, Mr. Metcalfe has my resume. This is the kind of situation I've been looking for."

"Your family?"

"My wife has passed." He raised his right hand and sketched a cross, the first sign that she had seen of his Hispanic heritage. "My children, three boys, grown now, living their own lives, are doing well. I have assured Mr. Metcalfe that he will be pleased with my work, and you also, Miss Seever."

That's right, I must be pleased also because, you know, I pay your salary. On the whole, though, she thought that she had conducted the brief interview in quite an adult manner. A sudden thought struck her. "Jack, are you from Mexico? Do you speak Spanish?"

"My parents came from Mexico. I grew up bilingual."

"There is a Mexican man I tutor in English, Juan Umberto. I think he'd be glad of a part-time job for a few weeks, maybe all summer. A helper for you—rake leaves, mow, while you get the grounds shaped up. He's legal. And, Jack, he wants to learn the language, become a citizen, you know."

"You want me to help him learn?"

"Exactly. Teach him the names of all the garden tools—shovel, trowel, rake, and everything else he handles. He's a busboy, full-time, in a swanky restaurant, where he doesn't have to talk. And so he doesn't. He needs to talk. You can help him."

"Of course, Miss Seever. Whatever you wish."

There it is again. Whatever I wish. She felt triumphant.

Mr. Metcalfe spoiled it. "Where can I reach Juan, Lori? I'll see if he's interested."

"I'll handle it." She immediately realized that she had spoken rashly. She didn't know what hourly rate to offer Juan nor how and when he'd be paid. Mr. Metcalfe knew. "I need to talk to you," she said to her factor, "before the next tutoring session tomorrow evening."

It's almost funny because I'd like to pay Juan, and I can afford to pay Juan, twenty dollars an hour, but, rich as I am, I'm not free to do that. I know enough to know that Juan's salary has to be proportionate to Jack's.

"When can you start, Jack?"

"Immediately. I'll move in day after tomorrow, if that's all right with you, Miss Seever. I'm eager to get going. I've already put my house on the market."

"Good. I hope this works out for both of us."

Lori thought that it would be good to have a man living on the premises once again. Jack wouldn't be Munchkin, she knew, but it would be good.

Chapter 55

JULIAN TOLD VICKI THE FUNNY STORY about Lori not having any spending money. They laughed together. "Actually, I felt remiss. I should have realized…"

"Yes, there are a lot of gaps in what Lori knows, things that she hasn't lived long enough to learn."

"The poor little rich girl didn't have money to take a cab to see Maria and Elena. Imagine how she felt not knowing how to get hold of her money."

"You straightened that out?"

"Easily. We looked in the desk, found Mrs. B's checkbook, and Mr. Carpenter had it changed to Lori's name. Found a few other interesting things, too."

"Like what?"

"Most interesting was a list of the assets that are held in the Rosen Trust. And another list of investments outside the Trust, like real estate that produces quite a cash flow but can vary wildly from year to year. Also income bonds that are steady. I talked to Mr. Carpenter about how everything is managed. As executors of Mrs. B's will, you and I should know how the estate functions. Mr. Carpenter's been on top of it all for years. I think he's a very careful man. Handsomely paid, of course. We're lucky to have him."

"And Mr. Metcalfe too. They're loyal to Mrs. B's memory and to Lori. We need that loyalty while we get familiar with the size of her inheritance. It sounds enormous, Julian, and it'll keep us busy. Our girl's not the only one with a lot to learn." She changed the subject. "Julian, do you know why Lori went to visit Maria and the baby?"

"Somehow, Lori feels responsible for Elena because we were the ones who found her abandoned on the ferry. By extension, she's responsible for Maria. She hopes Maria will come work for her when she completes her stay at Take Heart House. Did you know that 'Take Heart' is what they call the program she's in?"

"Nice. When is the program over for Maria?"

"In October. Lori says it will be a blessing to have a baby in the house at Christmas. Her face lit up when she said that."

"I can guess. Lori will want to plan something special, I'm sure. Do you know if the Take Heart program has helped Maria? Has she liked it?"

"Yes to both questions. And her social worker praises her highly."

"Elena's Daddy? Where's he in all this?"

"Gone back to Mexico. Seems he has a wife there."

"What a bum! But good because that does leave Maria free to build her own life. Lori has offered to send her to the Munchens' school, and Maria seemed open to that idea. Another question, Julian. I've been wondering why Mrs. B chose us as executors. Surely, she had many more capable people to choose among. Had that thought occurred to you? It's a bit strange."

"I asked Mrs. B that myself, and she said she knew I was smart and honest, but, most of all, she had observed that I love Lori. Maybe the same for you?"

Vicki's eyes widened. "Do you? Love Lori?"

He drew a slow breath. "Yes. Could we talk about that next time?"

"Of course. But one last question; really, this is the last one. How is Melissa?"

"How should I know? These days we just wave when we're both at the Club."

"You don't go to her dinner parties anymore?"

"Made up an excuse for one last month and haven't been invited since. I think she's found someone who likes pink ties." He grinned and she grinned back.

"You okay with that, Julian?"

"Absolutely." Just as Vicki started to smile, he added, "Lori 's pleased about it too."

Chapter 56

"Do you have lots of money, Julian?" Lori asked.

"Enough."

"I need a more exact answer. Are you a multimillionaire, like I am?"

"Indeed, no."

"A millionaire then?"

"Close. I make a good salary at Reliance, more than I need. I am well invested. Why do you ask? This some sort of game?"

"Not a game. I just wanted to be sure about your circumstances. Julian, why don't we get married?"

They were driving home from Tuesday tutoring. Her abrupt questions had amused him and intrigued him as to where they were leading. The proposal left him speechless, hollowed out with sudden, swift desire. *Darling Lori...my dearest, darling Lori...*

She waited but not very long. "Well," she spoke tartly, "you have to think it over? I've thought it over, and I would like to have a husband, and you are the husband I would like to have."

"But do you realize, Lori, that you are on the rebound from Bill?"

"I've thought that over too. I had a lot of fun with Bill. I was terribly hurt when he ditched me. I still miss him sometimes, but I really think I've outgrown him. I hope he and Rusty have a happy marriage. I truly do. If I had married Bill, we probably would have been bored with each other after a few years. A boring marriage. Wouldn't that be awful?"

"Lori, this is a crazy idea. You're at loose ends. I'm too old for you."

"You're forty-three. Maybe you haven't noticed, but, since Grandma died, I've been aging quite rapidly. I figure I'm about thirty-five by now, which makes us perfect for each other."

Her argument reminded him of the way Julie reasoned, and he had to laugh. She pinned him with a cross look. "You think this is funny?"

He sobered instantly. "Lori, I am flattered, overwhelmed actually, that you would ask. There is nothing I would like better than to marry you."

"Well then, is it settled?"

"Hardly. There are problems."

"Name them." She drew a small notebook from her pocketbook. "I'll write them down, and you'll see how easy it is to solve them."

He drew a long breath. "Lori, the 60s were a watershed in this country. I grew up in the pre-1960s. I mean it when I say the Pledge of Allegiance; I love America from sea to shining sea. I've always respected my elders. I knew from the get-go I was responsible for myself, so I finished school, got a job, and stuck with it. Julie and I believed that World War II was the war to end all wars. When it was over, we were safe. That was the slogan: *America has made the world safe for democracy.* Still, I knew it wasn't safe to use a credit card to buy whatever struck my fancy, I knew it was part of my job to protect women and children, and I didn't have sex until I was married.

"You grew up in the 60s and 70s, Lori. A whole different landscape. Social mores I valued were dumped. The birth control pill, and then technology, changed all our lives. I'm saying we really come from different worlds."

She tapped her pen against her teeth, and his heart constricted. Julie used to do that. *Is it a sign? Probably not,* he realized. For she immediately said what Julie would never have said.

"You're a dope, Julian, a big idiot. We've spent a lot of time together in the past months—it's almost a year—had a lot of experiences together. Some cool stuff, like Elena on the ferry, and some tough to handle, like Bill's visit and Grandma's death. I never noticed that this 60s hang-up of yours was a problem before now. If it ever becomes one, we'll compromise. All married people compromise. And we have the money to do it.

"For your information, in case you wondered about Bill, I haven't had sex yet—though I think I'll like it—and I don't intend to have sex until I'm married. I have the standards of a 40s girl. I even respect my elders, even someone slightly elder, like you." She laughed, her blue eyes crinkling at her little joke. "You got that?"

He reflected that the fact that she would speak so easily and openly of her sexual history underlined the difference in their backgrounds. He parked the car and followed her into the house as he always did to make sure that Mrs. Barnes was on duty, that all was secure. It gave him time to put his thoughts in order.

"Listen to me. It's this way, Lori. I loved being a daddy, and I think I was a good one. I changed diapers. I wiped snotty noses. I clapped when Joy's dancing class put on Swan Lake, no matter that the kids—twelve eight-year-olds in pink tutus—made an oval rather than a circle, no matter that Joy kept hitching up her tights. I applauded and Julie did too even though we thought that Swan Lake was Duck Pond.

"I pitched balls to Miles in the backyard. I was a Boy Scout leader. We went camping together. I advised him and bought tools when he built his soapbox racer. I did all that. It was a special time. I loved being married, loved being a daddy.

"Now," he said carefully, "I want to be a good granddaddy, and, since I'm here in New York, I want to see plays and real ballet. You want babies. Elena is a substitute, but you want your own babies ASAP; I've had my babies."

It took her only about twenty seconds to answer. "No problem. This time around, *our time*, you won't be on the diaper or snotty nose detail. The nannies and I will take care of all that. We'll have a day nanny and a night nanny, whatever we need. You'll never have to get up from your sleep to walk a baby with colic. You'll just have the fun part. We can go to the kids' Christmas play on Friday and to the Metropolitan Opera or the theater on Saturday, see? You'll love our kids; I know you will. Anything else on your mind?"

"Why did you ask about my money?"

"It's good that you're rich. If people said you married me for my money, you wouldn't like that. Neither would I. Will you think about it, Julian, about marrying me?"

"I don't dare think about it. I honestly don't dare."

"Why not?"

"It would be too easy to tell myself it would be okay, that the age difference doesn't matter."

"It doesn't to me."

"It matters."

"Oh, Julian. You are a hard-hearted man."

"I hope not, Lori, but I have looked into my heart. I see myself at the ebb of my life, in a wheelchair maybe, growing feeble, maybe with Alzheimer's, a burden to you when you're still in your prime. That thought sickens me. Someday—maybe soon—you'll be swept up in a young love, maybe someone you meet at college, the kind of grow-old-along-with-me love that I shared with Julie. Darling Lori, I wish from my soul that I could be your young love."

"Julie was your young love, but you didn't grow old together. It didn't work, did it? She died. You're crazy, worrying about things that *might* happen in forty years. You know that I could die before you, cancer or something."

"The percentages are against that. Listen, Lori, when you meet the guy you think is the right guy, I'll be your godfather. I'll vet the guy. I'll check him out, hard."

"Big deal."

"I would like to be your husband, Lori, believe me, more than anything. Don't say another word about it; I'm not that strong. It's better that we be friends, loving friends. Your grandmother and I grew to be friends, and it was good for both of us. And, notice, she never asked me to marry her." He had tried for a laugh, and, when that didn't work, didn't produce even the faintest of smiles, he tried for normalcy. "May I pick you up for tutoring Thursday?"

"I'll drive myself. I know the way."

"Of course you do. But we always go together, and we've already invited Roz to dine with us at Reuben's afterwards. I'd like to pick you up on Thursday, Lori. Say it's okay."

"I suppose."

"Lori, don't do this to me. Don't be peeved."

"Peeved? What kind of a word is that? I'm furious," she flared. "I propose to you. You turn me down for no good reason. And you say I shouldn't be hurt. Well, let me tell you, I *am* hurt."

He ran his hand through his graying hair. "Ye gods, Lori. This is hard for me, too. I want to say, 'Yes, I accept. It's my dream come true! Yes, I'll marry you and we'll live happily ever after.' Instead, I guess I said all the wrong things."

"You certainly did."

"Then hold on to this one thing. Whatever I said, I said it because I want the best for you. I don't think I'm the best."

"A lot you know."

"Lori, I'll pick you up Thursday for tutoring. As usual. That okay?"

"Maybe yes, maybe no. I'm tired of things as usual."

"Lori, you know I keep to a schedule, a routine. I'm dull like that. Thursday at five, okay?"

"Oh, all right, all right. As usual then."

"Thank you."

"Oh, Julian, maybe you are a little dull, but I always know I can count on you." Her sudden quirky smile, *like a rainbow*, he thought, was an apology. She picked a beautiful red and yellow apple from a bowl on the kitchen table and tossed it to him. "I *can* always count on you, can't I?"

"Always. I'm glad you know that. Thank you."

"You're welcome, I guess." He started to leave.

"Don't go yet. We'll talk about something else—not about getting married." She spoke to the back of his head, then to an empty room. Surprised, she heard his car start, and, mocking him gently, she said with a sigh, "Ye gods!"

Chapter 57

JULIAN WAS RELIEVED TO SEE THAT LORI came running to his car in high spirits on Thursday. All thoughts of marriage seemed to have been put aside, at least for the time being. He knew her moods pretty well by now, and he knew that she was elated.

"Oh, Julian," she cried, "the most wonderful thing, just voted today! The Trust has established a new program, a 'Dreams Come True Scholarship Fund.' I thought up the name. Names are important. Do you like it?"

He barely had time to nod before she rushed on. "It's an opportunity for ambitious, young immigrants, like Roz, men and women, to get more education or job training after high school. There will be ten recipients every year. Tuition and a cost of living stipend. Roz will be the first. I can't wait to tell her."

He wasn't surprised at all to hear that the Rosen Trust had approved of Lori's proposal. Nevertheless, he joined in her enthusiasm. "We'll have a real celebration at Reuben's after class. I'm glad the Umbertos will be with us. Will you save the news until then, or tell Roz right away?"

They discussed how best to announce the good news. Julian noted that the Umbertos would not only be happy for Roz but they would tuck away the scholarship information for the future use of their own three children. Their eldest was already in third grade, while their little girl was in first.

Lori commented once again that it helped to be rich.

"You've done a good thing, Lori. It's win-win," Julian complimented, and they went to their tutoring stations, glowing with satisfaction.

Fifteen minutes later, Lori came into Julian's classroom with a worried look on her face. "Roz hasn't shown up, Julian. Juan, do you know why? Is she sick? Has something happened?"

Julian caught the uncomfortable look that Juan exchanged with his wife, Nita, and was instantly alert. "Tell us, Juan."

"Rosita," Juan said carefully, "Rosita, she is married."

"Married?" Lori was unbelieving, even as she saw Nita nodding. "She never said a word about a boyfriend."

"Husband now. Big, important man from Mexico. Rich." Juan delivered the news.

"In U.S., family business. Businessman, see?" added Nita. "Good-looker too. Good-looker couple."

"I can't believe it." Lori was dismayed, aghast. "It's so sudden."

"Yes, quick." In an age-old gesture, Nita cradled her arms and rocked a baby.

"Oh no. Roz is pregnant?" Lori was astonished. Nita nodded and smiled broadly, expecting Lori to be pleased. Lori sank into a chair. "I suppose," Lori said slowly, thinking out loud, "she'll want to continue learning English, maybe her husband too. What's his name? Maybe Roz will still want to learn data processing, don't you suppose, Julian?"

He looked dubious. "How should I know?"

Juan shook his head firmly and explained, "Live in Mexico now. Guadalajara. She asked we tell you." He added, "Husband is Miguel, call himself Michael, Michael Mono. He speak English very smooth. Is big, rich businessman."

"Is 'Mono' his family name?" asked Julian in surprise.

"Something like."

Ah then, a few more syllables in Mexico but cut short for American business use.

Lori asked, "Are they really going back to Mexico?"

"Gone. Right after little wedding. Big wedding in Mexico coming."

"Big wedding in Mexico *later on*." Julian made the correction softly.

"Roz didn't even tell me goodbye. I don't know what to say," Lori wailed. Tears suddenly filled her eyes, and she stood up and left the room.

Julian was worried about Lori, but he turned to his students and took up the lesson again, trying to carry on as if nothing had happened.

They were a rather subdued group at Reuben's, but they studied the menu, as students should.

"Chicken a la king, what means that?" Nita asked.

"Chicken, chopped up in small pieces, in a sauce. Maybe something that Joey could eat," said Julian.

Joey was intent, at the moment, on beating his spoon on the highchair tray. But Nita, pleased to show that she had come prepared, pulled two jars of junior baby food from the diaper bag: one lamb stew and one applesauce. She tied a bib around Joey's neck and started to feed him.

Well, I suppose it's easy to catch on to the conveniences of the supermarket, thought Julian. *Nita doesn't need English for that.*

"Mr. Elsmore, what means this?" Nita pointed to "griddle cakes" on the menu.

Stumped for a description, Julian said, "I'll order some. You'll see."

Letting Julian deal with the explanations and ordering, Lori turned her attention to Jim and Estella. The children, having been in the country for two years and in the ESOL class in their school, were easily bilingual. "I want to learn Spanish," she told them. "Think you can teach me?"

Delighted, they told her the names for table, tablecloth, chairs, dinner, water, and bread. When Jim deemed her accent correct, he exclaimed, "Far out, Miss Seever! Gimme five."

Lori laughed and slapped palms with both children. Winsome little Estella then climbed down from her chair and went around the table, held up her chubby hand, and said to each adult, "Gimme five."

Lori laughed again but then seemed to lose interest in the game and, turning to little Joey in his highchair, took the cloth napkin from the breadbasket, shook it out carefully, and draped it over the baby's dark curls.

"Where's the baby? Where's Joey?" she said. Joey reached up and, after several twists and shakes of his head, pulled the white cloth away. "There he is," cooed Lori. "There's Joey." She played the game several more times, and the toddler, his eyes bright with success, favored them with his gap-toothed smile.

It was all quite genial, almost normal, but, throughout dinner, it had been clear to Julian that Juan was distracted and working something out in his mind.

Now, clearing his throat, the man began his statement in careful English. "Miss Seever, Mr. Elsmore, is much poverty in Mexico."

Julian remembered that Juan had recently added the word "poverty" to his vocabulary list and was pleased. "We understand that, Juan."

"Rosita, her family—four little brothers and sisters—all poor."

"Yes."

"Michael Mono not poor. Now Rosita not poor. Good."

"Well, yes."

"Good, yes. Nita say women say they very much in love Rosita and her man. So, more good. And good for Rosita family. Big businessman help, pull strings, get jobs. You know?"

"Juan," Julian spoke slowly, giving Juan time to keep up with his words, "you're telling us that Roz has made a good marriage, a good choice. We should be glad for her. Is that right?" Juan nodded vigorously, and Nita, catching most of her husband's speech, also nodded happily.

When they left the restaurant, after final good-byes and high-fives, Julian started the Le Sabre and, with a glance at Lori, commented, "That went well, don't you think? Wonder if Nita will ever have use for 'griddle cakes'? Maybe the kids will."

A hiccup told him that Lori was crying. He went on with his monologue, hoping to turn it into a conversation when she was calmer. "They're so between cultures. It must be hard. They call their boys solid American names but have a lovely Hispanic name for their dear little girl. They work hard at learning to speak English, all that crazy grammar and spelling. And did you notice how easily they pick up English idioms? I was surprised when Juan said 'pull strings;' I never taught him that. He must have heard it at the restaurant and somehow figured the meaning. And the children with 'gimme five.'"

"Roz never even knew she was going to have a scholarship. I was busy getting that for her, and she was busy getting married."

"Lori," he said, "don't cry. Even though you're rich, you can't run other people's lives."

"Right. I'm finding that out. I can't make things happen or change things that have happened. Grandma's dead, Bill dumped me, Roz doesn't want my scholarship, I can't pay Juan more than I pay Jack, and I don't even know how much I pay either one of them. I'm caught in a spider web."

"Would you rather be poor? Ask anybody and they wouldn't hesitate a second. Rich is better than poor."

"I know, I know. I sound ungrateful."

"Worse. You sound stupid."

"Stupid! Julian!"

"Listen, Lori, sometimes only your best friend will tell you when you're talking crazy, sounding stupid. You'll learn, you'll figure out this business of being rich. I thought you handled the news about Roz in a very adult fashion."

"I *am* an adult," she snapped. "Don't be condescending. Don't pat me on the head."

"Sorry about that. I'm just saying you proved you're an adult. Lori, Juan says this is a good move on Roz's part. We have to be happy for her."

"I *am* happy for her. I'm just disappointed. Hurt, I guess. It's been a rotten week."

"Not everything. You'll get another student right away, if you want one. I know there's a waiting list, a shortage of tutors. And once people hear about the scholarships, there'll be lots of applicants. The Rosen Trust has done a mighty good thing."

"It's been a rotten week," she repeated. "Just when I decide that being rich is going to be great, that I'll have a lot of fun and forget Bill, just when I make up my mind that I won't let anyone turn me into a sad little King Eddie, just when I'm feeling pretty darn powerful, it turns out that Roz doesn't want my scholarship. Of course not. Why should she? She's got a good-looker husband, and she's going to have a good-looker baby. And you, Julian Elsmore, you won't even *think* about marrying me."

He ignored the last. He heard another couple of hiccups and mentally threw up his hands. *Ye gods. What a tough time she's having. Maybe Vicki can help her.* He turned all his attention to driving.

It was over a week before Lori received a note from her former pupil. It was brief.

> *Dear Miss Seever,*
> *I am married and live in Mexico. I say goodbye to you*
> *and to United States.*
> *I say thank you for all help. I remember.*
> > *Rosita Mono*

The signature, Lori thought, summed up the end of the relationship. It was not Roz, but Rosita Mono, who wrote the stiff little letter. Roz, for whom she had dreamed such bright dreams, had disappeared from her life forever.

"I think it's going to take me awhile," thought Lori soberly, "to get used to being rich."

Chapter 58

THE SUMMER WORE ON, and, even as she mourned for her grandmother and her broken engagement, Lori found her life returning to normal.

The Downstairs Club adopted a poor family, and a group of ten volunteers spent two Saturdays repairing and cleaning their rundown house in a rundown area of the city. The conditions there were pretty appalling to the young people, who were all from middle-class or better backgrounds. They hauled out bag after black plastic bag of trash and cleaned out a refrigerator that was overstuffed with decaying food, much of it half-empty boxes of take-out. They had been told that these people were poor, so they had expected the refrigerator to be empty. One of the girls made matters worse by upchucking, and Lori herself stepped out on the back porch for a breath of fresh air.

"How can people live that way?" a young volunteer asked Pastor Wellington when they met after the first Saturday to evaluate their charity project. "We cleaned up stuff they could have cleaned up themselves."

"Sometimes poverty and hopelessness have the effect of paralyzing their victims. They just give up," the pastor explained. "It's not your place to judge them. Help as much as you can. Give them a fresh start. Let them know someone cares."

"I feel they're taking advantage of us," a bronzed, seventeen-year-old boy muttered. "I don't mind giving up my Saturday to help the elderly or someone in a wheelchair, but this woman we're helping isn't old. She seems able-bodied, and her teenaged kids hang out at the house but don't offer to help with the clean-up."

"The sheets and blankets are disgusting," added an earnest girl. "Disgusting. And the washer is broken. When you turn the faucets on, the place floods. There's no detergent anyway. I looked."

"Gen," asked the pastor easily, "who does the laundry at your house?"

"Well...my mom or we've a maid who comes in twice a week." Gen fell silent.

"Picture this," said Pastor Wellington. "You can't turn on the washing machine because there's a split in the water hose. You manage to get that taped closed but you've no detergent. Somehow, your mom comes up with two dollars and sends you to the store but you're hungry so you go to a fast food place and get two of those 99-cent burgers and a glass of water. No detergent. Your mom yells at you. No laundry. No clean clothes. Not even clean dish towels. Maybe no hot water. So why bother?

"Our handyman is going over this week to replace the leaking hoses," the pastor continued, "and I'll send along a couple boxes of detergent. Remember, our goal is to help these people, not criticize them. They've had some tough breaks you don't know about."

Lori spoke, "If the kids are there next Saturday, can we ask them to pitch in?"

"Well, don't order them around. Ask them to help *you* do a job. You guys willing to go back there Saturday morning?"

Somewhat reluctantly, all ten volunteers agreed. Obviously, the project was not what they had expected. Where was the warm, fuzzy, do-good feeling? Where was the family's gratitude? Could that family ever get on their feet again, Lori wondered. She reflected that she had the money to give them a completely fresh start, set them up in a new house even, but then there were probably thousands of similar families right in this area who also needed help, and what about them? Well, it certainly wasn't simple.

Gabriel Wellington was satisfied that his young parishioners were learning about the hard work and disappointments of doing good.

When Lori told Julian about the Downstairs Club and their charity project, she also asked if he thought she should make a private contribution, maybe a new washer.

"About that," he advised, "ask Pastor Wellington. I myself never donate on impulse. We should help the less fortunate, yes, but I check out any need or non-profit before I give a dime."

"How? How do you check?"

"Every non-profit produces an annual report. That's the law. Look at their overhead. How much of what you give actually benefits their cause? How much is spent on big-wigs in the organization for first-class travel to conferences held at luxury resorts, for bonuses, benefits?"

"Really? Is that what I should do?"

"If you're asking for advice, yes. Learn all you can about business in general and about how the Rosen Trust operates."

"My trust? You think I need to investigate my own trust?"

"I think you should know every last thing about it. But don't just tinker, Lori. Either take the responsibility of running your trust, or leave it all to Carpenter and the Board."

July 26 was Lori's twentieth birthday. Julian had always wanted to take her to an elegant restaurant, and this was his opportunity. Both Dr. Glazers attended the party with pleasure. It was a delightful occasion. Lori blew out her candles with one powerful whoosh, which meant she would get her wish. She smiled mysteriously, and, whatever she longed for, she kept secret.

A few days later, Lawyer Carpenter's son, whom Lori had never met, wrote her a little note, identifying himself as Bram and inviting her to an end-of-summer pool party. The note read "We're just a couple of miles out of the city. Follow the enclosed map. Casual attire. I look forward to meeting you."

"What does that mean, 'casual attire'?" Lori asked her psychiatrist and confidant.

"Shorts, preferably denim, but not torn ones. Flip-flops. Paint your toenails. It's a pool party, so take along a bikini and a towel, although there will probably be a stack of towels in the bathhouse. Put your tennis racket in the trunk of your car."

"Back home, everyone would bring some food, like pretzels or a pan of brownies."

"Not expected in New York. There'll be plenty of snacks."

"Well, tell me about this Bram," said Lori.

"He just graduated from college. Headed to Harvard for an MBA. There's another son, about your age, I think. I forget his name."

"Will it be a big crowd? There won't be anyone I know."

"Probably not, but they'll know who *you* are. They'll be friendly."

"It's the money thing again, isn't it? You're saying they'll know I'm Mrs. Bellington's granddaughter who inherited all her money and they'll like me and my money bags before they even meet me."

Lori sighed but Dr. Glazer was reassuring. "Lori, you can relax; you'll be fine. It's not a big deal. They're rich, too."

Lori did enjoy the party. Bram and his brother, Ward, were good hosts. They saw to it that she met everyone and was welcomed into the circle. The tan young men, horsing around in and out of the water, eyed her with approval, and she eyed them in return.

Standing by the pool with Ward, Lori observed, "You and Bram have unusual names."

"He's Bramwell. That's for our mother's family. My dad and I share the name Edward. He's Ed; I'm Ward."

"Cute," she said.

"Why, thank you, ma'am," he drawled. "I appreciate the compliment."

"Well, you're some conceited lad." She pushed him into the pool and jumped in after him with a great splash.

When she surfaced, he dunked her, and when she surfaced a second time, he asked, "Friends?"

"Friends," she confirmed.

Within a week, one of the girls invited her to a picnic, and Ward asked her to go with him to hear a folk singer.

"It's James Taylor. He's pretty famous," Lori told Vicki. "Ward says he's singing at Sheep Meadow. Some farm, I guess, like Woodstock."

"Sheep Meadow is part of Central Park."

"Oops. Glad you told me that. Anyway, it sounds like fun.

"You know, don't you," Lori asked Dr. Glazer, "that Lawyer Carpenter managed to get me into Columbia U. for the courses I want to take. I'm looking forward to that, big time. The summer's almost over."

Chapter 59

———

Lori and Julian were at the kitchen table, just finishing their dinner one mellow Friday evening in October, when they heard hammering.

"It's Jack Salvo," Lori explained. "He asked if he could do a little carpentry work."

"Why?"

"Because he's very careful about things like that. He gets an idea about some change or improvement he'd like to make and then he asks my permission. You see, I'm the boss, the one who pays the bills. He knows it and shows it. He's very respectful. That's how it works." She gave Julian a smug look. "I'm learning how to be rich. There *are* advantages to being rich, besides having lots of money."

"You're pretty pleased with yourself these days, aren't you? I'm not asking why Jack asked your permission; I'm asking what is the carpentry project?"

"Julian, don't tell me you've forgotten. Just like a man!"

"Forgotten what?"

She explained patiently, "It's almost a year since we took that ferry ride and found little Elena. That's an anniversary for us, Julian. And soon for Maria. She's nearly completed her year of training at the Take Heart House. She won't have to ask for a continuance there. Mrs. Barnes wants to leave, and Maria and Elena will be moving in with me in just a few weeks."

"What's Jack Salvo got to do with any of that?"

"Well, you know the stairs right up the side of the carriage house to his apartment? He's putting a gate, one of those folding gates, at the bottom of the stairs to keep Elena from climbing up."

"He doesn't like little ones? I'm surprised."

"He *does* like children, but he knows that Elena isn't very steady on her feet yet. Julian, Elena will be seventeen months old when they move in. She isn't a baby in a crib or playpen; she's a toddler with unlimited curiosity about everything, but with no sense about what's dangerous. The twins are like that. We have to protect Elena. Jack doesn't want her to try to climb those stairs and fall and hurt herself."

"Good for him. Let's walk out and inspect the gate."

The carpentry, Julian saw, had been competently done. The gate was well chosen. Of stained wood and with brass fittings, it blended nicely with the surroundings. He wondered if Mr. Metcalfe had told Jack to put it on the estate bill or credit card. *Maybe Mr. Metcalfe picked it out himself.* He still didn't know how those things worked, but gradually he was learning.

When they walked up, Jack was just putting his tools away and cleaning up a few spills of sawdust. He looked up with a slight smile and accepted their compliments. "Can't be too careful with a one-and-a-half-year-old." He paused a moment and then said, "Miss Seever, a young man stopped by when you were gone. He asked a lot of questions."

"Who was it?

"Said he was Dan, a friend of yours from Columbia."

Julian shot a questioning look at Lori, and she nodded. "There's a Dan I know in my Economics 101. Nice fellow. What kind of questions, Jack?"

"Well, he was friendly. Said I should call him Ol' Dan. That's what his classmates call him because he's older than most of them. Twenty-five, he said, as if it mattered to me. Took him awhile but all his chatting boiled down to he wanted to know if I'm employed full-time. Do I live on the grounds? Any other live-in help? Asked about you too, Mr. Elsmore. Wanted to know if you lived here. Were you a relative? Or what?"

"Did he say how come he dropped by?"

"Said you had told him about the place, Miss Seever, and he was interested in American architecture of the nineteenth century. He was disappointed you weren't home." Jack changed the subject. "I was wondering, Miss Seever, are there any other things you need done to get ready for the little girl?"

"I'm making lists, Jack, thanks. Mr. Elsmore and I plan to buy some baby furniture next week. Some of it will need to be assembled, I suppose."

"Whatever you need done like that, just let me know." Jack picked up his tool kit and went into the garage to put it away.

"Lori," Julian asked, "how well do you know this Ol' Dan? How did he know to ask about me?"

"We've had a soda after class a couple of times. Just chatting. He doesn't have family himself. His dad raced cars in Australia and was killed in a big crash before Dan was born. Carridan Keegan was his name. You ever heard of him?"

Julian shook his head. "I don't follow racing."

"Dan's real name is Carri*dan*, see?"

"I'd like to meet the guy."

They went back to the big house and washed the dishes. When Julian left later in the evening, he saw Jack still puttering in the garage and stopped to talk.

"Jack, anything else about the guy who stopped by? It sounds odd to me, his nosing around that way."

"That's what I thought. Handsome fellow, nicely dressed college boy."

"You think he's interested in architecture?"

Jack considered. "Miss Seever drives a new top-of-the-line car, lives in a big house, wears expensive clothes and sometimes expensive jewelry. There are fellows who are quick to add those things up, you know. And she's pretty too. A catch. That's why I told her. I didn't really trust that young man."

"Jack, if Ol' Dan shows up again, if anyone like him shows up, let *me* know right away." He pulled out a business card. "Here's my phone number. See, Miss Seever's grandmother named me executor of her will, so, officially, I'm sort of Lori's guardian." Jack nodded.

Julian was disturbed. The next morning, he called Lawyer Carpenter and explained the situation.

Carpenter understood at once. "We have a man on call at our firm who checks on people like that. Can you give me a name?"

"Dan Keegan. Said his friends at the University call him Ol' Dan because he's twenty-five and some of them aren't even twenty yet."

"That name's spelled K-e-e-g-a-n?"

"I guess. Incidentally, his first name is actually Carridan, Carridan Keegan. He's a junior. He told Lori his dad raced cars in Australia some years ago. Implied Dad was a big star, died in a crash before Ol' Dan was born. Might be a starting point. Anyway, that's his story."

"Um," said Mr. Carpenter, "have you met him?"

"Not yet."

"Meet him if you can. Probably be a few days before I have any information. You'll keep tabs on Lori? Call me if there's anything to report, but don't let her know we're checking. She's young but she likes to be independent."

"I know."

Julian hung up the phone thinking, *She's protected, as safe as Lawyer Carpenter, Jack Salvo, and I can make her. I'll tell Vicki too. Always good to have Vicki in the circle. The four of us can certainly protect Lori from the Ol' Dan Keegans of this world.*

AT THE CEMETERY

October 7, 1979

Julie, it's almost eighteen months since you died.

I've read all about the stages of grief. For me, acceptance of your death, of the death of our marriage, wasn't the final step. It was immediate. I identified your battered body, and my heart broke. I knew.

Now I'm accepting another reality. I want to be married again. In a strange way, that's a compliment to you because I was so happy when we were married. I want to be happy again. Please understand that I can't mourn forever.

Without being vain, I think I can say that Melissa viewed me as a candidate for marriage. But we weren't ever in sync. That I know.

Lori reminds me of you when we were both just out of high school and in love for life. It would work with Lori— at least for awhile. But there's that age difference— twenty-three years. I love Lori. I wish I could marry her. If I were her age...But I'm forty-three. I can't steal all the excitement and exploration of young romance from her. I can't rob her of that.

Ever since I first talked to Dr. Glazer, I've intended to tell her I came to her thinking that since all her patients were women, she'd see one among them who was just right for me and she would introduce me...a crazy notion. I must have been nuts.

That's all I have to say, Julie. I hope you understand.

❧ ❧ ❧

Chapter 60

Lori and Vicki Glazer were having a conversation.

"There's this guy in my economics class," said Lori. "I've had a Pepsi with him a couple of times, and he asked me out to dinner and a movie tonight, but I told him I already had plans. You know, Julian and I have dinner together at the house after we see you, just as we did when Grandma was alive. I'm learning to cook."

"What about this economics guy? Do you want to date him?"

"Sort of yes and sort of no."

"Why the 'yes'?"

"Well, he's good-looking and fun, and, over the summer, I stopped thinking of myself as an engaged girl. I've had some real dates."

"Then why the 'no'?"

Lori sighed. "He likes me because I'm rich."

"What makes you think that?"

"He walked me out to my car and was impressed."

"Any guy would be."

"But most guys would say, 'Wow, what a buggy! You rich or something?' That's what Bill would have said, just blurted it out. Ol' Dan didn't let on he was impressed, but, the next day, when I came from my history class, there he was sitting cross-legged on the hood of the car, and he asked me,

'I know a neat little snack bar close by. How about we drive down there and have something to drink?'"

"Did you?"

"Yes. He wanted to drive, but I said I would. It was just a Pepsi, but he's fun."

"Sounds normal to me."

"But we didn't just happen to run into each other. I have to wonder did Dan hang around all afternoon, waiting for me to show up? History's a three o'clock class."

"A young man attracted to a pretty girl might do a crazy thing like that. Are you maybe a bit paranoid, Lori? Too sensitive about being wealthy?"

"While we were chatting, I mentioned how much I liked my History 221 course. He could just take a look in the catalogue and make sure that it was a Monday, Wednesday, and Friday class. Then, Dr. Glazer—and this is what made me suspicious—last Friday, when he knew I was at class, that's when he showed up at my house."

Immediately, Vicki was on high alert, her eyes sharpening. "He came to your house when he knew you were away? Why?"

"Jack Salvo said he was very friendly, hung around to talk, asked a lot of questions. And he told Jack he was disappointed I wasn't home, but see, I *know* that he *knew I wouldn't be home.* That's why I don't trust Dan. I think he was reconnoitering. I think he likes to hang out with rich girls."

"Maybe, but don't leap to conclusions." Vicki's smile was grim. "Since you want to date, it still might be fun to go out with him, keeping all you know in mind, sort of like a detective game."

"No, I don't want a date where I have to be watchful, be suspicious. What fun would that be? I trust Julian. We're comfortable together. Did I tell you Julian's going to meet me Saturday morning after I get my hair done at Rosen's, and we'll buy baby furniture? He's picking up Elena and Maria to shop with us. They're moving in week after next."

Although she had suggested it, Vicki didn't really want Lori playing games with good-looking Ol' Dan, a man whom she had already put on her get-rid-of-him list. She was pleased that Lori had rejected her advice so readily. *Chalk one up for reverse psychology. Chalk one up for Lori*, she thought.

During their conversation, a week earlier, Julian had told Vicki about Carridan Keegan and had said, "Lori's so innocent. Too trusting. We're her guardians, and it's our job to protect her. I'm glad that Lawyer Carpenter is checking the guy out. I have bad vibes about him."

She had agreed. Now she thought, with wry pride, *Lori doesn't have a lot of experience, but she's not dumb. She did a pretty smart job of sizing up Ol' Dan, of protecting herself. Good for her.* Dr. Glazer would have bet her framed license that Ol' Dan was already, in Lori's mind, a has-been.

Now she followed Lori's change of topic. "So Maria's going with you to buy baby furniture?"

"She is. I wanted it to be a surprise, but it's for *her* baby. I could tell she was tickled when I asked her to go along."

"Since she has no money, she'll realize that you're paying for all the stuff, but will it be *her* stuff or *your* stuff? You need to have a clear understanding about that."

"Hers of course—a gift. Okay, I'll make that clear. And I've a surprise for Maria. When I was in the store last week, I scoped out the baby department, and, Dr. Glazer, they have this darling crib, white wood with drawers underneath and a four-poster canopy of white lace with a pink silk lining and puffy pink bows at each corner. I asked them to hold it for me. Well, for Maria. She'll love it; any mother would. Matching sheets and a comforter too. Everything is washable. Expensive but really practical because it converts to a youth bed later on."

"Sounds lovely. What else do you need?"

"Babies need lots of stuff. I got a list from a baby book. Not just big stuff that you'd think of right away, like a playpen and a stroller and a chest of drawers, but diaper bags and potties and car seats. And toys and clothes. It will be cold soon. They had the cutest little snowsuits at Rosen's. I could hardly tear myself away."

"Why is Julian going with you and Maria on this shopping trip? Is he just for transportation?"

"Well, he likes shopping for baby stuff—we've done it before—but mostly because he'll be the practical one. If he's not along to put the brakes on, I won't be able to stop. I'll buy every stuffed animal they have and half a dozen mobiles to hang over the crib, especially since I don't have to worry about how much I spend. Of course I'm trying to remember most all of it has to fit into Cook's old room. Even there, I've been thinking, you know, there's a big butler's pantry right next door. I could see about having the connecting wall taken out or maybe have a door cut through." She stopped, breathless. "You know, Dr. Glazer, when something like Dan happens, it's the pits to be rich, but when I'm buying stuff for Elena, *wow!*"

Once again, Dr. Glazer recast her thoughts. *Well, maybe in some ways Lori does need to be guided and protected. Just until she gets more experience. Just until she learns the negatives of being rich. Dan has been one such experience. Thank Heaven Julian will be here soon. We'll talk.* To Lori, she said benignly, "Happy shopping."

"Dr. Glazer, another reason Julian agreed to go shopping is because he has a granddaughter just about the same age as Elena. Did you know that? He'll probably buy stuff for little Julie. He's a sucker for babies."

"Yes, I know about little Julie. You think he's a sucker?"

"Absolutely. Stubborn, too. He won't marry me."

"Marry you? That's new." Vicki, who seldom registered surprise, registered surprise. "You asked him? Did you actually ask him?"

"Anything wrong with that? He'd be a perfect husband. He liked me before I was rich. That's important. And I like him."

Dr. Glazer's eyes snapped, but she managed to keep her voice professional. "Time's up, Lori. We'll discuss Julian later. Send him in."

Chapter 61

NOT REALIZING THAT A SUDDEN STORM had blown up, Julian entered the "conversation" room with a friendly "good evening."

Vicki eyed him angrily. "Julian Elsmore, your appointment is canceled."

He was caught off balance. "How come? Is something the matter, Dr. Glazer?" He usually addressed her formally when he was in her office.

"Don't you 'Dr. Glazer' me. I'm Victoria. And that's the woman you'll talk to this evening, or we won't talk at all."

"Well, sure, all right. What's the matter, Doctor…I mean, Victoria? What…?"

"Julian Elsmore, are you so woebegone you're thinking of marrying a child? Lori's a child, who just had a number of major changes in her life—a broken engagement, her grandmother's death, all that money, Ol' Dan showing up. She needs time. You and I are supposed to be helping her."

"I know, I know, Doctor…I mean Vicki. But Lori isn't really a child. She's twenty."

"She's a child, and you're a foolish man. Go away."

"Ye gods, Vicki, what are you talking about?" He was bewildered.

"I'm talking about you even thinking about marrying Lori. Are you insane? We're supposed to help her. Do you think you'd be doing one hell of a job of helping her by marrying her?"

He was shocked at her vehemence. *She's really upset. Why is this woman, usually so calm, swearing?*

"Listen, Vicki, it's not polite to say this, but it was her idea. I know she's on the rebound from Bill. No girl likes to be dumped. She's in a muddle, confused by her sudden wealth. She needs time to get used to being rich. We should just be standing by. I told her I'm not the answer. She's too young for me."

"Can't you say that you're too old for her? You can't, can you?"

"Victoria," he said, speaking firmly, "be quiet a minute. This isn't like you. Yes, I can say I'm too old for Lori, if you want it that way. But I'm not too old to get married. I don't like being single. I've been single long enough. I'd like to be married again."

"But not to Lori. *Never.* To whom then?"

"That's why I came to you in the first place. I know I should have made it clear. I intended to. See, Stan told me that all your patients were women, and I thought there'd be one just right, you'd introduce me and… Well, I know I was half-crazy then. When I met Lori, that night when Dempsey had the accident, it seemed preordained. She filled a hole in my life, she and her grandmother."

Vicki was indignant again, close to anger or maybe tears. "You thought I was running a lonely hearts club?"

"Ye gods, no! I was half out of my head with grief. I know that. You know it, too."

"If you are thinking of marrying Lori, you're still out of your head."

"Please, Vicki, listen to me. That's your job, isn't it, to listen to me? Lori brought the subject up. I love Lori in a special sort of way, but I know, like you said, I'm too old for her. That's what I told her."

"But you do want to get married?"

"Of course." Now *he* was irritated. "That's what I just said. Someone near my own age, someone I'm comfortable with, like you. I want a partner, a companion, a friend. Well, more than that really. I want to be in love. I want…" A surprising thought stopped him. *What did I just say?* He blinked twice. *Someone like you.*

It was an epiphany.

"Why, Vicki," he said softly, wonderingly, "I never saw you. Or I saw you as my doctor. Suddenly I see you…well…differently."

"Julian Elsmore, go away. I mean it. You are an exasperating man."

"And you are…Why didn't I see it sooner?" He was half-dazed. "You are exactly…"

"And don't come back, you ex-patient, you. You're permanently cancelled."

"All right, I'm not your patient any longer. But expect me back, Victoria." He left her without saying good-bye, repeating the question to himself, *Why didn't I see it sooner?*

Bewildered but with a growing sense of exultation, he took Lori home. They ate dinner and chatted about something or other.

"What's wrong?" she asked.

"Not a thing," he replied. "Not a single thing is wrong."

His heart was alight.

AT THE CEMETERY

November 1979

Julie, the darndest thing has happened. I'm going to court Victoria Glazer. I'm going to fall in love again.

Julie, you know that I wish our marriage had been forever. I've heard people speak of single bliss. "Single" isn't bliss for me. I yearn to be connected to someone, to be committed to a loving person.

It was very tempting to say yes when Lori proposed because I love her. She says she loves me. It would have been so simple, made us both happy at least for a time. But there's twenty-three years between us! In my heart, I know it wouldn't be right.

Vicki sent me away. I don't blame her for being mad. I've been a dunce, but I'm sure I can eat crow and get my courtship in gear. That's exciting. I'll try to be a good husband, just as I tried with you. I'm getting ahead of myself, I guess, assuming Vicki will marry me...but...

It helps to talk to you, Julie, to tell you my hopes, to get my mind straightened out.

He went back to his apartment where the only things in the kitchen cupboard were coffee, crackers and peanut butter.

He could be lighthearted about that because change, it was a-comin'.

Chapter 62

VICKI HAD AGREED TO SEE HIM. "Yes, usual time, Friday evening after Lori's appointment," she had said.

"Victoria," he told her formally when he entered her office on Friday evening, "you dismissed me as a patient. I'd like to take that a step further: You're fired."

"You don't need a psychiatrist any longer?" Her voice was tightly controlled, but he thought it was less hard than it had been the week before.

"I don't need a hired listener. I need a friend, a confidant. Can we talk together? Will you tell me about you?"

"I can't be Julie's stand-in."

"No one could be a stand-in for Julie."

"I had to say that, Julian, had to be clear about it. I'm not Julie. She was your first and forever love. I could never be Julie. I'm Victoria."

"I know who you are. I know who Julie was. Julie was the main character in a book I used to love to read. But now I've put that book on the shelf. It's a good memory, but can't there be a new story for me?" He looked at her, a question plain on his honest, hopeful face.

"So, Victoria, since you've cancelled me, and I've fired you, will you have dinner with me tonight?"

She regarded him silently for a very long moment. Anger had faded from her face, to be replaced by a light flush. He thought, but couldn't be sure, that he saw pleasure in the brightening of her eyes.

His voice was tentative. "Did that reach your ears the way I meant it? Will you have dinner with me?"

She took her time but finally said, "Yes. Wait right here? I won't be long." She disappeared into the office bathroom.

He stepped to the outer office and asked Lori if she had plenty of cash because tonight she would need to take a taxi home. He had other plans. "Call a cab now," he told her.

When Vicki returned, she was wearing a slim, black skirt and a blouse of some creamy, sheer material. The flowing sleeves gathered tightly at her wrists, and the V-neck was trimmed with a double ruffle. Over her arm, she carried a black shawl that had been knit with occasional glints of silver in the yarn and then finished with long, silky fringe. She had loosened her hair from the professional bun, and it fell softly to her shoulders. She was scented with an exotic Oriental perfume.

"Ah."

Around her lovely neck hung a rope of turquoise beads. The first loop circled her throat. The longer loop disappeared between her breasts, and his mind followed the beads. *If I held them in my hands now, they'd be warm.*

Aloud, he said carefully, "You are full of grace."

"Thank you." She handed him the shawl. It was folded into a triangle, and he put it carefully around her shoulders. Julie had never worn a shawl.

"Is that right?"

"Perfect." Suddenly, she squeezed his hand. "Let us go somewhere beautiful, Julian, good food, soft music, long tapers. I know just the place. Give me a minute to phone. They'll find a table for us." A moment later, she hung up the phone. "All set."

"Let's go then, Victoria." He opened the office door. "You have your key?"

"I do. I have the key."

"Victoria, right now you know where we're going and I don't, but we'll go in my car. I'll drive, you navigate. And, wherever we're going, I feel that we're turning a corner. Does it seem that way to you?"

"Yes, we're on a new street, one I like." Again, she reached for his hand.

Julian Elsmore smiled. With pleasure he clasped the hand she offered. *My friend, my dear*, he thought, *my very dear*.

Aloud, he quoted Mrs. Bellington, bless her, "Now let us go forth, Victoria, and dine together."

Epilogue

Readers of *Full Measure of Love* will want to know about the weddings that ensued.

Victoria Glazer and Julian Elsmore were married on a Friday evening in early June, 1980. Dr. Henry Glazer blanched at the thought of "giving his daughter away." Instead he stood as Julian's best man.

Lori was the bridesmaid. If she shed a few tears when the man she had hoped to marry wed another woman, she shed them in private. At the wedding and reception, lovely and flirtatious in a gown of light jade green, she showed only a smiling face. The morning after the wedding, however, a fierce Lori sat for her final exam in Corporate Finance 202, and she aced it. That afternoon she bested Ward Carpenter, who adored her, in a hard-fought game of tennis.

It was a long grind before Lori earned her college diploma. Every semester she collected more credits until, at age twenty-seven, she finally graduated. "That's okay," she told Vicki and Julian. "I've been busy with tutoring, busy with Maria and Elena, and, more and more, I'm on top of the Rosen Trust."

She laughed that she had also devoted quite a chunk of time to her social life. "That Ward Carpenter," she observed, her voice tender, "hangs in there. He's my best guy."

She had scarcely laid her cap and gown aside before she put on her bridal dress and married her best guy. It was a big white wedding. The reception included a table of old friends from The Downstairs Club, a table of present and former ESOL students, a few of her grandmother's surviving cronies, her parents more relaxed than she ever remembered them, Carpenter relatives, and a host of other well-wishers, including of course the Elsmores. Mr. Munchen and his handsome Elsa were proudly present. Charming little Elena was the flower girl.

The marriage produced four children. Two boys and a girl were chock full of self-esteem, an outgoing, exuberant trio, sure of their place in the world. Lori and Ward were proud of these boisterous offspring but also struggled to keep a lid on them.

Because genes will out, their fourth child was a timid little boy, slight in stature, diffident in manner. With tender and constant love, Lori coached, praised, and encouraged young Julian into thoughtful and confident manhood.

When the kids were grown to young adults, Lori overheard one of her older sons say, "Jules is quiet but sometimes the rest of us do dumb stuff, kind of thoughtless stuff, you know. Then he's our family go-to guy for sensible advice and peace of mind."

That's good enough, Lori thought. *That's certainly good enough.*

I DIDN'T START WRITING NOVELS until I was eighty-five years old because I was always busy with many important things. Bob Marshall and I raised ten energetic children, we both earned graduate degrees, we built a six-bedroom home (lots of sweat equity there). Bob (God rest him) was a college professor (Latin); I taught and supervised adult education in Frederick County, MD.

My new career as an author has been exciting. I feel as if I'm seventy again.

Most gratifying outcome: *Crooked Lines* put me in touch with many old friends.

My second novel, *Full Measure of Love*, is published as part of my ninetieth birthday celebration. I hope that reading it gives you pleasure.

A signed copy of *Full Measure of Love* may be ordered directly from the author. Send $20 (includes postage) to:
Ann Hall Marshall, PO Box 826, Emmitsburg, MD 21727.

Full Measure of Love will be available on Amazon and Kindle.